SILENT SHADOWS

A PETER BLACK THRILLER

DAVID ARCHER

VINCE VOGEL

RIGHTHOUSE

ISBN-13: 978-1-63696-164-4

ISBN-10: 1-63696-164-9

Cover design by: Damonza

Printed in the United States of America

www.righthouse.com

www.instagram.com/righthousebooks

www.facebook.com/righthousebooks

twitter.com/righthousebooks

PRAISE FOR THE PETER BLACK SERIES

PETER BLACK THRILLERS

PROLOGUE

OSAKA, JAPAN

A PRICKLE OF EXCITEMENT WRIGGLES THROUGH the robust figure of Kujira Iwasaki as he waddles down the bustling Dotombori Arcade, flanked by his bodyguards. The sights and smells of the narrow enclave flood the powerful businessman with memories of childhood. Of his mother's warm hand guiding him through the busy crowds to one of the many udon noodle bars that line the edges of the popular thoroughfare. The smells take him to a time when the simple treat of a bowl of kitsune udon would be enough to fill that boy with contentment for the rest of the day.

The crowded alleyway eagerly parts for the men, not just for the two imposing bodyguards but for the sweating, lumbering figure they protect. Adorned in a suit large enough for three men, a mobile Kujira is something akin to a human wrecking ball.

They arrive at Dotombori Imai, a modest, traditionally

fronted udon bar in the arcade's heart. Secluded from the bustling throng, its entrance lies beneath a low-roofed veranda. It is there that a young hostess in a red kimono and oshiroi face paint respectfully greets them and leads the way inside.

Kujira prefers to dine alone, so the entirety of the noodle bar is reserved for him. He certainly has no desire to share his experience with the common rabble who usually frequent the establishment.

Once the men are settled, preordered dishes start arriving promptly. Kujira begins with a bowl of kake udon, its aromatic broth reminding him of his mother's pride-filled gaze as she used to watch him eat. He indulges himself absolutely, his eating reminiscent of a feeding frenzy at a pig farm. From the sidelines, the bodyguards, abstaining from eating themselves, grimace as they observe their corpulent boss devour the udon with the fervor of a giant sea creature indiscriminately vacuuming up fish in the ocean.

A procession of dishes follows, each one consumed with the same unyielding pace. On the third cycle of food, the hostess disappears into the kitchen with a tray of empty dishes. Closed off from the main restaurant by a solid screen door, it is a good thing that Kujira and his men can't look inside. Otherwise, they'd see that the cooking area contains two armed men, a stressed chef, and a gagged and bound hostess. Within the stench of cooking, they patiently wait for Kujira to finally finish, the meal promising an imminent and dramatic climax.

"Is that fat pig not finished yet?" one of the gunmen complains to the hostess.

"No. He wants his next dish."

"You heard her," the other gunman snaps at the chef, while at the same time poking him in the back with a pistol.

The nervous chef nods and begins bowling up another dish of udon.

"We could be here all night at this rate," the first gunman complains.

The hostess turns sharply on him. "All night, Tatsuo?" she retorts, her green eyes beginning to burn.

Tatsuo averts his own gaze and studies the greasy tiles between his feet.

"All night?" she goes on coldly. "We have waited fifteen years, and you worry about one night, brother."

"I am sorry, Yūki," Tatsuo says obediently. "I just want this pig dead is all."

"And I told you. Not until he's finished the last dish. Not until he's had his fill."

She bores into Tatsuo with her stare. Feeling it, he raises his eyes to meet hers, witnessing the burning desire of this woman writ large all over her face: a true dragon.

The chef comes over and holds out the bowl of udon. "It won't be long now," he says cautiously.

They turn to him.

"What?"

"He usually finishes after three lots," the old chef continues. "He's two more dishes to go until the kitsune. That's when he finishes. After that, they'll order coffee and smoke for an hour or two before leaving. So it won't be long."

Yūki carries the steaming dishes from the kitchen to Kujira, drawing the attention of the three patrons. The trio scrutinize her movement from kitchen to table, their smirks revealing unspoken desires. Kujira, in particular, watches her with the same hunger he reserves for the food.

She sets the tray down, arranges the dishes before the imposing figure, and begins clearing the remnants of his previous course. As she moves to retreat with her tray of discarded plates, Kujira stretches out a moist, cold hand and grabs her arm in his sweaty grip.

Yūki freezes.

Her face, turned away from him, contorts into a silent grimace. She suppresses the urge to reach into her kimono and draw the hidden wakizashi inside, to sever the intrusive hand and paint the room with a crimson spray.

Restraining herself, she pushes aside the revulsion and turns to him with a façade of sweetness, meekness personified.

"Kujira-san?" she asks, her voice a gentle murmur.

"You have the most beautiful jade eyes," he slurs, his whole chin glistening with the grease.

"Thank you, Kujira-san," she replies with practiced gratitude.

His wet lips part into a smile, showing off his yellow teeth and the remnants of the feast stuck between them.

Yūki looks down at his hand on her arm, then back at him.

"You're new, right?" he asks.

"Yes, Kujira-san."

"But, still," he goes on, the stench of his breath making her nauseous, "I feel like we've met before. Have we?"

"No, Kujira-san," she lies. "Not to my recollection."

He continues to stare at her with that dumb look on his

face. Her fingers itch for the sword tucked beneath the kimono.

The kitchen bell rings, and Kujira lets go. After all, the food is important, too.

Yūki bows and leaves.

Inside the kitchen, Tatsuo ushers her aside.

"What was all that about?" he asks.

"He thinks he recognizes me."

"Even with the oshiroi makeup?"

"He doesn't know it's me," she assures her brother. "Only thinks he's seen me before."

Tatsuo gazes at the screen door. A narrow gap at its edge allows him to spy into the restaurant. His eyes settle on Kujira as he shovels another bowl of thick noodles into his gob, moving his chopsticks like a stoker on a steamboat moves his shovel when feeding coal into the furnace.

"We should just go out there and murder them all," Tatsuo says in a hushed tone, gripping his pistol and tightening his jaw.

"And we will, brother," Yūki assures him. "But in the right way. Just like with Watanabe. Just like we will with all of them."

She places a soft hand on her brother's shoulder and gazes longingly at him. The look softens Tatsuo, just as it always does. He could never say no to her when they were little; he can't say no to her now. If she says it has to be done a certain way, then it has to be done a certain way.

"Hey, you two," their companion says.

They turn to him.

"You'd better get out there. The pig's finished. He'll want the next course."

Yūki fetches the next dish and carries it out.

Soon the last kitsune is served, and as Kujira finishes his meal, Yūki serves him coffee. Kujira leans back on the bench seating, the backrest creaking under the strain, and lights a cigarette. His shirt is undone over his belly, revealing the pink gut that lies there on his lap like a sleeping bull calf.

Yūki hands out the cups and serves the coffee. She then backs off while they add cream and sugar. As she observes them from the side, she pays special attention to the two bodyguards. She watches them sip the brown liquid. Frown slightly. Sip it again. Make further faces. Try a third sip. Then ask each other whether they think the coffee is salty.

Good, Yūki thinks. *Three sips is more than enough.*

She steps forward right at the moment the two men begin to feel odd. She comes to a stop before Kujira, whom she keeps her eyes fixed to as the two men get up from the table, grabbing their stomachs.

"What's up with you two?" Kujira asks, frowning at them.

One of the men is seized by such a tearing, ripping pain that he screams out. The other is not far behind, and Kujira watches as both men turn deathly pale. The next thing, they are convulsing on the floor, pink foam frothing from their mouths, and finally, they lie still, their final breaths coming out as rattling hisses.

Kujira watches in horror. He looks sharply over at Yūki.

"Call an ambulance," he demands. "Don't just..."

It is then that he notices the self-satisfied smirk on Yūki's face.

"I don't think it will help," she tells him, her obsequious

geisha mask replaced with the iciness of a predator. "A priest would be more useful than a doctor."

The ice-cold tone of her voice sends shivers down the spine of Kujira Iwasaki. A flicker of recognition sparks fear in his eyes.

"Poison," he stammers. "It was *you*."

Yūki casually takes a seat across from him, her silence more chilling than any words. She unhinges the floral kanzashi from her lustrous black hair, shaking it loose until it cascades down over her shoulders. From her kimono, she extracts a packet of wipes, methodically removing the oshiroi makeup and geisha façade and revealing the warrior beneath.

All the while, Kujira stares in disbelief. "What is going on?"

She speaks with chilling calm. "Do you know," she says as she wipes the paint from her forehead, "Watanabe asked the same thing."

The wrinkles on Kujira's wide brow fold over one another, pinching together in a gathering of skin at the top of his nose.

"Watanabe is dead."

"I know," she says right in his face. "It was me who put him in the ground."

"You?"

When the last of the makeup is off, a wicked smile is revealed. "One down," she says in a hollow tone. "You will make two."

Kujira sits there, bloated and weighed down with food, staring at her, trying to figure out for sure where he knows her from.

As gradual realization washes over him, Yūki feeds him

another clue. "I've aged, and you... you've grown significantly."

And then he knows.

"Tanaka's bitch," Kujira mutters under his breath. This triggers Yūki's wrath, her fury ignites, and she vaults up from her seat, echoing his vulgar words.

"*Tanaka's bitch!*"

"You're supposed to be dead," Kujira whispers, aghast.

"Yet here I am," Yūki retorts.

Kujira plants his hands on the table and hoists his hefty body to stand. Once he's upright, Yūki promptly flips the table to the side. Now, only a three-foot chasm separates them. Taking the lapels of her kimono, she tears it open to reveal her breasts.

Kujira's eyes burst in shock.

"This will be the last thing you ever see, Kujira Iwasaki," Yūki hisses, withdrawing her wakizashi from its hidden holster. The blade slashes through the air at him as Kujira stands there paralyzed. He looks down, a diagonal gash appearing across his bloated abdomen. The cut is so precise that it takes a moment before it begins to seep blood. Then it gushes.

Kujira falls back onto the bench, grabbing at the cut line as it opens from the pressure, his intestines starting to push through the gaping wound. His hands scramble, attempting to contain his insides as they spill from him.

"You, Kujira Iwasaki, took everything from me," Yūki declares. "Yet you left me my life. Today, I leave you with nothing!"

And with a mighty two-handed swing, she brings the

sword down, severing his head from his bloated body. Her revenge is one step closer to its ultimate completion.

ONE

HOKKAIDO, JAPAN

Nestled in the wilderness of the Soya Subprefecture, at the very northern tip of Hokkaido, the two assassins find themselves in a barren landscape reminiscent of Alaskan summers. Indeed, the nearest semblance of civilization is the fishing village of Higashiura, a quaint settlement of just over six thousand souls.

This morning, their run carries them through quiet roads bordered by cherry blossom trees, along low cliffs overlooking the raging sea, and across sandy beaches, past jagged volcanic rocks piercing the waves. The run finally ends at their hillside home, a two-story wooden cottage surrounded by a thicket of tall Sakhalin spruce trees that keep it hidden from prying eyes. Except someone has managed to find it. A black sedan sits ominously outside their cottage, heralding uninvited guests.

As the assassins near their home, two men step out from

the vehicle. The younger of them, dressed in a black suit, exudes the unmistakable aura of a bodyguard. His gaze never strays from them as they come to a stop. The elder man, leaning on a cane with a handle carved in the shape of a duck's head, introduces himself as Akechi Akiyama, the chief of security for Tanaka-Corp.

His egg-shaped head is as bald as the duck on top of his cane, and white stubble decorates the very end of his chin like icing sugar. His eyes are two slits across his stern and serious face.

Nobody says anything after the introduction. Certainly not Peter or Michael.

"I'd better get straight to it," Akechi adds in a gruff voice. "May we go inside?"

"No, we may not" is Peter's curt reply. "Whatever you have to say can be said out here."

Akechi Akiyama nods. "Then I will proceed. I am here to speak with you today about a lucrative opportunity, Azrael-san."

"A job?"

"Yes."

"Then no."

"No?"

"No," Peter repeats.

"I heard you both recently lost almost all of your money."

Peter turns to his son. "Mikey, go inside. I'll handle this from here."

"You sure you don't need me?" the kid asks.

"No. Go inside. Start breakfast."

Michael leaves the scene, locking eyes with the bodyguard as he moves off. Opening the front door of their wooden house, he steps inside and is gone.

Peter swivels his gaze to Akechi Akiyama. "Look," he begins in an icy, detached voice, "I don't do jobs for people who just turn up out of the blue."

"An associate of mine called you yesterday," Akechi tells him in a flat tone. "You told him no."

Peter leans forward, keeping his voice low, regardless of the remoteness of where they are. "Then," he seethes, "I guess that would mean you've wasted your journey."

"But my boss wants to hire the best: He wants to hire *you*, Azrael-san."

"The 'best' is down to opinion, always will be. There are other 'bests' out there, especially in my game. If your boss can afford to pay you to go on wild goose chases, he can hire someone good enough to get your job done."

"We've already hired others," Akechi retorts dryly. "In total, we have employed fifteen different entities to complete this job, and only a single four-man team of Australian commandos remain in the game."

"What happened to the others?"

The old man's eyes darken. "They are either dead or missing."

Peter shakes his head gently, a sardonic grin rising on his face. "Sounds like a *great* job."

Akechi Akiyama's look hardens. "The man I represent," he practically growls, "will not take no for an answer, Azrael-san."

"Well," Peter says, leaning forward and adding the next part in a hushed tone, "I'm afraid that's something he'll have to learn."

Akechi's brows narrow at him. "You and your son are ronin, are you not? Killers without masters. I have come here to offer you both a job that will pay more money than every other contract you take for the next five years. And yet you say no."

It is Peter's turn to pierce his eyes. "That's exactly what I'm saying."

Akechi sighs, then angrily mutters, "Then so be it."

Before parting, he hands over a business card, urging Peter to reconsider and contact the number on it if he changes his mind. Then, after the men depart, Peter goes inside and finds Michael peeking through the curtains at the retreating sedan.

"They left their card," Peter says, handing it over to the kid.

"Old school," Michael comments as he looks it over.

"That's what I thought."

Michael hands the card back and meets his father's eyes, seeing the worry in them.

"What is it?"

"Are you sure you're ready for what comes next?" Peter asks, the words hanging heavy in the air.

TWO

ARASHIYAMA BAMBOO GROVE, KYOTO, JAPAN

THE AUSTRALIAN COMMANDO WIPES AT HIS EYES with a sweat-soaked sleeve, attempting to clear his vision from the blood dripping down from his hair. The planned ambush had turned into an utter disaster. His three comrades, now reduced to lifeless bodies, had been caught in an unexpected onslaught when a ruthless yakuza death squad arrived just after they had engaged their target at a local tattoo parlor. Three mercenaries, at least six yakuza, a tattooist, and a pair of hapless bystanders are all now dead. But not the target, no. She had managed to escape, disappearing into a nearby bamboo grove—the one he now stands in.

Submerged in the tranquil sanctuary of towering green bamboo stalks, he feels like he's been transported to an alien world, a stark contrast to the rugged bushland of Northern Australia where he grew up. The bamboo shoots seem to extend indefinitely, providing ample cover for their elusive target.

A snapping twig underfoot shatters the eerie silence.

Quickly pivoting to his right, he catches a fleeting glimpse of a shadowy figure about forty yards away. Without hesitation, he unleashes a hail of bullets from his Sig MPX PCC 9mm carbine, showering the vibrant bamboo canopy in lead. As quickly as she appeared, however, she vanishes into the foliage.

A hollow click signals the end of his ammunition. As the mercenary ejects the spent mag, he instinctively reaches for a fresh one, only to be met with the cold realization of his dwindling arsenal—he's out of ammo. Abandoning the now useless MPX, he utilizes his last resort, the Sig Sauer P320 Legion holstered at his hip.

Bracing himself for the uphill pursuit, he maps out an arc in his mind, aiming to intersect her anticipated route. His intuition suggests her destination—the Tenryu-ji Temple nestled at the peak of the grove.

He edges his way through the endless reeds of bamboo toward the wooden temple, through a tight alley of green shoots and—she's there. Grabbing the wrist with the gun. Driving the hand into the hard bamboo, knocking the P320 out of it. He blocks the punch that comes. Then the kick. Pulls himself clear of her as she reaches into her kimono and pulls from it the wakizashi short sword she keeps underneath. The Australian pulls the only weapon he has left: a K25 eight-inch hunting knife with a serrated back. He holds it out to her one-handed as she circles him in the jōdan-no-kamae fighting position with the wakizashi held above her head as though she is preparing to cut him in half.

The Australian cat-foots around, eyes on the raised short sword, body low. The meaty blade of the K25 is an extension of his arm. They enter a small clearing in the bamboo—a fighting ring.

"Hey, darlin'," he says. "Are we gonna dance or fight?"

He likes to talk, Yūki thinks. *Good. My silence will make him uneasy.*

"You not gonna join the convo, sweetheart?" he jabbers on.

She continues to circle in silence, her glowing green eyes concentrating on the man and not the knife. For it is the man who moves—the knife only goes with him by default.

"Come on, darlin'. Don't be like that. The least you can do is speak to me. After all, you and your gook mates just killed three of the best blokes a fella ever knew."

Yūki smiles.

It makes the Australian mad.

He rushes at her, feigning with his right but shifting the blade to his left, slashing it through the air at her.

Yūki dodges it with ease, tipping her body to the side, never once lowering the wakizashi from its raised position.

"You here to fight or what?!" the Australian cries out in frustration as he pulls up hard and whirls around.

Yūki resumes her silent circling, the smile never leaving her lips. The words of her father come back to her, long-ago words of training from the practice floor: "Use the opening moments of a fight to study your opponent. Let them make their moves and watch for weakness. You may miss out on a quick victory, which is always to be sought, but these moments of study help bolster your chances for eventual success. Take your time. Be sure."

"Bugger this!" the Australian exclaims. "I haven't come here to DANCE!"

He leaps at her.

Yūki almost gets her feet wrong, almost fails to escape the downward flash of the K25, feeling its tip run along the length of her left forearm as she twists away. And they're circling each other again, the Australian wearing a grin, his eyes on her arm. Yūki looks down as blood begins to dribble from the cut.

Her father's voice fills her mind once more: "Don't over-think it. Only ever expect what actually happens in the fight. React to that and nothing else. Live the moment."

As he moves, the Australian takes a low crouching position like a tiger about to pounce. Yūki stays with him, keeping the distance between them a continual three meters, the blade of the wakizashi hanging over the top of her head like the sting of a scorpion.

"Did that hurt, sweetheart?" he says, goading her.

Blood drips from her elbow onto the ground. Yūki witnesses a level of elation in her opponent. The scratch on her arm clearly signifies some point of satisfaction for him. *Well, it won't last.*

The Australian comes at her again.

Yūki dodges the thrust of his knife at the last second so that she can meet the stabbing arm with her own blade as she spins away. The Australian ducks sideways and escapes, but not before taking the razor-cut of her blade across his own forearm.

When they are once more facing each other in the clearing, he checks the arm for a second and winces at the deep gash she's opened up along it.

His eyes glare rage at her.

More circling, more probing.

The Australian closes the space between them, edging toward her, the K25 held out, the anger showing in his squinting eyes, the clenched jaw. He feints left and under, and suddenly they are pressed together. He goes to thrust the knife into her abdomen, but she twists away and back, and as he falls forward with the weight of his own body, he's pulled onwards toward a target that is no longer there. It is then, as she lithely glides away, that Yūki brings the short sword down onto the back of his neck and severs it at the spine.

The Australian sags and drops to the ground, the knife spilling out of his limp fingers.

Breathing deeply, Yūki restores calm to her muscles and sheaths the wakizashi, pulling her kimono closed over the top.

The man sent to kill her is on his front. He is a large man, and it takes all Yūki's strength to turn him over.

The Australian's eyes are open. He's still alive.

"No," he pleads weakly as she lowers herself and takes a seat on his chest. "Please..."

Placing a hand over his mouth and nose, she squeezes off the oxygen, gazing all the time into the dying man's eyes as they gradually go blank, recalling at the same time her father's words: "He who cannot stare into a man's eyes as he dies will never learn to exist inside the void. And, therefore, will never learn to kill with any great skill."

THREE

SHINOSHIMA, RYUKYU ARCHIPELAGO, JAPAN

Nestled in the East China Sea lies the starkly inhospitable Shinoshima, or "Death Island," the second smallest of the Tokara Islands. A hundred miles from Japan's southern tip, Shinoshima is a volcanic island clad in sheer cliffs and sharp rocks—a testament to its last eruption some three hundred years ago. It stands unique among Japanese islands, having been purchased from the government in 2001 by the country's wealthiest man, Koji Tanaka, leader of Tanaka-Corp. The price? A hefty two hundred million US dollars.

The island's appeal for Tanaka lies not in its rugged terrain, however, but in its hidden depths: an extensive underground fortress built during WWII by the Japanese government. Originally intended for storing military equipment and munitions, this sprawling subterranean structure fell into disuse after Japan's surrender. Inherited by the government in 1952, the fortress remained untouched until Tanaka took ownership. Viewing the nuclear-blast-resistant facility as a canvas, Tanaka commissioned architects and designers to transform it into a high-end survival complex. The result was an underground haven akin to a cruise ship for the elite, boasting an opulence akin to a mega-yacht. It is here, in this palatial bunker on Shinoshima, that Tanaka currently resides—waiting for her to make her next move.

It started less than a month ago with Ishi Watanabe. Poor Ishi. His one weakness had been his vanity. He had been handsome as a young man and desperately wanted to remain so in the prime of his sixties. His need for endless surgeries, though, had made him vulnerable.

What *she* did was savage.

Three days after his mutilated corpse had been discovered in a surgical bin not far from a well-known plastic surgery, a package had arrived at the headquarters of Tanaka-Corp's Kobe offices. Inside was an organ transplant container, and inside that was the carefully removed face of one Ishi Watanabe. She had used a scalpel to cut it away from the tissue underneath, and she had done it while he was still alive. Tanaka knew this because what had killed Ishi was not the injury itself, but the heart attack he'd suffered while she'd done it to him—skinned him alive.

Then, three weeks later, Kujira Iwasaki was murdered in an Osaka noodle restaurant, the killer leaving behind his headless, eviscerated corpse, as well as the bodies of his two poisoned bodyguards.

Next will be Haiko, Tanaka is sure of it.

He hopes to have things in place by then.

As he delves into his thoughts, a chime from his tablet disrupts Tanaka's quiet contemplation. It is a Zoom call from Akechi Akiyama, his trusted security chief.

"Akechi-san," Tanaka says in a harsh voice that cuts through the still air of the bunker.

Akiyama bows reverently and low before raising himself and speaking into the camera. "Tanaka-shachou," he begins, using the respectful suffix *shachou*, meaning *president*. "I have unfortunate news. The four Australians are dead."

"Fools," Tanaka says under his breath.

"We also received this only moments ago."

The camera zooms out. Someone hands Akechi Akiyama an organ transplant box. Koji Tanaka already knows what's in it. He watches with blank interest as Akechi opens the container and tips the box forwards so Tanaka can see its contents.

It is a big fat tongue, and Koji Tanaka can't help thinking of the old markets of his youth, where the Chinese laborers used to buy all sorts of strange things. Cow tongue had been one, and he had always been amazed at the sight. Kujira's tongue is just as dark colored as a cow's. After all, he was a heavy smoker.

"So long, my fat friend," Tanaka says.

They had known each other a long time. Had built empires together. Shared a hunger for consumption.

"Send it to his family," Tanaka says with a wave of the hand.

"It will be done immediately, Tanaka-shachou."

They move on to fresh business.

"What about your visit to our American friends?" Tanaka asks.

"I'm afraid Azrael refused the job."

"It was expected. Is everything in place for the secondary proposal?"

"Yes, Tanaka-shachou."

"Then it is time to act."

FOUR

HOKKAIDO, JAPAN

Michael spots Mayu the second he walks into the Big Echo Karaoke Bar, one of only two bars in the whole town. She's the only person in there dressed like she's come straight off Harajuku Street in Tokyo rather than Higashiura fishing village. Her attire, characterized by platform boots, a leather miniskirt, a black and red striped jumper, and vibrant two-toned hair, starkly contrasts with the plain dress of the locals.

"Michael-san," she breathes softly into his ear as they greet each other with an awkward hug, "these people are so strange."

He can't help imagining that they're probably thinking exactly the same about her.

Mayu is also a temporary inhabitant of Higashiura, having arrived only a week ago as part of her job in IT programming. Their paths had crossed the previous day during Michael's run when Mayu had gotten lost along the shoreline. After he'd kindly guided her back to town, she had asked him out on a date, resulting in their current rendezvous.

At the karaoke bar, Mayu and Michael keep their distance from the enthusiastic performers, taking a booth farthest from the stage. There, they sit watching the locals wail out songs for a while before Mayu plucks up the nerve to speak.

"This is a strange town," she comments.

The kid can't help smiling.

"Yes. It's very strange," he agrees.

Mayu giggles, and when she smiles, the dimples on her cheeks sink in. She's very pretty. Beautiful, in fact. But, then, she's supposed to be.

"You are quiet," she points out.

"Am I?"

"Yes. This is not like American supposed to be. You Americans always like to talk. My father always say that American is afraid of silence. He always got to fill it with his voice."

The dimples sink in farther.

Michael laughs. "I guess that would be a fair assessment. Of most Americans, anyway."

The kid loosens up. Starts chatting. She's easygoing— plays the part. Laughs at all his jokes, no matter how lame, or even if they're a joke. At one point, he asks her if she'd like another drink, and she bursts into giggling. Obviously something lost in translation.

Or just another part of the act.

Three drinks in, she asks him to sing with her. They put

their names down at the bar, and ten minutes later, they're up on stage performing Elton John and Kiki Dee's "Don't Go Breaking My Heart." They have an absolute ball at it, murder the song royally, practically falling off the stage laughing by the end. Then, as they slink back to their table, Mayu grabs ahold of Michael, and they kiss.

This part of it he doesn't mind. He plays his role as she plays hers, and they enjoy a long kiss with a bit of grab-ass.

Another two drinks and they're walking back to the motel she's staying in, a two-story rectangular building that looks like it was made out of a Lego set. They go straight to her room. He takes a seat by the window while she makes him a drink. Whiskey and Coke.

"Thank you," he says when she hands him the glass.

"Jim Beam," she says.

"You like American things?"

The dimples practically glow. "Yes," she says with a little smile curling her bright red lips.

They knock glasses together and drink.

Mayu's eyes watch him closely from over the rim of hers as he gulps down a mouthful.

Michael tastes the bitterness of it right away. It shouldn't take long. The room begins to sway from one side to the next, and then it is rolling over him like a wave and crashing down on top.

Once he's out, Mayu takes the zip ties she has hidden in the waistline of her skirt and secures Michael's hands behind his back. Next, she secures his ankles, wraps duct tape around his mouth, and places a cloth bag over his head. Finally, she takes a cell phone from a pocket and makes a call.

"*Tāgetto ga sagatte imasu,*" she says when it is answered.

The target is down.

———

PETER SITS enveloped in darkness listening to the sounds that surround him. The house, old as time, groans under the strain of the wind, a haunting harmony with the distant crashing waves. Closer to home, there's the creak of the spruce as they rock. And then something else. In this orchestration of nature, a jarring note stands out, so alien it shatters his solitude, catapulting him back to the world.

On the arm of his chair, his phone is ringing.

"Hello?"

"Ah, Azrael-san," a man says, his voice oozing smug satisfaction.

Peter instantly recognizes the voice of Akechi Akiyama—the stranger who showed up this morning wanting their employment.

"I told you no," Peter says firmly.

"And I told you that no is not a word Koji Tanaka accepts. Something you will shortly find out—I have just sent you the required video. You should watch it first before this conversation continues."

The phone chirps, and Peter removes it from his ear. Finding the message, he begins watching the attached video. It is only eight seconds long, but, then, it doesn't really need to be any longer.

The footage is taken from the inside of a panel van that is being driven at speed. The time on the dashboard clock says nine-thirty. That's fifteen minutes ago. A man in a white kabuki mask with red and black detailing drives. The camera pans left to the back of the van. A hospital bed has been bolted to the floor. On it lies Michael. He's unconscious, arm and leg restraints contain his limbs, and thick leather straps hold him on his back.

The video ends. Simple message. They have his son.

Peter places the phone back to his ear. "I really should warn you, Akechi-san," he says in a tone as cold as a razor blade, "that you're playing a very dangerous game. You do know who you are playing with, don't you?"

"A wild animal," is the reply. "But even a wild animal can be tamed. All you need do is take away its cub."

Smug prick, Peter thinks.

"Go on, then," he says. "Get on with it. Tell me your proposal."

"Gladly, Azrael-san. A car will arrive shortly. You are to get into the back of it. Your son's life depends on your complete cooperation. If you refuse or become violent or we feel you are not cooperating fully at any stage, Michael-san will be terminated with immediate effect. Every second you do as we say is a second your son lives without being harmed. Do you understand, Azrael-san?"

"I get the format," Peter says in a bored tone. "I'm now, essentially, your bitch."

"Essentially, yes."

FIVE

SHINOSHIMA, RYUKYU ARCHIPELAGO, JAPAN

THE CAR WHISKS HIM AWAY TO A PRIVATE HANGAR at nearby Wakkanai Airport. There, a Gulfstream G650 awaits, its sleek body gleaming under the airport lights, ready to transport him to Kagoshima. That's only a stopover, however, a stepping stone in his odyssey.

From Kagoshima, he is ushered into a Mitsubishi SH-60J Seahawk helicopter. Its rotors cutting through the air, it carries him hundreds of kilometers southwest across the churning East China Sea, toward a desolate speck of barren rock named Shinoshima.

Upon landing, he is met by Akechi Akiyama and three armed men, and they all board a monorail that takes them deep into the island itself. Beyond a set of blast doors, a self-sufficient complex emerges, complete with greenhouses, livestock, and essential amenities.

The journey concludes at an auditorium-like room.

Devoid of a stage, it does, however, boast floor-to-ceiling glass paneling at its front. Whatever is on the other side remains unilluminated and hidden, leaving Peter with nothing to see except their reflections off the black glass as they enter the room. Rows of lavish leather armchairs stare down at the screen, and Akechi directs Peter to the front row. The security chief takes the neighboring seat, and the trio of armed bodyguards settles behind them.

As they get comfortable, Akechi leans toward Peter. "Would you like some refreshments, Azrael-san?"

"No. Just make this quick," Peter retorts.

Once the men are all settled, the room dims. Concurrently, the lights behind the glass reveal a minimalist room featuring a cream leather sofa and a small table. Amid the room's stark concrete walls, only a single door breaks the monotony.

It swings open, and in strolls a middle-aged man clad in a charcoal suit, exuding an air of austere grayness from his hair down to his pallid skin, which doesn't appear to have been touched by the sun's rays for some time. He is accompanied by a diminutive man with white hair who wears a black samue. His physiognomy carries the serene air of the Buddhist monks who usually wear the samue. Yet, the ominous gleam in his dark eyes silently cautions Peter—this man is far from tranquil.

With an air of silent authority, the first man takes his place on the sofa, a predator settling into his lair. He leans forward, his gaze penetrating the barrier of bulletproof glass and locking onto Peter with unsettling intensity. His companion, the monk-like figure, assumes a discreet position behind him, poised and alert.

It is clear: the first man is the formidable Tanaka, the second, his personal bodyguard.

Koji Tanaka, with his silvered hair and cruel eyes, resembles an old wolf, an alpha in the twilight of his reign, securing himself against the onslaught of eager betas. He addresses Peter in his deep, guttural Japanese, filling the room with a voice carried by speakers. Akechi leans in to translate. "Tanaka-shachou says he wishes to employ your specific services. See, there's a woman…"

As Peter listens, he scrutinizes Tanaka. The mere mention of "woman" triggers a visible grimace in the modern-day industrialist. It appears this "woman" resonates with him like a bitter jolt.

"…This woman is the daughter of a formerly influential yakuza *Wakagashira*. Now leading her own band of criminals, she poses a significant threat to Tanaka-shachou and his associates. Two of his closest allies, men he considered family, have already been murdered by her…"

Peter raises his hand, signaling Tanaka and Akechi to stop. "And what are you expecting?" he interjects. "That she'll eventually come for you?"

The wolf-man stares at him hard for a while, then nods and speaks, his voice translated by Akechi, "That is correct."

"But you live here with all this security. What's a handful of yakuza against this fortress?"

The man of steel, Tanaka, simply stares, taking a moment before answering.

"Nothing," Akechi translates. "Tanaka-shachou is fortified with trusted personnel, all meticulously vetted and none having direct access to him apart from his loyal bodyguard,

Jin. His security team is well-trained, ready to defend this place. If they attack, they will all perish."

"So why doesn't he just wait for that to happen, then?" Peter asks, his voice carrying a note of skepticism.

Akechi seems taken aback by Peter's blunt question. He glances toward Tanaka for guidance before responding.

"Because Tanaka-shachou is not a man to wait for things to simply happen," he explains, his voice steady. "He's a man of action. A man who believes in taking control of the situation rather than sitting back. Plus, there's the matter of reputation."

"Reputation?" Peter echoes, arching a brow.

"Indeed." Akechi nods. "In our world, reputation is everything. If Tanaka-shachou simply waits for an attack, it may be seen as a sign of weakness. But if he acts first and eliminates the threat, it sends a message. A message of strength and power. Besides," he adds, "why wait for a mosquito to bite when you can swat it out of the sky?"

"And I take it," Peter says, "I'm to be the fly-swat."

"You are," Akechi agrees.

"And why is this woman coming for your boss?"

Turning to face his superior, Akechi respectfully holds his gaze just shy of direct eye contact. Behind the screen, Tanaka gives a solemn, singular shake of the head. Then he goes on, Akechi translating.

"Whatever Tanaka-shachou did or didn't do changes nothing. The deal is simple. You are a killer. Your son is in our possession. Kill this woman or your son is dead. Honor your son by personally bringing Tanaka-shachou the head of Yūki Yokashina."

And with that, Tanaka gets up and begins leaving the

room, the bodyguard trailing behind him. The lights in the anteroom go out the second he's gone, and, consequently, the lights brighten in the auditorium.

"Right," Peter says, turning to Akechi Akiyama. "Now that's over with. Take me to my son."

———

IN THE DEEP SUBTERRANEAN REALM, Peter enters a second room separated from another by a pane of glass, though significantly smaller than the auditorium-like chamber they'd previously occupied. It's more akin to a conference room or a storage area. With a flicker, light fills the compartment beyond the glass, revealing an even more confined space, one resembling a sparse prison cell.

The harsh light illuminates the raw austerity of the next-door room: the stark, bare concrete walls; a thin, rolled-up mattress tucked away in a corner. Bolted to the floor, a desk with a computer and a chair stand out, their starkness amplified by the stainless steel toilet attached to one corner wall. An air vent on the ceiling breathes conditioned air into the space, and amidst this austere setting, another figure comes into focus, standing by the glass: Michael.

Choosing to forgo the offered seat, Peter approaches the screen. Their voices shimmer in the hollow silence, amplified by hidden microphones.

"Nice place you have there," Peter quips, his tone dripping with sarcasm.

"Hilarious," Michael retorts, unamused.

"At least you've got a computer."

"One that they watch constantly."

Even though Michael can see no more than his own reflection on his side, their gazes meet through the glass, a father-and-son moment punctuated by grim circumstances. Peter's voice breaks the silence.

"How rough did they handle you?"

"Not the gentlest," Michael admits, lifting his shirt to expose a harsh mosaic of green and purple bruises that lattices his ribcage.

"Any fractures?"

"No, just this technicolor of bruises."

"Probably dropped you during the transport."

"Yeah, probably. Anyway, they want me to tell you that I'll be acting as your handler. You need anything, or anything comes in from this end, I'll be in contact with you."

"So that's what the computer's for."

"What did you think? They installed it so I could keep up to date with my social media?"

Peter's grim features soften at his son's jest. A sense of humor will be a valuable asset in the grueling days and weeks to come. As he prepares to respond, the door creaks open, and Akechi Akiyama's face appears.

"Time's up, Azrael-san," he announces.

Peter spins back toward Michael. "Hang in there, Mikey," he says. "I'll try and get this done as quickly as possible."

Michael's response is a silent nod.

SIX

TOKYO, JAPAN

DIRECT FROM KAGOSHIMA, PETER IS FLOWN TO Tokyo, accompanied by Akechi Akiyama. Throughout the journey, Tanaka-Corp's chief of security assures him that he can provide virtually anything necessary for the mission. Peter enumerates his needs, and Akechi confidently guarantees everything.

"How about operational expenses?" Peter probes.

A JCB platinum corporate card is promptly presented to him. As he eyes the gleaming plastic card, he quips, "That ought to do it."

"No need to go to extremes," Akechi chides lightly. "Just the standard expenses."

Next, he extends a cell phone toward Peter.

"For communicating with your son," he elucidates.

Without a word, Peter slips it into his pocket, his gaze

shifting to the aerial view of the cityscape outside the jet window. "Why are we heading to Tokyo?" he inquires.

"Yūki's next target resides in Tokyo," Akechi reveals.

"And are you going to tell me who that might be?" Peter puts to him.

"Patience, Azrael-san. First, you need to familiarize yourself with Yūki, understand her. On the phone I just gave you is a series of files. Read them. Then, once everything is arranged, I'll be in touch."

"What exactly is being arranged?"

Reclining on the lavish cream leather interior of the Gulfstream G650, Akechi's demeanor turns serious. "One of the primary reasons Tanaka-shachou was so adamant about recruiting yourself, Azrael-san, is your intelligence background with the CIA."

"Mostly, I handled pest control," Peter retorts, "quick in-and-out assassination missions."

"Nevertheless, you are skilled at assuming roles, correct?"

"If the job demands it."

"Well, this mission might require you to play a particular character."

It is then that Peter interjects with a telling question: "Is *he* aware?"

The question catches Akechi off guard. "Is who aware?"

"The target. Does he know Yūki's coming for him?"

Akechi's twitch reveals more than his silence.

"So he doesn't," Peter surmises, "and your boss is planning to use him as unsuspecting bait?"

Akechi offers no response.

Sighing in disbelief, Peter diverts his attention back to

the scenery outside. As dusk cloaks the sky, city lights flicker on below, setting Tokyo aglow with life.

———

Within minutes, they touch down in Tokyo International, at Tanaka's private hangar. A vehicle awaits them. "My driver is at your service. However," warns Akechi, "you must stay within the city limits."

Peter gets into the car, directing the driver to take him to the Shibuya ward of the city, and by the time they reach the fashionable district, it is awash with neon light and human traffic.

"Here is good enough," Peter says as they reach a busy intersection where the lights are red and a mass of people cross all at once, resembling a crashing wave washing across the road.

Peter gets out. When he closes the door, the driver calls to him. "Where will you be staying?" he queries tersely. Peter grins in response. "That's not your concern," he answers and strides away without waiting for a retort.

He vanishes into a nearby alley, weaving through the narrow pathway sandwiched between towering buildings, eventually arriving at a street filled with noodle bars. Neon signs blaze across the façades of the eateries while hostesses solicit passersby with enticing offers. He finds his preferred canteen, slips into a seat at the back, and watches the city workers as they kick off the weekend with merry camaraderie —beer, sake, and bowls of noodles.

Ignoring the spirited crowd, Peter places an order for

ramen, crispy chicken wings, and a bottle of Sapporo Gold. As he waits, he studies the data on Yūki, examining the extensive files on the phone while sipping beer and eating his food, getting acquainted with his target.

The file is remarkably detailed—even including a copy of Yūki's birth certificate. The 43-year-old Yūki Yokashina has a tragic backstory. As an infant, she was the lone survivor of a brutal home invasion in which her mother and grandparents were murdered when gunmen looking for her yakuza father sprayed their home with bullets. Her quick-thinking mother had hidden her under floorboards during the assault, thus saving Yūki when most of her family had perished that day.

Peter imagines the baby girl wriggling under the floor as blood drips down on her from between the gaps in the boards.

Her father was the notorious yakuza hitman Takashi "The Gun" Yokashina, a man who played a crucial role in the infamous Yama-Itchi War, a brutal gang conflict that lasted four years from 1985-1989. When the leader of the Yamaguchi-gumi, the largest yakuza family, died unexpectedly, a power vacuum emerged. The ensuing struggle culminated in the murder of their interim leader, sparking a four-year war. Amid the chaos, the Bosozoku Clan's best soldier, Takashi, was enlisted to resolve the conflict, and, so the legend goes, in a month, Takashi had single-handedly ended the war, leaving a pile of bodies in his wake and thus earning a legendary reputation.

Takashi's subsequent status elevated the family's standing, making Yūki akin to yakuza royalty. Among the data, Peter finds an address for the now blind Takashi, living a quiet life in Osaka. He commits the address to memory, sensing it might prove useful further down the line.

The data also includes details about Yūki's half-brother, Tatsuo Yokashina, the child of a fleeting relationship between Takashi and the hostess of a drinking den. Tatsuo has made his own mark in the yakuza world as the boss of the Bosozoku Clan, a group with a significant network and muscle power.

Peter is on the brink of diving into Yūki's file at Tanaka-Corp when his cell buzzes. It's Michael.

"Hey, Mikey. How's life treating you in the big house?" Peter says, trying to lighten the mood.

"About as good as being locked up twenty-four hours a day can be. Anyway, just to let you know, they've assigned me a crew," Michael changes the subject.

"A crew?" Peter sounds interested.

"Yes. Tech guys, stuff like that. I have direct access to them. They can infiltrate security systems, scan hotel registers, scrutinize police files, you name it. Plus, they have a team of mercenaries on standby, in case you need some muscle."

"That's reassuring," Peter replies, his voice heavy with sarcasm.

"You're in Tokyo, right?" Michael inquires.

"Yeah."

"Because that's where your next assignment is."

"Akechi did mention that. Have they told you who it is?"

"Nope."

"Typical."

"Where are you holing up?" Michael asks, trying to paint a mental picture.

"The streets of Tokyo for now. I need to stay on the move." As Peter answers, his eyes scan the street through the restaurant entrance. A car is parked opposite, two men sitting in the front keeping a close eye on the restaurant, occasionally checking their phones, probably tracking Peter through the Find My Phone app.

"Have you had the chance to review the file on the target yet?" Michael's voice snaps him back.

"Yeah, you?"

"Not much else to do in here. Thoughts?" Michael prods.

Peter mulls it over, watching the throng of people pour into the noodle bar.

"Haven't finished yet," he finally answers.

"Did you get to the part about her and her father hunting down the people who killed her mother?"

"Not yet. Just learned about her father and brother's ties to the yakuza."

"Just wait till you get to the revenge part. It gives you an idea of what shaped this woman and how far she'll go for vengeance."

"Can't wait," Peter replies dryly.

Michael sighs into the phone. "What do you reckon Tanaka did to her?"

"I don't know. Probably double-crossed her somehow."

"I searched her on the Internet."

"Oh?"

"Yeah. I found a local news report with her name on it about a car accident up in Hokkaido. She wasn't involved, but her husband and daughter were killed. They were hit by a truck on a bridge. Their car plunged into a river. Both bodies are missing. Swept away by the current. The reports, including the official police ones, all point to an accident. You think she blames Tanaka for it?"

"Be careful, kid," Peter warns. "Tanaka's people are watching our every move. Don't ruffle feathers."

"*He* brought *us* on board," Michael snaps back. "Not the other way around."

"Remember, he's also the one who can switch off the oxygen supply in your cell. So keep that in mind."

"I'm sure he'll give us a heads-up if we're crossing a line. So far, they've let me snoop around online. Maybe Tanaka has nothing to hide. Maybe she's just pissed because her severance package wasn't good enough."

"Maybe."

"But then why kill all the others?"

Peter rolls his eyes. The kid's insatiable curiosity is going to land him in hot water.

"Can't you let it rest?" he urges his son.

"No," comes the blunt reply. "Do you buy that she's killing them to get back at Tanaka? Or do you think she's got direct beef with these other guys?"

Peter mulls it over. No, he doesn't buy it. But he knows too little to form a concrete opinion one way or the other.

"I haven't really delved into the other murders yet," he replies.

"You should."

Peter orders another beer, passing the order slip to the passing hostess with a polite nod. The noodle bar is morphing into a bustling, noisy pub. The doorway is now obscured by patrons.

"Look, Mikey," he says, "our job is to neutralize this woman, not empathize with her. She's a target, nothing more. Let's get this done, go home, and steer clear of Tanaka's affairs. Understood?"

"Yeah, I get it. But it's boring in here. At least you're out there in the thick of it."

The beer arrives, and Peter tips the hostess a crisp ¥10000 bill. The largest denomination in Japanese currency, it equates to about seventy dollars. She is visibly thrilled. Peter leans in and whispers in her ear in broken Japanese that he'd like her to keep his phone while he uses the restroom. She seems taken aback, but the generous tip soothes her concern, and she nods in agreement.

"Mikey, I gotta bounce," Peter says into the phone. "Stay low."

"You too."

Peter ends the call and hands the phone to the hostess.

"I'll keep it behind the bar," she offers.

"*Arigatō*," Peter says.

He doesn't really care where she puts the phone. He has no intention of coming back for it.

With the front door a no-go, Peter swiftly downs the remainder of the beer, rises from his seat, and navigates his way toward the rear of the bustling eatery. The narrow hallway, a forgotten artery amidst the restaurant's life, takes him past sign-laden restroom doors. His journey ends at the swinging entrance to the kitchen, a round window showcasing a cramped culinary arena beyond.

Directly opposite, he spies the door of an open fire

escape, its position burned into his memory from previous visits here during his CIA days. He takes advantage of the busy hostess pushing through the swing door, laden with a tray of steaming udon and sizzling teriyaki beef. As she maneuvers her way out with a deft back push against the door, he presses his body into an alcove beside it. His face is hidden as the door swings toward him, his presence unnoticed by the hostess through the round window. She trudges forward, oblivious to him, before she is out the other door, blending back into the restaurant's hustle.

Once the flapping door settles into a still silence, Peter peeks through the window. The chefs are engrossed in their culinary ballet, their backs shielding his path toward the fire exit opposite. Seizing the moment, Peter threads himself through the kitchen like a phantom wind, and he's free.

Dim streetlamps punctuate the murky alleyway, the edges lined with garbage cans, the ground shimmering with puddled reflections. The pulsing neon heartbeat of the city seeps in from both ends of the passage, but Peter resists the allure. Instead, he propels himself up the grimy brickwork of the opposite building, fingers finding purchase in the narrow crevices. After scaling two stories, a rust-eaten service ladder guides him to a flat roof, one leap away across the alley. He takes a run up and jumps the gap. His landing rattles the metal stairwell attached to the noodle bar building. Unfazed, he ascends to the top, the seventh floor.

Remaining discreet behind the protection of a large neon sign advertising a nearby Uniqlo store, Peter monitors the entrance to the noodle bar directly below. One of the men in the parked car grows restless as the crowd inside reveals Peter's vacant table. After a hasty call, a third man materializes from the crowded street, confirming a three-man operation.

An exchange of words at the car, and the newly arrived man forays into the noodle bar. He returns minutes later, the search party now three strong, and they march in together. Less than a minute later, Peter watches them emerge into the back alley, their tactical movements indicative of seasoned operatives. One of them brandishes the phone Peter left behind, an obvious tracker since it was handed to him on the plane by Akechi Akiyama.

From his eagle's nest, Peter observes the men scatter. Two of them go off in separate directions, while one lingers in the alley, engaged in a phone call. Despite the drone of the busy street, Peter deduces the operative is informing their superior about the evasive Azrael.

Five minutes tick by, and a call summons the lingering man back to the alley entrance. Peter tracks his exit onto the street and his return to the car. As the vehicle leaves, blending into traffic, Peter concludes that the remaining two operatives are still lurking in the vicinity. With this in mind, he makes his eastward escape via the rooftops.

Shibuya City wasn't his chosen location for its culinary offerings, but for its low-tiered rooftops. Unlike the towering edifices of Minato or Shinjuku wards, Shibuya features five and seven-story structures—residential and commercial—that enable easy rooftop navigation. Six blocks from the noodle bar, Peter descends into a quiet residential street fringed by clubs and pubs. The glow of a nearby 7-Eleven calls to him.

Inside the store, he retrieves a prepaid cell phone from a rack near the counter, purchasing it with cash to avoid using

Akechi's traceable credit card. Outside the store, he dials a number he's committed to memory.

"Who is this?" a voice questions after a few rings.

"It's me," Peter says.

"Hello, you," responds the man on the other end, his tone shifting. "What have you got?"

"The kid is in place."

SEVEN

NEW YORK CITY, ONE MONTH PRIOR

ONLY FOUR WEEKS AGO, PETER AND MICHAEL WERE spending their days in relative anonymity. That was until there was an unexpected knock at the door of their Brooklyn apartment. Early evening, the kid was out, so it was Peter who answered it.

"Oh, great," he muttered under his breath the second he saw through the spyhole who it was standing in his hallway. Reluctantly, he swung the door open.

Standing outside his door were two familiar faces. Their names were Ben Knight and Kirsty Lang. Knight, a tall, graying figure from the CIA, was one of the few individuals from Peter's time in espionage who had earned his trust. Lang was his youthful prodigy fast-tracked into the CIA's Unit-Seven while still working on her Master's in Computer Programming at MIT. Her distinct dyed-gray hair had a strand matching the pink shade of the bubble gum she was chewing.

"Hey, Peter," she greeted.

Peter didn't respond. Instead, he fixed his gaze on Knight.

"Peter," Knight began, his voice carrying the tone of an apology. "May we come in?"

"Why didn't you call ahead?" Peter retorted.

"Would you have answered if we did?" Knight countered, to which Peter responded with a noncommittal shrug.

"So can we?" Knight added. "Come in?"

Peter had three words: "What's this about?"

Knight went deadly serious. "We need your help."

Peter sighed long and hard. Despite his misgivings, he stepped aside and allowed them in, if only to hear what they had to say. Why they needed his help.

The apartment was modestly sized—comprising a living room with an adjoining kitchenette, two bedrooms, a bathroom, and a hallway complete with a closet. As the guests settled in, Knight's eyes wandered to the book Peter had left open on an armchair, Miyamoto Musashi's *The Book of Five Rings*.

"That must be a coincidence," Knight murmured, glancing up from the book.

"What's that?" Peter asked, settling down across from his guests in the armchair.

"Never mind," Knight waved off the question. "Where's the kid?"

"Attending community college."

"Cool," Kirsty Lang chimed in. "What's he studying?"

"His high school diploma," Peter informed her in a dry undertone.

She had nothing to say to this, and the room fell silent. Despite the closed windows, the low hum of city life permeated the apartment. Located in Brooklyn Heights, the street outside was bustling at this hour.

"Nice place you got here," Knight remarked.

"It's tolerable," Peter responded tersely. "Hardly Sorrento. But then, after the government took all our money, we had to come here and get regular jobs. Didn't we, Ben?"

"That wasn't my call, Peter," Knight defended himself. "The powers that be saw fit to scrub your records clean, consider Paul Adams and Michael Henderson as deceased, and provide new identities and citizenships to you both. Nevertheless, they weren't willing to let you keep the wealth gained through illicit activities."

"We earned that money," Peter snarled.

Lang chuckled beside her boss, remarking, "By assassinating people."

Peter turned a frosty look on her. "You mean the same job I used to perform for the US Government? The same job you've probably come here to ask me to perform?"

Caught off guard, Lang recoiled.

Attempting to dissolve the tension, Knight asked, "What work are you into now?"

"Construction," Peter informed him. "Seems to be the only job we're qualified for apart from killing."

"And where are you working right now?"

"On Manhattan Island. You know the redevelopment project on East 34th Street?"

"I do. You like it?"

"Like I said," Peter replied dryly, "it's tolerable."

"And," Kirsty Lang interjected, "Michael works there, too?"

Agitated, Peter sat forward in his armchair, his eyes narrowed on his former boss. "Look, if you really want to know, he's part of a painting crew, and I man a jackhammer all day. It gives me pains in my arms, and he can't ever get the smell of paint out of his nose. But that's not what you've both come about. So please, for the love of God, get to your point."

Knight sighed. "You're right. We are here to ask you to kill someone. Possibly more than one. But let me assure you..."

Peter raised a hand to cut him off.

"No jobs," he said.

The two CIA operatives could do little more than gawk at him.

"Peter," Knight resumed, his voice dropped to an almost grave register, "this isn't any ordinary run-of-the-mill job we're asking of you."

"I made myself clear to both you and Nash after our little escapade in Rome: The kid and I are done. You and your government cronies pardoned me. You swept under the rug a laundry list of crimes that could have seen me strapped to the electric chair. You seized all our assets. Fine. We're square. Just let us be. But this"—he leaned in, jabbing a finger toward Ben Knight—"this isn't letting us be."

"But Peter—"

"No, Ben. I stated plainly to both you and Nash that I was done. That *we* were done. Whatever predicament you find yourselves in, you have an arsenal of capable people at your disposal. Green Berets, Navy SEALs. You're the damn United States Government. Assign any one of your officially sanctioned killers to do it."

"We can't."

"Then find someone else. Not me. Not the kid."

"But you're tailor-made for this assignment."

"Why?"

"Because the target has specifically requested you."

The room's temperature seemed to plummet.

Peter found himself involuntarily scowling. "The target *requested* me?"

"You and the kid."

"But he's the target? How does he request his own killer?"

"May we explain?"

A tense silence filled the room as the two men locked eyes. Finally, Peter reclined in his seat and motioned for Knight to continue. Explain. "But I'm still not on board," he added.

It was Kirsty Lang who elaborated. "Have you ever heard the name Koji Tanaka?"

"Really rich Japanese guy," Peter returned.

"That's about the gist of it. Or at least, that's the extent of what any Internet-savvy individual would know from his Wikipedia page or the myriad of Forbes features. They hardly scrape the surface of the details I'm about to share. Peter, Koji Tanaka isn't just Japan's richest person. No, Koji Tanaka is the world's largest biological and chemical weapons manufacturer, as well as its second largest black-market arms trafficker."

"Is Japan aware of this?"

"It's irrelevant," Lang told him. "Tanaka reigns supreme in Japan. He is the primary economic benefactor to the country's ruling party, a party that, I should add, has been in power for the last seventeen years."

"But Japan is an ally of the United States, a global ally of NATO. If international law is being violated, they're obliged to intervene."

"No NATO member is in jeopardy. The sovereignty of a country isn't under threat. There's no feasible method of pressuring the Japanese in this situation, particularly not against their own interests. Tanaka-Corp is the third largest employer in Japan. Its tax revenue contributes almost ten percent to the country's GDP. The Japanese government has been, at best, uncooperative, claiming that the matter is beyond their jurisdiction."

"How can it be beyond their jurisdiction?"

"Because Tanaka's weapons labs aren't located in Japan. They're on an island privately owned by him. A loophole in local law situates the island outside the boundary of the nearest prefecture, and thus it isn't subject to Japanese law."

"Convenient," Peter dryly observed.

That was Knight's cue to interject.

Leaning forward on the couch, he fixed Peter with a sincere look. "Every attempt to open a case against Tanaka has failed," he confessed. "Our best shot is to infiltrate his operation and collect intelligence from within. If we can penetrate his facility, then we can acquire evidence of his criminal activities. That way, the Japanese will then be cornered into taking action, or at the very least, cede control to the United States."

"And you want me to infiltrate this facility?"

"No," Knight asserted, maintaining eye contact. "We want to get Michael inside."

Peter's eyes bulged at the proposal.

"Absolutely not," he snapped instantly.

"Please, just hear us out."

"No!"

"Peter, please," Kirsty Lang interposed. "Michael has proven his mettle in situations like this before. We're fully aware of his exploits in the Ukraine, Rome. If there's any eighteen-year-old who could hold his own on an island like Shinoshima, it's Michael Black."

"He's only just started to lead a normal life," Peter countered. "He's only just begun sleeping through the night without being woken up by nightmares. The panic attacks have dwindled to once every few months. I acknowledge that I'm as responsible for that as anyone, but now I just want us to live a..."

It was then that Ben Knight interjected with two words that congealed the blood in Peter's veins:

"Murak Din."

It had been years since Peter had heard those two words uttered—and with them, the visceral images they brought forth. Like an awful secret being revealed anew, Peter recoiled at the mental onslaught of sights, sounds, and smells.

Murak Din wasn't a person. It was a location. A small, jungle-enshrouded village in Myanmar's Rakhine district. Instantly, Peter was transported back there.

He is trudging toward the eerie stillness that has replaced the usual cacophony of life. When he'd been here the day before, the small village had been alive with the hustle and bustle of communal living. It has now fallen under an unnerving silence.

He approaches the edge of the village cautiously, his heart sinking as he takes in the scene. His boots crunch on the leaf-strewn ground, the only sound in a sea of silence. The rest of the world seems to recede, swallowed by the encompassing hush.

Homes stand empty, devoid of their usual vibrant life; a deserted playground echoes the laughter of children now lost. A tethered goat lies motionless on the ground, its eyes frozen in an eternal stare. Birds have fallen mid-flight, their colorful feathers dulled and splayed across the ground. The lush greenery around the village, once vibrant and flourishing, has turned into a lifeless gray, mirroring the cruel fate of its inhabitants.

As he moves farther into the village, he comes across a scene that stops him cold. A mother lies on the ground, her body curled protectively around her small child. Her eyes, wide and vacant, stare at the baby nestled in her arms, as if she had been trying to shield him from the invisible killer that has swept through this place.

Peter feels his heart tighten, his experienced, war-toughened exterior crumbling in the face of this overwhelming grief. The mother's fingers are entwined with her child's, a lasting symbol of their love, a poignant connection that even death has failed to sever.

The tragedy is palpable in every corner of the village, a testament to the unseen horror of chemical warfare. It is a sight that will be etched into his memory forever, a bitter reminder of the existence of evil.

"Are you saying," Peter started as the three of them sat in

the living room of his Brooklyn apartment, "that this Koji Tanaka guy is behind Murak Din?"

"That's exactly what I'm saying," Ben Knight confirmed. "Not only did Tanaka's company develop the weapon, but he personally brokered a deal with the country's junta for access to the region."

That's when Peter became aware he was gripping the arms of his chair. The leather squealed and groaned under the intensity of his violent grip. Murak Din had seared an indelible scar onto Peter's soul. A grim reminder of the profound depths to which human cruelty can plunge. Particularly the segments of humanity that we often revere the most.

And it wasn't solely the fact that these individuals could be so callous and brutal that rattled Peter. It was their blithe indifference. The way they could witness the world ablaze from their gilded perches and not feel an ounce of empathy. Their sole concern revolved around amassing power—dodging culpability. And because they wielded such immense authority, they were virtually invulnerable.

But not always.

"All right," Peter finally responded. "I'm on board. But I can't guarantee the kid will be."

———

AFTER HIS EVENING CLASS, Michael returned home, and Peter meticulously recapped the meeting's details, delving into the chilling tale of Murak Din. By this point, Ben Knight and Kirsty Lang had long since departed.

At the end of Peter's recital, Michael exhaled a lengthy sigh. Then, "Did she ask about me?"

"Did who ask about you?" Peter replied, perplexed.

"Kirsty."

Peter rolled his eyes, incredulous. "Jesus, Mikey. I've just relayed all of that grim stuff, and your first concern is skirt?"

Undeterred, Michael persisted, "Well, did she?"

Peter was blunt in his response: "No. Now can we focus on what's critical? What's your answer?"

Michael's expression shifted to a more solemn one. "This is incredibly dangerous."

"I'm aware," Peter replied. "The plan might not unfold as they envisage. There are countless variables."

"This Tanaka guy specifically requested us?"

"He did. His associates are already trying to locate us. He seems adamant about recruiting us to eliminate some woman, and apparently, he doesn't appreciate refusal."

"And Knight and Kirsty truly believe he'll resort to abduction if you decline the offer? That he'll take me as leverage?"

"It seems that way."

Knight and Kirsty Lang had thoroughly discussed the plan before their departure. At this point, Yūki Yokashina had only executed the first man, Ishi Watanabe. Only hours after receiving his friend's disembodied face, Tanaka had sent his operatives on a global search for Azrael and his apprentice. When Knight learned about this detail, he felt compelled to bring it to Peter's attention.

"And they're certain," Michael asked Peter, "that he'll detain me on his island? Not somewhere else?"

"He's resorted to the same thing before, and the island is

perfect for it. He's outside of any country's jurisdiction. Ben said there have been at least three such instances. Once, when Tanaka aimed to acquire a stubborn shareholder's stake in a company, he kidnapped the man's family and held them on his island until the shares were transferred to Tanaka-Corp."

"And Knight thinks he'll use me the same way?"

"That appears to be the assumption. However, you won't be alone in this."

"I won't?"

"No. You'll have help inside Shinoshima."

"Help?"

"Yes. The CIA has a mole in Tanaka-Corp who has been feeding them information."

"Then why doesn't Knight use *him* for this?"

"I don't know. I didn't ask. But whoever they do have on the inside will be helping you."

Michael pondered it all for a moment, biting his lip. Then he let out a long sigh and said, "After what he did in Myanmar, I don't think I can refuse. This Tanaka character certainly has it coming."

"Then I'll call Knight," Peter said, retrieving his phone from the arm of the chair. "Get the ball rolling. They want us established in Japan within a week. Make Tanaka and his cronies think they've found us hidden there. It will alleviate suspicion if it's them approaching us. It's like I always say: the best cons are the ones where you get the mark to do all the chasing."

EIGHT

SHINOSHIMA, ONE MONTH LATER

IN THE DARKNESS, MICHAEL LIES SPRAWLED across his bunk, ears finely attuned to the sounds of his underground prison. Over two weeks of meticulous planning with the CIA's elite—including lessons from an infamous escape artist with sixteen maximum-security prison breaks under his belt—has heightened his senses to an almost predatory level. Every noise, every smell, every subtle change is an opportunity to understand his environment better.

Michael spends these solitary hours familiarizing himself with the unique rhythm of his surroundings. The adjacent room, divided from his cell by several panes of one-way mirrored glass, often hosts a vigilant guard who persistently monitors him, despite the ubiquitous camera nested in the corner of his cell.

The clinking of the glass panels rattling ever so slightly in their frame signals the comings and goings of the watchman in the next room, a subtle dance dictated by changes in air pressure as doors open and close in the bunker's airtight environment. Even the ventilation system offers valuable insight, acting as an unintentional auditory conduit and olfactory channel. The murmur of conversation, the scent of a meal—these small pieces of information paint a larger picture of his captivity.

This is how he knows that when the watch changes, the room is often left unattended for a while, freeing him from prying eyes. During these brief intervals, he bides his time, cataloging the patterns and waiting for the perfect window of opportunity.

Just as a spider detects the faintest tremor on its web, Michael is currently tuned into every nuance of his surroundings. It's six a.m.—the time when the guards change shifts. A soft clinking emanates from the panels, punctuating the silence as the door in the adjacent room opens, then closes. Muffled conversation in a language alien to him trickles down from the vent above. Minutes later, silence reigns again.

Now is the time.

In a hurry, he bolts upright, crosses the cell, and activates the computer. A single press of the mouse initiates the prearranged program.

The lock on the door yields with an audible click. Freedom is just on the other side. Stepping into the narrow corridor, he takes note of the other cells. No time for peeking through spyholes; he needs to keep moving.

Pausing at a corner, he presses his back against the cool

wall and sharpens his senses. Above, the hum of the ventilation system is a constant drone that mixes with the soft buzz of the strip lights. He retraces the memorized map in his mind: a long corridor, a left turn, a right, then stairs spiraling down.

He rounds the corner and a set of double doors come into view. They are only accessible with fingerprint ID. His, supposedly, have been added to the system. Michael's heart hammers in his chest as he presses his thumb onto the scanner, a yellow line rhythmically scanning up and down. It blinks green, and the locks withdraw with a hiss.

"So far, so good," he murmurs to himself, stepping into the next stage of his daring escape.

Soon he reaches a stairwell. Level B-5 is printed on the wall in huge characters. He needs B-35, so he begins descending, making sure to go easy, keeping his ear to the wind. CCTV cameras stick out on every floor, watching the stairs; or at least they would if the CIA contact hadn't broken into the system and now has them playing footage from the last hour over and over on a loop. The same goes for the camera in his cell.

The contact had also managed to grant him unsupervised access to his cell's computer, providing a means to connect to an online messaging board. It was on this platform that he communicated with Kirsty Lang, who informed him that the contact would disable the security at six a.m. Furthermore, a package had been discreetly placed inside Shinoshima for him to retrieve.

Michael is heading to it now—the "something" left by their inside man.

Slowly and cautiously, he drops through the floors when

a door opens somewhere below, stirring the air. He presses himself against the wall as two men step into the stairwell a floor beneath him and begin ascending. Just as he considers retreating, another door opens, and a person enters from the level above.

Caught between two converging forces, panic bubbles within him as he tries to unlock the door with his thumbprint. The sensor flashes red twice, refusing to disengage the lock. He can see the men below approaching, and the one above is a mere ten steps away.

Taking in a calming breath, he slows his racing mind. The problem is simple: He needs to hold his thumb against the sensor for longer. As he adjusts his approach, the lock finally clicks open, and with heart-stopping timing, just as all three men converge on his level, Michael slips through the door, out of their line of sight.

Now he finds himself in a new corridor, wider and curving—a service tunnel. This part of the facility is uncharted territory for him, a place he hadn't spent all day memorizing from plans the contact sent to him via the computer. He is straying from the mapped route seared into his memory. It's unclear whether this detour will lead him to the contact's package, and the farther he travels, the stronger the feeling of being lost grows.

Despite his uncertain surroundings, Michael pushes onward, trying to recall the intricate details of the facility's map and the key locations Kirsty Lang had highlighted during their exchange.

Just as disorientation begins to mount toward frustration, a familiar sight emerges from the gloom: a hospital ward, its long window revealing a dormant world of medical machinery. Recalling the ward from his time going over the maps, Michael orients himself and finds his way toward a nearby stairwell leading to his desired location, the ominous silence of the service tunnel reverberating with the hiss of conditioned air and the buzz of artificial lighting.

Michael finally reaches B-35, a section distinguished by its heightened security measures. Blast-proof, hermetically sealed double doors stand guard, demanding a retinal scan for entry. Thankfully, the contact has placed those on the system, too.

They lead to another set of double doors, and he is shut in. Quarantine protocols douse him in a cloud of disinfectant from a network of grills, and after enduring the minute-long decontamination, a green light signals his entry into the realm of pristine laboratories.

The sterile environment of B-35 with its dazzlingly white walls, floor, and ceiling is momentarily blinding. It takes a few moments for his eyes to adjust, and when they have, Michael begins counting down the doorways until he reaches the one he seeks, an automatic, windowless panel.

It admits him into a room lined with hazmat suits resembling spacemen hanging in a dungeon. Amidst these sentinels of safety, he finds suit number eight, the one Kirsty indicated holds the essential item from the contact.

Hidden within the suit's left arm is a GoPro Hero Eleven, the world's most portable GPS camera, capable of capturing high-quality video and storing a vast amount of data, and which also embeds each file with a digital time-stamp and geographical location. There is also a USB lead for charging and data transfer.

Once Michael has familiarized himself with the GoPro,

he dresses in one of the hazmat suits and sets off. His understanding of Japanese characters is virtually nonexistent, so he resorts to counting the doors from the changing room, a navigational strategy engraved in his memory.

Finally, he arrives at the one he wants. The door is adorned with several warning signs in a medley of yellow and red. The most notable, written in Roman characters, reads *BSL-4*, which denotes biosafety level four—the utmost level of precaution taken in microbiological laboratories for handling deadly, easily aerosol-transmitted agents with no available vaccines or treatments.

After a clumsy attempt to maneuver the GoPro with gloved hands, Michael manages to take a photo. With newfound mastery over the device, he switches it to video mode and enters the room.

Inside, automatic lights flicker to life, revealing a pristine, white laboratory. Michael pans the camera around, capturing microbiological safety cabinets, a large fume hood in the center, and workbenches laden with petri dishes, glass vials, and test tubes.

Each detail he meticulously records.

With the mental blueprint of the lab firmly in mind from the planning phase, Michael heads straight to a Kirsch pharmaceutical refrigerator. Almost as tall as him, the refrigerator is filled with plastic drawers that house an array of dark contents—Yersinia pestis, botulinum toxin, aggressive kappa particles, lysins, ricin, smallpox, and countless toxins, each labeled meticulously. Every item and even the contents table on the door are captured on camera.

Suddenly, the GoPro's time display yanks Michael back

to the present. He curses as he realizes he has a mere seven minutes to return to his cell before the camera in there switches back to a live feed.

NINE

TOKYO

THE FIRST RAYS OF DAWN HAVE BARELY KISSED THE sky when Akechi Akiyama and his two associates storm a timeworn "love hotel" tucked away in a corner of Shinjuku ward. Bathed in the lurid glow of green and purple neon signage, the entrance invites them into a world garishly embellished in vibrant and surreal hues. They step into a lobby painted in an ultraviolet glow by the lighting, where a clerk remains concealed behind a curtained counter—an artful and eccentric dance of anonymity that characterizes these types of establishments in Japan.

Upon hearing Akechi's introduction, the clerk abruptly shoves aside his chopsticks and bowl of shabu shabu and rips open the curtain. Seeing the three stern men standing in his lobby, he gives a polite but hurried bow before scurrying away from his post.

"He's in room five on the third floor," the clerk discloses

in a whisper, handing Akechi the key. "I switched the elevator off, and all the fire escapes are locked."

With the hotel on lockdown, Akechi and his team ascend to the third floor. The two men with him are ex-SOG operatives. Highly trained, they approach the room with their Heckler & Koch USP pistols ready. Taking positions either side of the door, one of the men takes the keycard and taps it on the sensor. A click of a lock, and they flood into the room.

The lights are on. The room is modest—a lounge area, an ensuite bathroom, and a double bed. It is here where Peter Black lounges on a stack of pillows, nursing a cup of coffee. The sight of him is greeted with the deadly points of the operatives' guns.

"What took you so long?" Peter quips as Akechi joins them.

Despite the question, Akechi remains silent, coming to a stop at the end of the bed, leaning with both hands on his cane.

Peter shrugs. "You want coffee? I brought enough for everyone."

Silence is still Akechi's response, his men's guns unflinching.

"You think," Peter begins, "I'd book into one of the busiest hotels in the whole of Japan under my own name if I didn't want you to find me?"

Akechi finally speaks, commanding his men to wait outside and leaving him alone with Peter. After helping himself to a cup of coffee, he pulls up a chair beside the bed.

"Why did you run?" Akechi asks.

"I didn't exactly run," Peter responds with a hint of defiance. "I merely ditched your surveillance team. I don't like being followed."

He retrieves his cup from the bedside table and nonchalantly sips it.

"You must understand things from our end, Azrael-san," Akechi says, his voice like iron. "You are a dangerous animal. A tiger. And when you take the tiger's cub, you must be wary of it coming after you."

Peter speaks just as firmly. "No more following. I'll do your shitty job, but only if you leave me to do it."

Akechi drinks a little more of his black coffee, pressing the cup to his thin lips. Then, "Okay. I can agree with that. Now"—his tone changes, becoming darker—"pay attention, Azrael-san. I'm about to give you Yūki's next target. It is a man named Haiko Shusaku."

"Tell me about him."

Akechi explains that Haiko is a notorious playboy with an equally infamous reputation as one of Japan's most celebrated stockbrokers and investors. He has a knack for the markets, yet his real passion is his pursuit of the opposite sex.

"And I take it Haiko knows nothing about what's coming for him?" Peter asks.

"No. And you are forbidden from telling him. The more obvious a target he makes, the more easily Yūki can be drawn into the open."

"And how do you suppose I'll be around this Shusaku guy when that happens?"

The glimmer of a smile creeps onto Akechi's lips. "Haiko's personal security team has just had a position come available," he explains, "and you're in luck. Tanaka-shachou has personally recommended you for the job."

TEN

TOKYO

Peter arrives for his first day of work with Haiko Shusaku in a Mitsubishi Evo X. A beast of a car, it is agile and powerful and makes a statement. As he drives it into the city, he thinks about the day ahead, protecting a man who lives on the top three floors of Tokyo's most exclusive skyscraper: Toranomon Hills Residential Tower in Minato ward.

Peter doesn't leave the car with the building's valets. Instead, he parks on one of the surrounding streets. He gets out, pops the trunk, opens a small carry case that sits inside, and retrieves the FN 509 Tactical 9mm pistol sunk into the foam mounting within. Tucking it into an underarm holster he wears beneath his charcoal bespoke suit jacket, he adds a spare mag, a tiny can of mace, a compact taser, and night vision goggles to his arsenal, the inside of the Savile Row-made jacket fitted out to carry each item as inconspicuously as possible.

Prepared for anything, he heads inside the towering glass edifice of Toranomon Hills. Crossing the checkered marble floor of the lobby, Peter takes in the minimalist elegance of the space. When he reaches the service desk, the pretty clerk sitting behind it asks him to wait, and as he settles into a comfortable armchair, he is about to ask himself what he is even doing here when a tall Japanese man saunters up and says, "Peter-san?"

And so his first day begins.

Peter gets up from the chair, stepping forward to extend a hand in greeting. However, the man before him doesn't take the hand. Instead, he bows respectfully. Peter, slightly taken aback, withdraws the outstretched hand and gives a subtle nod instead of returning the bow.

"Follow me," the man instructs, guiding Peter toward the elevators.

Inside the lift, he introduces himself as Shin Ishimora, the head of Haiko Shusaku's personal security. "I understand you do not speak Japanese," he inquires as the elevator ascends toward the top of the building.

"That's correct," Peter confirms.

A faint grunt escapes Shin's lips, followed by a muttered curse in Japanese. "Most of my team do not speak English," he complains disdainfully. "Only myself and one other do. This will complicate matters. It's a pity that the boss can't say no to Tanaka. No matter how dumb his suggestions."

"Listen," Peter interjects, eager to set the tone early, "I'll do my best to comply with your directives and to safeguard Shusaku-san, but..."

"Shachou," Shin corrects him gently. "He prefers 'shachou.' It's more respectful than 'san.'"

"All right, I'll do my best to protect Shusaku-shachou."

Shin sighs, clearly skeptical. And he has every reason to be; Peter, of course, doesn't intend to defend Haiko Shusaku's life. His primary role is to be vigilant for any threats to it, much like a fisherman patiently waiting with a baited hook—and just like the fisherman, he feels nothing for the worm or its life.

"How come Tanaka was employing you anyway?" Shin says before adding, "I never knew he took on *gaijin*."

Gaijin: foreigner.

"I was more of a subcontractor," Peter responds.

"Curious. First a woman, now an American. Tanaka-shachou certainly has eclectic tastes."

"A woman?"

"Yes, Koji Tanaka's personal bodyguard used to be a woman. A beautiful woman. And she was pretty tough, too," he says, fixing Peter with a less-than-impressed look. "Tougher than you, I bet," Shin states nonchalantly before returning his gaze to the ascending numbered lights. They're close.

Reaching forward, he punches the stop button, the elevator obediently grinding to a halt.

"Why have we stopped?" Peter inquires.

Shin turns to face him, an expression of gravity etched into his features. "Before you meet the boss," he declares, "there's something I ought to tell you. The guys upstairs will likely make you sign a non-disclosure agreement, but I think it's important you hear this straight away. The boss has certain... eccentricities."

Akechi had vaguely mentioned this during his briefing on Haiko Shusaku back at the love hotel, but Peter still prompts Shin to elaborate.

Shin's mouth twists into a hint of a smile. "Our boss is a remarkable individual," he says. "He has a keen eye for business opportunities and a knack for empire building. But his discerning eye doesn't stop there."

"Where *does* it stop?"

"You know the boss is seventy-two, right?" Shin's fleeting smile returns.

Peter nods in agreement.

"So despite his years, his taste in women hasn't aged since he was a much, much younger man. And his appetite... well, let's just say it's hearty. You're going to encounter a lot of unclothed women."

"So it's not all bad, then."

Shin shakes his head solemnly. "Don't even think about it. The boss is remarkably possessive. One lingering glance at his women could land you in hot water."

"One of *his women*," Peter mutters to himself.

"And that's not all. There are other aspects that could be detrimental to the boss's image. Our responsibility extends beyond physical security. We must also prevent the outside world from discovering certain... practices."

"Practices?" Peter questions with raised eyebrows.

Shin grimaces, seemingly uncomfortable with the ensuing explanation. "In certain intimate matters, the boss requires... assistance."

"Assistance?"

"Yes, there's someone who... facilitates." Shin's eyes bore into Peter's.

"So Haiko-shachou requires help... for sex?"

"More often than not, he's merely a spectator. But when he needs to... participate, then Benny steps in."

"Benny?"

"That's right. You'll meet him shortly."

"Is that everything?"

"Pretty much." Shin exhales a long, weary sigh before resuming the elevator's ascent.

The apartment is stunning, featuring a fish pond in the lobby replete with golden koi drifting lazily among waterlilies, set off by a charming little waterfall.

Shin guides Peter deeper into the luxurious residence. As they proceed, they encounter a series of stunning young women, casually draped about the premises. Arrayed across the furniture, they lounge or stroll about in an assortment of lingerie, some of them simply in the nude. Their languid movements are evocative of wildcats; they sip champagne, some of them snorting what Peter presumes to be cocaine off a silver platter. The sounds of sensual moans usher them into a grand lounge.

The room's design features a sunken central section in the shape of an oval, accessible via a few steps. Plush sofas line the edges, and a bed, seamlessly integrated into the floor, takes center stage. On it, three women are intertwined in various stages of intimacy, their bodies gleaming with perspiration under the soft light. They are an unlikely trio—a fiery redhead, a dark-skinned African woman, and a sultry brunette. It's an explicit scene that might be found in the fantasies of a hormonal teenager, easily accessible online. Yet men with as much wealth as Haiko Shusaku can bring such fantasies to life.

Peter scans their faces quickly.

None of them are Yūki Yokashina. Nor were any of the women he passed on his journey to this room.

Occupying a sofa with a clear view of the spectacle is an elderly man, Haiko Shusaku. His gaze, like that of a predator, is fixed on the performance while his fat-lipped mouth slackens, his tongue protruding. The image of a lecherous toad springs to Peter's mind. In one hand, Shusaku holds a fat cigar, in the other, a wineglass.

At the other end of the sofa, a muscular man with a well-sculpted physique lounges, engrossed in his phone, seemingly indifferent to the carnal display before him.

This, Peter concludes, must be Benny.

The women involved in the erotic performance seem oblivious to the newcomers. The lascivious scene continues unabated. Shin instructs Peter to halt at the top of the stairs leading to the central pit. Peter complies, and Shin goes to his master, proceeding to converse with Shusaku in hushed tones.

The elderly man glances up at Peter, smiling at the foreigner with the ashen hair and steel-gray eyes. "Come. Come." He beckons with a liver-spotted hand.

Peter makes his way to him, keeping his gaze locked on the old man and steadfastly ignoring the writhing dance of flesh. When he is within a few steps, Shusaku halts him with a raised hand.

With his English limited to "come," Shusaku relies on Shin to interpret. As the old man mutters, Shin translates. "The boss extends a warm welcome. If you are comfortable with the current arrangement, he hopes you will become an integral part of the household."

Both men pause as a crescendo of moans signals a climax in the ongoing performance. Shusaku grumbles, apparently miffed at having missed the full enjoyment of the moment.

Resuming his discourse, Shin adds, "Shusaku-shachou has a trial period of three months. If at the end of this period he deems the fit to be right, you will be welcomed as part of the family. However"—both Shin and his boss's voices go harsh—"if you so much as stare at one of his women, you will be cast out from his home. With that"—the voices brighten once more—"Shusaku-shachou welcomes you."

With the introduction concluded, Peter bows, and they leave, Shin escorting him to meet the rest of the team. They comprise six men, all appearing as reserved and indifferent to Peter as Shin. The most he receives by way of greeting are a few grunts and cursory nods.

In Japanese, Shin discusses the newcomer's duties with the others, and although Peter doesn't speak the language, he can piece together enough to understand that they've assigned him to patrol the perimeter—he'll essentially be a night watchman. There's a smattering of laughter when one of them jokes about providing him with a flashlight and a whistle.

They've chosen to keep Peter out of the way, to sideline him—a decision he finds perfectly agreeable. It will, after all, provide him ample opportunity to explore the grounds and to look for wrathful women with lethal intentions.

———

THE NEXT FEW hours of the day go by in a blur. Shin takes Peter on a tour of the property, pointing out key areas he needs to patrol, and introducing him to the small army of domestic staff who keep the place running. Peter, for his part, takes everything in with a studied calm. He notes the locations of cameras, alarm systems, potential weak spots in the perimeter, and other relevant details, essentially trying to figure out how Yūki Yokashina could possibly gain access.

Once this is finished, Shin leaves Peter to patrol several of the floors. The second he is left alone, Peter finds somewhere private and makes a telephone call.

Answering after three rings, Peter doesn't wait for Akechi to speak.

"I need something," he says into the phone.

"What thing?"

"How quickly can you source a one-parachute system?"

"What is that?"

"Basically the type of parachute a base jumper uses."

"I think that can be done."

Peter stands on the fiftieth-floor observation deck in Toranomon Hills, gazing at the Tokyo cityscape. Dusk is upon the metropolis, and evening invades the streets and avenues. Tokyo is just beginning to turn neon.

"How soon can you have it ready?" he asks into the phone.

"A couple of hours. You're at Toranomon Hills?"

"Yes."

"What's your impression of Shusaku?"

Peter's eyebrows furrow. "Are we being social now?"

"It's merely a question."

"Does it matter? I thought you Japanese didn't do small talk."

"You mean we don't speak endlessly like you Americans?"

Peter ignores the jibe. "Just ensure I have the chute by tomorrow."

"It will be delivered to your location."

"Call me when it arrives."

As Peter is about to end the call, Akechi interjects, "Azrael-san?"

"What now?"

"What's your guess on her approach?"

Peter ponders on it, having done so ever since he arrived.

"Given the circumstances," he muses, "she might blend in with the women. Shin, the chief of security here, vets them thoroughly. I've examined their files. None of them are Yūki Yokashina. Plus, Shusaku seems to have a particular taste that doesn't include Asians."

"She could alter her appearance to appear more European."

"Not without it being noticeable. Most of these women walk around butt-naked. Any overuse of makeup or prosthetics would be easily scrutinized. She isn't among them."

"And the security? Any infiltrations?"

"You mean like you've done with me?"

"Yes, like you. There could be another plant."

Peter is considering the possibility when he notices a figure approaching. It's another member of Shusaku's security detail.

"I have to go, Akechi. Ensure your man calls as soon as he drops the parachute off."

Peter ends the call and turns to his newfound colleague.

Like him, the man is clad in a charcoal suit, but unlike the others, he seems less hostile, perhaps even a tad congenial.

"You're on patrol duty, I see," the man comments in English, halting beside Peter at the window of the observation deck.

"Yes. Just enjoying the view on my break. It's quite a city," Peter muses.

His companion gives the sprawling city a cursory glance. "It's a city, like any other. And, like any, it is teeming with corruption."

"Get enough people together," Peter returns, "and you're sure to get corruption."

The man offers a faint smile and extends a hand. "Akira."

"Peter."

Their hands meet in a firm shake.

"Is the party still raging upstairs?" Peter inquires.

"You mean the incessant orgy."

"I do. I was pretty relieved when they assigned me foot patrol."

"I've been here six months," Akira tells him, "and it's still overwhelming. Anyway, we shouldn't chat too long. I've been sent to fetch you. Shusaku is leaving for his favorite nightclub soon. Shin wants you to learn the ropes when moving the boss."

ELEVEN

TOKYO

THE ROPES ARE PRETTY SIMPLE. TWO BODYGUARDS maintain a close physical proximity to Haiko at all times, while four others maintain vigilance on the periphery. Before they disembark from Haiko Shusaku's exclusive elevator, the men call ahead to the lobby. The room is cleared so that only the doorman and two clerks remain, bowing deferentially as Haiko passes, the billionaire paying them no mind as he strides past in platform shoes, adding height to his compact five-foot-three stature.

They don't take the women. They are to stay inside the confines of the huge duplex with a pair of bodyguards overseeing them. Peter surmises it's probably to make sure they don't wreck the place, having already witnessed several instances of the young women losing control during drunken antics.

The building's own security detail have cordoned off the

entrance, and a limousine is waiting. Inside the back of it, two young women in cocktail dresses await, their profession quite obvious. Neither matches the description of Yūki Yokashina. They're tall, blond, likely Russian or Baltic, and they squeal in excitement as Haiko approaches the car.

"*Redīsu*," he greets in Japanese, opening his arms wide before ducking into the vehicle and throwing himself into a pair of silicon breasts.

The two men who will be sticking close to him get in also. Peter and Shin head to a separate car, and soon they are departing in a three-car convoy. Their destination is WOMB, a nightclub famous for its international DJ roster and wealthy clientele. Inside, Shusaku is received warmly, almost like an old friend. He is immediately escorted to the VIP area, accompanied by the towering women and four of his bodyguards. Peter and Shin don't join them. Instead, they monitor the club's security cameras from a control room in the basement. Each bodyguard is equipped with a communication earpiece connected to Shin's radio. Well, all except Peter, who wasn't given one.

"Pretty pointless for you, *gaijin*," Shin had said. "Not with everyone else speaking Japanese."

Peter spends the next hour poring over video feeds with Shin and the club's security officer, hoping to spot Yūki Yokashina. He yearns to find her quickly and avoid an extended assignment. Both Koji Tanaka and Akechi hinted at more targets beyond Haiko Shusaku, targets that appear to stand between Yūki and Tanaka. Peter has no desire for this mission to stretch into weeks or months or to serve a man like Tanaka any longer than necessary, especially given the megalomaniac's role in Murak Din.

The night wears on without any sign of Yūki. Clubgoers revel and indulge, women exploit men and vice versa, and any outbreaks of violence are swiftly quelled by the club's own security team. As for Shusaku, the elderly hedonist oscillates between burying his face in women's chests or a mound of cocaine. At seventy-two, Peter marvels at his endurance, questioning if his heart is made of iron. With things drawing on, he finds himself returning to the question that has nagged him constantly: What did these men do to Yūki Yokashina?

"What's that?" Shin's sharp voice rouses Peter from his thoughts.

Shin is clutching the radio, firing off instructions in Japanese to the rest of the team. He turns to Peter and asks, "You see it? Camera six."

Peter has already noticed. "They've got a gun," he states.

Shin remains in the security room, maintaining surveillance and communication, while Peter sets out, navigating a long service corridor. The thumping bass from the club resonates through the walls, the light fittings above quivering in response. Since they've allowed him to carry his own firearm, he unholsters his FN 509 Tactical from beneath his arm, deciding to forgo the suppressor. After all, a loud gunshot in a nightclub may come in handy.

He strides into the club, stepping onto a walkway that skirts the dance floor, which sits recessed in the center of the multi-tiered venue. Strobe lights and green lasers transform the dancers into twitching, angular silhouettes. No one pays Peter any mind as he traverses the throng, heading for the spot indicated by the security camera footage—a passageway near the cloakroom.

But it's empty.

As Peter wishes he had one of the earpieces, he spots another bodyguard moving along a balcony overhead, a hand to his ear, his brow furrowed in concentration. Peter wastes no time, weaving through a group of club-goers, gun held low and securely gripped. He climbs a set of stairs and trails along the balcony, heading in the same direction as the other bodyguard. The dark passage they traverse is dotted with alcoves holding tables and patrons. The VIP rooms are just ahead, guarded by two nightclub bouncers.

Emerging from the passage onto another dance floor, Peter spots the other bodyguard threading his way through a dense crowd near the DJ booth. It's clear he's approaching someone, but as Peter takes a closer look, he realizes the bodyguard is targeting the wrong person. The clothing is similar—easy to misidentify over the comms—but it's not their suspect.

Then Peter sees the true target. They're entering a door marked *Staff Only*. Thanks to a nightclub map he studied earlier, Peter knows there's a service corridor behind that door, connecting it to the VIP rooms.

He plunges into the crowd, heading straight for the door, entering the corridor just in time to see the target exiting through swinging doors into the VIP lounge.

Head down, Peter sprints into a space filled with roped-off booths where hostesses cater to the club's elite. A quick survey of the room locates the target, her pistol clearly visible.

Without hesitation, Peter points his FN Tactical at the ceiling and fires off a couple of hollow-point rounds into the air-conditioning. In this quieter section of the club, the deafening blasts have the desired effect: sparking panic and drawing the attention of the armed woman. She looks surprised when she sees Peter, then spins back toward Shusaku and raises her pistol—

Only to scream as a hollow point strikes the gun, sending it flying from her grip and shattering several bones in her hand.

Shusaku, having taken cover behind the two towering women, is now standing in his booth. The attacker, now unarmed, is crawling toward her fallen weapon. One body-guard reaches the gun first, while the other stays close to the boss.

Peter approaches, seizes her shoulder, and flips her onto her back.

Terror and hatred twist her features as she stares up at him. But one thing is certain.

She is not Yūki Yokashina.

————

THEY HAUL the girl out of the club, using the service corridors to slip unnoticed into an alley before shoving her into the back of one of their cars.

They're now driving through Tokyo, the woman wedged between Peter and Shin in the back seat, with two other men up front, one at the wheel. Meanwhile, their boss, Haiko Shusaku, rides in a limo back to the safety of the Toranomon Hills Residential Tower—back to his harem.

"We need to get her to a hospital," Peter insists for what feels like the hundredth time.

"No, we don't," Shin retorts.

"She needs someone to take a look at her hand," Peter argues.

The woman sits quietly, cradling the injured fist. Though her face is pale and sweat beads on her brow, she gives no sign of the intense pain she must be in.

"She'll live," Shin says dismissively.

The man in the passenger seat turns to them, grinning, and cracks a joke in Japanese that elicits laughter from the others. Peter understands enough to know the punchline: "Not for long."

"Look," Peter says, "we should at least take her to the police."

Shin doesn't respond.

To Peter's surprise, the woman smiles at his suggestion. She must understand English. She turns to Shin and, speaking in Japanese, queries if the *gaijin* realizes why they won't call the police.

Shin reacts swiftly. His hand flies out, striking her cheek and sending her sprawling into Peter's lap. Shin then roughly yanks her back up, hurling curses in her face.

She appears to be a strong, resilient young woman. There's no crying, no pleading—just silent defiance as she sits with her hair a mess and blood trickling from a split lip. She licks at the blood, a fiery smile spreading across her face, and Peter swears he sees flames in her eyes.

"I was fifteen," she declares in Japanese.

Shin moves to hit her again, but Peter's quicker. He grabs Shin's wrist, stopping the blow mere inches from her face.

Shin's glare is icy. He pulls his hand back and the two men lock gazes.

"You can let me out at the next corner," Peter says.

After a tense silence, Shin nods. He speaks to the driver in Japanese, and the car pulls over to the side of the road. They're on the outskirts of Tokyo, heading toward the Kawasaki docklands. The residential street they stop on is lined with tidy four-story apartment buildings, their miniature gardens and hedges impeccably manicured.

"This is gonna upset the boss," Shin sneers as Peter leaves the car. "You know that, right?"

Peter says nothing. With the door slamming shut behind him, he watches as the car speeds away. He notes the license plate, then heads for a residential parking lot nearby, pulling his phone out as he crosses the street.

"Mikey?" he says as soon as the call is answered.

The voice on the other end sounds groggy. "What time is it?"

"Nighttime. Look, I need you at the computer."

"Okay. Give me a second."

Peter strides into the bustling parking lot, a mosaic of cars and motorcycles. His eyes are drawn to a line of cars, where he locates a Toyota Prius, a model emblematic of Japanese roads. With the assistance of Akechi, he'd earlier obtained a universal digital key, a device capable of granting access to any Toyota Prius. This common, unassuming vehicle pervades virtually every parking lot across the country, the key transforming each into a vast, unofficial car-sharing network at Peter's disposal.

"Okay," Michael says into his ear as Peter gets into the Prius. "I'm ready. What do you need?"

"You said earlier that you can access Japanese CCTV.

Can you tap into the automatic license plate recognition system in Kawasaki Ward?"

"Easy," Michael replies. "One of Tanaka's guys showed me how to do it yesterday."

"Then I need you to trace a car for me."

"Let me take a look. What's the license plate number?"

"It's..."

———

THE GIRL'S name is Hana. Now twenty-six, she was ensnared by Haiko Shusaku at the tender age of fifteen.

She had been the daughter of a former boarding school friend of Shusaku's, an acquaintance that he exploited. From the moment he saw the young girl at a dinner party hosted by her parents, the letch became fixated on her. At that time, he was sixty-two and made it his mission to seduce her. Initially playing the role of a father figure, he feigned interest in her studies, leveraging his enormous wealth to provide opportunities her own parents could not.

As a gifted pianist, Hana was granted access to Juilliard through Shusaku's generosity, where he paid for world-class teachers to hone her talent. His limitless resources elevated her until she was adrift in a world far beyond her youthful comprehension. And then—Shusaku claimed his prize.

During her time at Juilliard, Shusaku cunningly proposed that she should reside in his Manhattan penthouse on Fifth Avenue. Unbeknownst to Hana, he planned to share this luxurious space with her. By the time she realized his true intentions, it was too late.

Over the weeks and months as her musical abilities

improved, her resolve weakened to the point where the spider saw it was time to bite. One week before her sixteenth birthday, Hana lost her virginity to a man forty-eight years older than herself. The experience had left her feeling numb.

After claiming her innocence, the old man's demeanor had shifted almost instantly into cruelty. Her private piano lessons, Juilliard, every privilege she enjoyed was held over her head as both a lure and a threat, and stranded in a foreign country, Hana was forced to comply with Shusaku's malevolent desires or face being cut off from everything.

The emotional toll proved too much. This relationship —her first venture into something resembling love—left Hana hollowed out. As her spirit diminished, so did her music. By seventeen, Hana's passion for the piano was extinguished; she stopped attending classes and began experimenting with drugs. It didn't take long for her to be expelled from Juilliard and for Shusaku to discard the shadow of the girl he'd broken. At eighteen, Hana was directionless. She returned to Japan only to be rejected by her family. From then on, she drifted aimlessly, falling into a recurring cycle of toxic relationships.

That was until three weeks ago when she spotted Haiko Shusaku in WOMB nightclub, the same club she'd just been dragged from. He was lounging in the VIP section with two young women, sipping champagne and laughing carelessly. Rage ignited within her, fueling a resolution for revenge. She took a job at the bar, ensuring her presence every night, waiting for Shusaku to return. She also procured a pistol from a yakuza contact, bringing it to work every night, waiting for her moment of retribution. Now that moment lay in ruins.

"We're here," Shin announces.

The car veers off the street into a warehouse parking lot, the distant lights of Kawasaki harbor and the clangor of unloading cargo ships filling the night air. They yank Hana from the car, marching her toward the warehouse. The windows are barricaded with corrugated iron sheets, suggesting the building is under renovation.

Shin produces a key and unlocks a set of double doors. They quickly guide Hana inside, plunging into near total darkness. A pungent mixture of mildew, decomposing fish, and pervasive dust taints the chilly air.

"Go start the generator," Shin instructs one of his men.

Acknowledging the order, the man vanishes into the dark. Hana hears the shrill protest of a rusty door hinge followed by the grating roar of a diesel generator sputtering to life.

As fluorescent strip lights stutter on overhead, they briskly escort her down a long corridor. Until now, Hana has been trapped in a fog of shock, but as they proceed, dormant panic gnaws at her insides, quickening her pulse and prickling her skin. Despite herself, she asks what they intend to do. Their response is chilling laughter.

The corridor ends at the main part of the warehouse. They usher her through another set of double doors into a vast space that amplifies her fear. A shipping container stands in the middle, its doors wide open, its interior resembling a prison cell.

Realization crashes over Hana like a frigid wave. She understands their intentions now.

"No!" she shrieks, wrenching her arm free of Shin's grasp.

She attempts to flee, but Shin's men swiftly intercept her. Her struggle is desperate but futile. One secures her upper body, the other her legs. Their combined strength easily carries her to the container.

"You were warned," Shin says coldly. "Now you will vanish. But not before we've had a little fun."

They carry her into the container, tossing her onto a dingy mattress. She tries to escape immediately, but they're ready. One man lifts her over his shoulder, undeterred by her flailing resistance, and returns her to the bed. As she tries to bolt a second time, he delivers a brutal punch to her mouth.

Dazed, Hana can only sit on the mattress and stare at the blurry, star-filled image of the three men, their ugly smiles piercing the fog of her concussion.

Shin seizes her by the arms, forcing them over her head. With a pair of handcuffs retrieved from his suit pocket, he secures her wrists to the bed's headboard, all while she watches in a stunned, vacant stupor.

Stepping back from their catch, Shin allows his mouth to form a sinister grin. Then the lights go out.

All of them.

The container, the warehouse, all of it is plunged into darkness. Hana can't help wondering if she has passed out, and it is as this thought crosses her hazed mind that the hum of the warehouse generator also winks out, leaving an oppressive silence in its wake.

The men begin to swear. Hana hears Shin's voice.

"It's probably out of gas," he says. "Go fill it up. You help him."

His two companions disappear, their diminishing footsteps following them across the warehouse and out the door.

There is silence once more. In the darkness, Hana can sense Shin there, watching her from the doorway. Panic claws at her chest, her heart pounding like a drum in the deafening quiet. Her breaths come in sharp, desperate gasps.

Then she hears it. The faintest of sounds, like the rustling of leaves in the wind, followed by a low, cautious tread on the floor. Hana freezes, her entire body rigid with terror.

The men are shouting now, their voices bouncing off the warehouse walls.

"What?!" Shin shouts back.

Hana can't quite make out what they're saying.

Shin shouts back to them, "What do you mean the generator is..."

There's the sound of scuffling, of something heavy hitting the floor, and then... silence again.

Suddenly, a hand covers her mouth, and she lets out a muffled scream. The hand is firm but not threatening, and a quiet voice whispers, "Don't scream. I'm here to help."

The hand releases her, and Hana gradually makes out a shadowy figure in the darkness. It's a man, his face obscured by a pair of NVGs, which he lifts up to show two eyes shining with a determined light. In the dimness, she can see he's holding a small device, which he quickly uses to pick the lock of her handcuffs.

The sounds of running footsteps and angry shouts resonate from somewhere outside the container. The men are coming back.

"There isn't much time," her rescuer says.

Pulling her up, he guides her out of the container to a back corner of the warehouse, where a door leads outside.

With a swift kick, he knocks it open, revealing a narrow alleyway.

Hana doesn't hesitate. She slips through the door, the man following close behind. They edge their way along the passage, the sound of their pursuers growing fainter and fainter by the second.

By the time the men reach the container, they find it empty. Hana is gone, swallowed up by shadow, leaving the men to curse and sputter in the empty warehouse. They've lost their prey in the darkness, and now, all they have is an empty cage and a feeling that someone has double-crossed them.

Shin lies unconscious just outside the door, snoring heavily and already sporting a swollen eye. Meanwhile, Hana and her mysterious rescuer disappear into the night.

———

It isn't until she's in the passenger seat of the Toyota that Hana realizes it's the same guy who shot the gun out of her hand.

As Peter aims the Prius down the dimly lit streets of Tokyo, Hana's heart surges with the adrenaline of their daring escape. She sits there trying to catch her breath, her arms wrapped tightly around her body, as if she is trying to hold on to her sanity. Her face is a battlefield of cuts and bruises, a testament to the torment she has endured.

Peter's seen enough in life to know that physical wounds are not the only ones she carries. Checking the hollow look on her face in the mirror, he can see a depth of pain in her eyes that goes far beyond skin and bone. It is a pain he knows all too well. A deep-seated wound that eats at the soul, inflicted by the worst kinds of monsters.

He pulls up outside a nondescript building, its façade barely more than a faded sign that reads *24 Hour Veterinary Clinic* in Japanese characters. Inside, a man named Hirako runs an illegal operation, patching up those who don't dare go to a regular hospital. Peter's knowledge of the place is a throwback to his years working for Pat Hughes' securities operation.

Peter helps Hana along, supporting her weight as they walk into the clinic. The interior is clean and well-lit, a stark contrast to the dingy exterior. Hirako, a lean man with sharp eyes, looks up from his desk.

He recognizes Peter right away. He doesn't ask any questions, doesn't even speak. He never does. With a nod, he ushers them into the back room, where he begins to tend to the broken bones of Hana's hand while she sits on an aluminum table usually reserved for animals.

As Hirako works away in silence, Peter takes a seat beside her. He offers her his hand, and she takes it firmly with her good one, grasping her fingers into his.

"I'm sorry," he says.

Hirako fills a syringe with a local anesthetic, and Peter watches Hana flinch as the needle pierces the skin, the pain momentarily flashing in her eyes before she quickly suppresses it. He squeezes her hand in a silent promise that he is there for her, that she doesn't have to endure this alone.

After a long silence, Hana finally speaks, her voice barely more than a whisper. "I was fifteen," she begins, "when Haiko first noticed me. My parents were so proud, so flattered that such a wealthy man would take an interest in their daughter."

Her words flow like a bitter stream, the story of a young girl with dreams and aspirations, gradually twisted and corrupted by a man of power and influence. How he had seduced her, manipulated her, and ultimately ruined her life. And how her parents, blinded by their ambition and greed, had let it all happen.

She tells him about the life she had lost, the music that had once been her passion, now a painful reminder of a more hopeful time, before Haiko, when her future seemed destined for something so much more than *this*.

As she speaks, Peter feels a rage begin to bubble and boil within him. A rage against the man who has destroyed this young woman's life, who has caused such pain and suffering. But along with the rage, he feels a profound sadness, a grief for the girl who has been robbed of her innocence and dreams.

When Hana finishes, she looks at him, her eyes glistening with unshed tears. "I'm sorry," she murmurs, "I didn't mean to…"

"Hana," Peter interrupts, his voice gentle yet firm, "you have nothing to apologize for. None of this is your fault. You should leave Haiko in the past." Squeezing her hand, he adds, "And you should get back to the piano."

Their eyes stare fixedly into each other, and in that moment, an understanding passes between them. They are both victims, both survivors.

TWELVE

TOKYO

Next morning, Peter finds himself back at the Toranomon Hills Residential Tower, strolling across the expansive space of the lobby, his footsteps reverberating off the polished stone. He reaches the reception desk manned by a smartly dressed concierge.

"Good afternoon, sir," the concierge greets Peter, his expression a well-practiced blend of professionalism and friendly familiarity. "How may I assist you today?"

"I'm here to collect a package," Peter replies, his gaze scanning the rows of neatly stacked parcels behind the desk. "It should be under the name Peter Johnson. I'm with Haiko Shusaku's staff."

The concierge nods. His fingers dance over the computer keyboard in front of him as he checks the system. "Ah, yes," he says a moment later. "We received a package for you yesterday evening. Just one moment, please."

He gets up from his seat and fetches a medium-sized box wrapped in plain brown paper. There is no address, only the name P. Johnson written in neat black letters.

"Here you are, Mr. Johnson," the concierge says, setting the package down in front of Peter. "Please sign here for receipt."

Peter scribbles the signature of Peter Johnson—whoever that is—on the electronic pad the concierge holds out, thanking him before picking up the box. His cargo tucked securely under his arm, he leaves the building and returns to the Mitsubishi Evo parked one block over. Sitting in the driver's seat, he unwraps the package and removes the flat backpack-contained single-use parachute.

He removes his suit jacket and places the chute on underneath, tightening the shoulder straps so that it is tucked neatly into the vertebral groove running along the center of his back. Then he puts the suit jacket on over the top. He's made sure to wear a size larger today, and thankfully, along with his large shoulders, the parachute is pretty much out of sight underneath. It doesn't look like he has a hunchback or anything.

Following that, he leaves the car and returns to Toranomon Hills.

Walking out of the lift into Haiko Shusaku's lavish penthouse, he is immediately set upon by Shin and the others. A man of imposing stature, Shin's every feature is hard and unyielding as his eyes narrow the second they land on Peter. He steps forward, aggression radiating off him like white heat. There is a cut running along the bridge of his nose that has received stitches, and the skin around his eyes is black.

"You," he growls, his voice echoing in the expansive

lobby of Haiko's place. "You come back here after what you pulled last night!"

There are three other men in the hallway with him. They immediately form a ring around Peter as their leader comes right up to him.

Peter meets Shin's burning gaze head-on, his expression calm despite the accusation. "And what was it that I did last night, exactly?" he says evenly.

Shin's lip curls. He shows his teeth and swears in Japanese.

Before the situation can escalate further, a door swings open on the far side of the room, and Haiko Shusaku himself appears. Though he is a much older man than the rest, his presence still commands absolute attention from the others.

"Enough, Shin," he commands in their native tongue, his voice carrying a quiet authority that silences the room instantly. He turns his gaze on Peter, appraising him with an unreadable expression. "If you hadn't forgotten," he says, refacing his henchman, "this man saved my life last night."

Shin looks like he wants to protest but falls silent under Haiko's stare.

"I have said enough," Haiko repeats, his gaze turning back to Peter. "I trust this man. And I suggest the rest of you do the same."

Peter can't help but feel a sense of grim satisfaction as he watches Shin back down. Haiko may be a monster in his own right, but in this moment, his faith in Peter is the only thing keeping him safe.

THIRTEEN

SHINOSHIMA

MICHAEL SITS ON THE EDGE OF HIS BUNK IN PITCH
black, still as a statue, eyes locked on the glass panels of the
one-way. The room is silent, save for the dull hum of the
ventilation system, and next door has just vacated, so he's
listening to make sure.

When he is, he goes to the computer, switches it on, and
clicks on the icon marked "run program," the one Kirsty
Lang has so ingeniously designed. His heart freezes in his
chest as he watches the screen, waiting for the familiar
loading bar to fill before soon, the Trojan horse begins infiltrating the system again, reaching out through the digital
veins of the facility.

The cell door lock emits a loud click, the sound reverberating in the small, concrete room. Michael stands up, the
tension leaving his body in a rush. Once more, he is free.

Stepping out into the corridor, he glances up and down it. The walls are sterile and white, the fluorescent lights overhead casting long, ominous shadows. He must move quickly.

He makes it to the first corner, presses himself against the wall, and listens. The sound of distant footsteps bounces along the passageways, but there is no immediate threat. Satisfied, he leaves the corner and moves, the soft-soled cotton plimsolls they've given him making no noise on the cold, hard floor.

Michael navigates the corridors with a renewed sense of urgency. He avoids the main passages, sticking to the less traveled routes. His heart thumps in his ears, a constant reminder of the ticking clock.

He reaches the stairwell, the sign for Level B-5 looming overhead. The stairs seem to stretch endlessly down into the dark abyss below. But there is no time to waste. He has to get to B-35.

Michael descends, his fingers brushing against the cold, metal handrail. The CCTV cameras watch silently, their electronic eyes fooled by the program. Stuck on a loop of footage, they see nothing amiss, just an empty stairwell.

As he nears B-35, his breath hitches in his throat. The door looms ahead, the retinal scanner next to it. Michael holds his face to it, presses his thumb to the pad below, and keeps perfectly still as a soft yellow light scans his eyes. The light turns green, the door clicks open, and Michael lets out a breath he didn't know he was holding.

There is more to Level B-35 than a few labs storing bad things. Much more.

Once Michael is sprayed down with disinfectant, he enters the bowels of B-35, edges along its maze of corridors with swift, measured steps, the feeling of the GoPro camera secure in his pocket a comforting reminder of his mission. Even in plimsolls, his footsteps sound loud in the sterile silence, the only other sound being the soft hum of unseen machinery.

It is as he nears a particular corner, however, that another sound emerges—a strange sound that freezes him in his tracks.

A chorus of ragged coughs and moans reverberates from behind a door, followed by a barely audible whimper. Michael's heart beats hard in his chest as he creeps closer to the source of the noise: a door at the end of the corridor that is unmarked, save for a small panel over the top with a red light glowing.

The sounds are undeniably coming from within.

His senses on high alert, every instinct screaming at him to turn back, Michael knows he can't. He presses his thumb to the scanner beside the door, the green light flashing a silent approval above, the door sliding open automatically with a soft hiss.

Inside is a sight that will forever be etched into his memory. It is beyond horrifying. The room he steps into is a gallery of human suffering. It is filled with rows of glass chambers, each housing a figure. Men and women, their eyes glazed over, their skin a sickly pallor, are encased within. Tubes and wires snake in and out of their bodies, connected to humming machines that pulse and churn with sickening rhythms. Some of the people shake violently inside their glass tombs. Others lay motionless, their faces contorted in pain.

A large central screen displays an array of live data—heart rates, temperatures, biochemical changes. Each of the poor, wretched souls is a living experiment, exposed to a cocktail of viruses and chemical agents.

Michael feels a cold dread seep into his bones. During their mission briefing, he had been told about the rumors regarding Shinoshima, about the experimentation they were supposedly conducting. But seeing it in person is a whole different level of horror. This isn't just a prison facility or the armored bunker of a megalomaniac. This is a torture chamber, a place where human life is reduced to mere data and experimentation.

His mind races, thoughts colliding with one another. He can hear his own heartbeat, loud and frantic in the deafening silence of the room. But he can't afford the luxury of shock. Not here, not now.

Tearing his gaze away from the helpless victims, Michael takes the camera from his pocket and, like in the lab the night before, records what he sees. It bites, the fact that there is nothing he can do for these people. He doesn't even know how to start to get them out of their chambers, let alone what to do with them afterwards. All of them are as close to death as a person can get. Most likely infected with things that have no known cure.

He hopes with all his heart that they expose this place for what it really is. With a final glance at the victims of this horrific enterprise, he pushes forward, the haunting tableau etched into his memory.

As he exits the room, the door sliding shut behind him

with a final, damning hiss, the weight of his discovery settles heavily on his shoulders. The corridors of B-35 are darker now, each shadow a reminder of the nightmare he has just witnessed.

But he is not done yet. Each step back to his cell becomes a testament to his newfound resolve. He has to escape, not just for himself, but for them. The world needs to know about this horror.

———

HAVING LEFT the atrocities of B-35, Michael finds himself standing in front of the cold, metallic door to his cell. An unease that he can't put into words nestles in the pit of his stomach. Something feels off, and a lingering unease creeps up his spine.

Prompted by a gut instinct for self-preservation, he tucks the GoPro into a discreet hiding spot at the top of a ventilation shaft running along the corridor outside his cell, hoping that the camera out there is still on a loop.

Pressing his thumb to the sensor, the green light flashes, and the cell door slides open. His heart drops.

There in the dim light, sitting on the edge of his cot is Mayu: the pretty young woman who had drawn him into this trap. She casts a dark reflection of her former self. A pair of cold, obsidian eyes stare at him, and a cruel smile tugs at the corners of her mouth, belying the softness of her features.

"Michael-san." She greets him in a voice as cold as the concrete walls around them. "You've been on quite an adventure."

The room, once his solitary refuge, now feels over-whelmingly claustrophobic. The buzzing fluorescent light above his head casts long, grotesque shadows up the walls. The hum of the ventilation system feels louder than ever, and the glass panels of the one-way continually clink in their holding.

"You like my home?" Mayu continues, a malicious gleam in her eyes.

Michael's heart rattles against his ribs, a wild animal trapped in a cage. He refuses to let her see his fear. He needs to stay calm, to think. His survival depends on it.

He steps farther into the cell, the door closing behind him with a chilling finality. His gaze never leaves Mayu. She stands up, and with imperceptible movements, braces herself.

A battle is about to begin, and Michael steels himself.

The cell is small, but there is enough space for a fight. As Michael and Mayu stare each other down, their tension fills it. He is aware that he needs to strike first, to take her by surprise, his muscles coiled tight and ready. Without a word, he launches himself at her, using the aggressive techniques of the Krav Maga his father has taught him. His fist aims straight for her face, his body already preparing for a follow-up knee strike, a signature move from Muay Thai. But Mayu is fast, her aikido training allowing her to fluidly step aside, using her opponent's momentum against him.

Caught off balance, Michael stumbles but quickly regains his footing, spinning to face her again.

Mayu laughs lightly. It is a chilling sound that fills the tight concrete cell.

Michael feints a right hook, only to launch a low kick

aimed at her legs, another Muay Thai technique. However, she predicts the move. Her judo skills come into play as she blocks the kick, simultaneously driving an elbow into his ribs. Michael grunts, the air rushing out of his lungs.

He staggers back but recovers quickly, shaking off the pain and circling her warily. He has to end this fast, knowing that in order to achieve that, he has to become unpredictable. He attacks again, throwing a series of jabs, mixing the Krav Maga and Muay Thai techniques. But Mayu is like water. Her movements flow seamlessly from one martial art to another. She blocks his jabs with karate's *uke* blocking techniques and retaliates with a swift jujutsu *osoto gari* throw, whereby she steps behind Michael's lead leg and sweeps it out from under him, while simultaneously pushing his upper body backwards.

Michael hits the cold, hard floor with a grunt, his breath bursting out of him in a winded gasp. There's no time to recover. Mayu is on him in an instant, her knees pinning his arms down, her fingers closing around his throat, throttling the very life out of him.

He struggles beneath her, his Krav Maga kicking in as he frees one of his arms, reaches up, and tries to gouge her eyes, a move designed to force an opponent to let go. But Mayu simply tightens her grip, his fingers not quite reaching far enough, so that all he can do is claw at her face, her training allowing her to maintain control even as he struggles. She is surprisingly strong. His vision starts to blur, his struggles weakening.

And then she lets go, standing and stepping back, her cruel smile returning. Michael lies on the floor, gasping for breath, his chest heaving. Mayu has most definitely won this round. But Michael isn't done yet. As his vision clears, he glares up at her, his resolve hardening.

This isn't over, he thinks as she steps over him and walks out of the cell, laughing as she does. *Not by a long shot. I will keep fighting, no matter what.*

FOURTEEN

TOKYO

Peter finds himself settling into a new routine. His night shifts consist of patrolling the grounds, observing the entrances and exits of the building, and noting the various security measures in place. At times, he feels like a ghost, unseen by the other members of the security team.

Throughout all this, he keeps an eye out for Yūki Yokashina, hoping she will come along and end this for him. But she remains elusive. He knows she must be somewhere within the shadows, lurking like a lion in the long grass.

Then, one evening, during another fruitless shift, Peter is walking outside along the edge of the building when something drops from the sky and hits the ground a few feet from him. He looks up at the tower and sees nothing—it must have come from there.

He finds what it was that's fallen. A stone with a small piece of paper wrapped around it and secured with an elastic band. Picking it up, he pulls off the band and unfolds the paper to reveal a short message written in English:

Meet me on the roof in fifteen minutes. I have information regarding YY.

YY must be Yūki Yokashina.

Peter has no idea who the message is from—it could be from an enemy, but he can't ignore the possibility that it could also be the breakthrough he's been waiting for. Anything to get away from this place and these people.

Peter quickly checks over his FN 309 and puts it back inside the underarm holder. Then he heads for the roof.

As he steps out onto the flat rooftop of Toranomon Hills, the cool night air rushes up and greets him. The city's skyline stretches out from every direction like a mural of lights. Scanning the area, he spots a figure standing near the edge, silhouetted against the backdrop of Tokyo.

As Peter approaches, the figure turns, and he is surprised to find that it is Akira, the member of Haiko's security team who came and got him from the observation deck on his first day. The one who can speak English.

Akira wastes no time, cutting straight to his point. "I know why you're here, and I know you're looking for Yūki Yokashina."

Peter eyes him cautiously. "How do you know that?"

"I know things. Like I know that she intends to kill Haiko."

"Who told you that?"

"I have sources inside the yakuza. That's how I found out about you."

"What about me?"

"Well, for one, I know who you're really working for."

Peter's heart shudders in his chest as he wonders whether his real purpose in all this hasn't been exposed.

"And who is that?" he asks.

"Koji Tanaka," Akira announces.

Peter is relieved.

"Okay," he says. "So...?"

"So I think we can help each other."

"How?"

"For that, I'll need to show you."

Peter feels a spark of interest ignite.

"Follow me, Azrael," Akira adds, his eyes glinting with mystery. He leads the way down from the roof and into a dimly lit service corridor that runs along an outer edge of Haiko's penthouse, the walls resounding with their heavy steps. Akira moves with a sense of purpose, his steps measured and confident. A feeling of unease tugs gently at Peter's guts, but he pushes it aside.

Eventually, they arrive at a nondescript door, identical to countless others they have passed. Akira turns toward him, his face illuminated by the stark overhead lighting. "It's in here," he says, gesturing toward the door.

Peter hesitates, his gaze flitting between the door and Akira. "What exactly am I supposed to be seeing in there?" he asks, searching Akira's face for any sign of deception.

Akira merely smiles, a gesture that fails to reach his eyes. "You'll see," he replies cryptically, pushing the door open. "And when you do," he goes on, "you'll understand how it will help you in your search for Yūki Yokashina."

Peter steps into the room, his senses immediately alert. It is a small, bare room, save for a lone chair in the center. He turns back to Akira, a question on his lips, but the words die in his throat as the door closes.

"Wait!" he calls, rushing toward it, but it is too late. He hears the unmistakable sound of a lock engaging and realizes he is trapped.

Peter pounds on the door, his calls for Akira shaking the dusty air of the small room. But there is no response. Only the oppressive silence of betrayal. Akira has trapped him, and for what, Peter is about to find out.

———

IN THE LIVING ROOM, Haiko Shusaku sits perched on a throne of rich leather and embellished metal, watching the writhing bodies of his own private spectacle unfold. The orgy is a feast of skin, an indulgence of hedonism that only a man of his influence can afford. His rheumy eyes feast on the sight, tracking the display of carnality unfurling before him, a perverse smile lifting the corners of his weathered lips.

He is about to turn to Benny when, in an abrupt, heart-stopping moment, the room is suddenly plunged into darkness as the lights flicker and die out. The lingering echo of laughter and pleasure is immediately replaced by a deafening silence. A second later, the usual lighting is replaced by the harsh, pulsating glow of red security lights. The room, now bathed in a foreboding scarlet, is no longer a place of carnal pleasure but a chamber of impending doom.

"Shin?" Haiko shouts out.

Showing his face at the doorway, Shin says reassuringly, "It's okay, boss. Just a fuse, we think."

"You think?" Haiko shouts back, annoyed that his pleasure has been interrupted. "Why don't you..."

An ear-piercing scream arising from somewhere in the distance interrupts him, reverberating throughout the room. The women, no longer entwined in the throes of pleasure, are now writhing in fear. The spectacle of bodies untangles hastily, fear propelling them to scramble away, their sensual moans transforming into cries of panic that resound hauntingly through the expansive room.

"Wait here," Shin says as the penthouse descends into more screams.

Amidst the pandemonium, a new chorus of sounds reaches Haiko. Gunshots, men crying out, others shouting at each other, an explosion of rapid gunfire, the unmistakable thud of falling bodies, each one sending a fresh wave of dread washing over him. His men, the loyal protectors of his domain, are being picked off.

As his gnarled, veiny hands clench the armrests of his throne, the soft leather now slick with his nervous perspiration, his heartbeat becomes a relentless, deafening thump that matches his growing fear. He is not accustomed to this emotion. It is alien, it is cold, and it is unrelenting. The fear slithers up his spine, coils in his stomach, and claws at his throat. The screams of his men, each more chilling than the last, ring out in the otherwise silent room as one man at a time, they are silenced, their assailants steadily making their way to Haiko through the various rooms and spaces of the penthouse. The once-powerful Haiko Shusaku is now a feeble, frightened old man, waiting for his reckoning in the heart of his own iniquitous paradise.

Just outside the door, Shin, his suit stained a dark, wet

crimson, faces the onslaught with grim determination. Sweat dripping from his brow, he fires off round after round at the intruders. He's managed to take down a few of Yūki's men, but their numbers seem endless.

Despite their training, Haiko's bodyguards are being overwhelmed. One by one, the eight-man team fall. With every fresh man downed, Shin's desperation grows. His loyalty to Haiko pushes him to fight to the last breath, but he can feel the odds stacking against him.

Yūki Yokashina, the vengeful matriarch of the Bosozoku yakuza clan, has finally made her move against Haiko. Let into the building by her mole Akira, her intention is clear and brutal—total wipeout of Haiko and his men. In the midst of the mayhem, she moves like a ghost, her motions swift and precise. Her black clothing blends with the shadows, making her nearly invisible as she stalks through the penthouse, taking down Haiko's men with lethal efficiency, her cold eyes filled with a fierce determination.

By the time Yūki reaches Shin, the last of Haiko's bodyguards, she shows no signs of fatigue. Shin, however, is near the breaking point, his body trembling from the adrenaline coursing through it. The penthouse resounds with the final cries of the dying, each one a testament to Yūki's ruthless pursuit of vengeance—and Shin finds himself out of ammo and cornered. With his back to the end of a hallway, he tosses down his pistol. Throwing his gaze to the side, he spots an antique tantō on a plinth. He grabs the ten-inch blade, draws it from its bamboo sheath, and holds it out to her.

Yūki smiles. With her pistol securely returned to her hip holster, she reaches down to her right thigh, where a wakizashi short sword is strapped. Carefully withdrawing it from its magnolia *saya*, she prepares for what lies ahead.

The short sword gleams crimson under the penthouse's security lighting, her eyes mirroring its cold, lethal sheen. The last of her men, totaling only six now from the twelve who'd originally stormed the building, Akira amongst them, come to a stop behind her. Seeing their matriarch holding her wakizashi, they hold back.

Yūki's voice, cold and unwavering, slices through the silence as she squares up to Shin in the wide hallway. "You are willing to die for your master?" she asks.

"Yes, bitch," Shin hisses. "I am willing to die for him."

"Even though you surely know what he is." Her eyebrows rise up her forehead—the gesture meant to show Shin that he is as guilty as the man he protects.

The bodyguard says nothing to this, his face etched with determination, gripping the hilt of the tantō knife tightly, the small but deadly weapon held ready in a low guard position.

Opposite him, Yūki stands with an eerie calmness that seems to permeate the air around her. In her hand, she holds the wakizashi, its sharp edge glistening in the red glow as though it is already covered in blood.

With a sudden burst of energy, Shin lunges at her, his tantō aimed straight at Yūki's midsection. She sidesteps the attack with ease, her movements fluid and controlled. Shin spins around, trying to keep her within his field of vision, but Yūki is already on the move. She closes the distance between them in a blink, her wakizashi swinging in a tight arc toward Shin's exposed flank.

Shin barely manages to raise his tantō in time, the clang

of steel on steel resonating through the room. He grits his teeth, trying to push Yūki back, but she is immovable, her stance firm and her grip on her weapon immovable.

Surely this isn't the strength of a mere woman, the bodyguard thinks. He senses a force of will in her that far surpasses any human abilities she may have. The need to avenge herself gives her the strength of the devil.

Yūki takes a quick step back, creating a small gap between them. Shin, seeing an opening, lunges forward once again, his tantō aimed at her chest. But Yūki is faster, her wakizashi meeting Shin's tantō mid-lunge, and with a swift motion, she twists her wrist. The force of the movement, as Shin tries desperately to regain his balance, sends the tantō flying out of his hand.

Unarmed and off-balance, Shin is at Yūki's mercy. She moves swiftly, her wakizashi slicing through the air in a horizontal arc. The cold steel grazes Shin's chest, a thin line of red appearing in a diagonal slash across his shirt.

Shin falls back against the wall, clutching the five-inch cut. He looks up at Yūki, his eyes wide with a mix of fear and respect. Yūki, standing over him with her wakizashi still in hand, meets his gaze with a calm, impassive expression.

Shin's eyes widen with desperation as he manages to choke out a single word. "Wait..." His hand reaches out, a desperate plea in his eyes. Yūki, her gaze cold and resolute, does not hesitate. With one swift, sure motion, she plunges her wakizashi into his heart. Shin's eyes widen, his final breath escaping his lips as the life fades from them.

All this time, Haiko Shusaku has been cowering in a corner. He is still there when Yūki enters the living room, the remains of her yakuza hit squad following closely behind. Now alone and defenseless, Haiko trembles in fear as Yūki saunters over to him, her eyes displaying an unforgiving and icy sternness.

His robe hanging loosely around him, Haiko finds himself the center of a very different kind of attention than the one he was enjoying just minutes ago. The six yakuza surround him.

"No... No!" he protests, his voice weak and raspy. His aging, bloated body struggles against their iron grips as they grab him. One of them, a hulking mass of muscles with a scar running down his left cheek, takes hold of Haiko's flailing arms. Another grabs his legs. The remaining men move to support his weight, their hands firm under his back and thighs. Together, they hoist the struggling man into the air, his cries bouncing off the walls.

They carry him toward a large, wooden table that sits at the edge of the room. His protests turn into desperate pleas that fall on deaf ears. The men, their expressions never changing, move with a calm, deliberate pace, Yūki following behind with her wakizashi.

With a rough, unceremonious thud, they lay Haiko on the table, his body sprawled across the surface. His breaths come out in ragged gasps, his body shuddering from the shock and fear. As the men hold him down, the reality of his situation hits him.

He is no longer the watcher, the one in control. Now he is the one being held down, the one under control. Fear bubbles in his veins, terror coursing through him.

Yūki comes over him. The cruel smile on her face is a grotesque mirror of his past indiscretions. She raises the short sword, his eyes fixing to it. She nods at one of the men.

As the others keep him held to the table, the yakuza with the scar uses a yanagiba knife to cut away the old man's underwear.

Now Haiko really struggles.

Yūki bends down to him and, in a voice as cold as the steel of her blade, tells him, "Struggle all you want, Haiko, old friend. But I am taking what I came here for."

And with that, she performs the violent act of castration and penectomy, essentially turning Haiko Shusaku, old letch that he is, into a eunuch. His screams reverberate throughout the penthouse, a haunting soundtrack to his downfall.

———

PETER FINALLY MANAGES to bust down the door, his shoulder numb from the effort, aching all the way down to the fingers on his right hand.

As he staggers into the service corridor, a gruesome sound comes from the penthouse, a strangled scream from Haiko, and then silence. Peter's blood runs cold as he realizes what has just happened. Yūki has finally taken her ultimate revenge against Haiko Shusaku, and Peter is late for the party.

When he steps through a back door into the penthouse, the FN 509 gripped firmly in his hand, his eyes take in the grim tableau. The wreckage of the penthouse lies strewn around, a macabre testament to the violence that has unfolded. It is eerily quiet. Remnants of the gruesome battle are everywhere—the bodies of Haiko's guards, spent bullet casings, blood up the walls, soaking into the plush carpet.

In the heart of the abode, its master, Shusaku, is conspicuous by his absence, his silent presence made all too tangible by chilling artifacts of a recent act of terrible violence. A ghastly pool of blood seeps over the edges of a once-pristine table, each drop landing onto the floor with an almost deafening tap. A trail of bloody footsteps weaves a grisly path across the once welcoming expanse of the living room, culminating at an ajar balcony door that swings gently in the evening breeze, its threshold serving as a chilling invitation to the unseen horrors beyond.

Just as Peter is absorbing the scene in the living room, he hears the sound of the elevator doors opening in the lobby.

He rushes down a hallway, stops at a corner, and tucks himself against it. Peeking out from the nook, he is just in time to see Yūki and her band of men stepping into the elevator, making their exit. He catches a glimpse of Yūki's cold eyes as she turns around, an unspoken warning in them that she is not to be messed with.

Peter lifts the FN Tactical and aligns his sight on the target just as the elevator doors begin their inevitable reunion. His mark, Yūki, seems to possess a sixth sense for danger. In the fleeting sliver of visibility before the doors finally kiss, her gaze locks on to his, a victorious smile playing on her lips. Then, swallowed by the elevator, she vanishes. Azrael has missed his chance.

Peter emerges from cover, his eyes instinctively shooting upward to the digital display above the elevator doors. The numbers are a blur, rapidly descending, mirroring Yūki's swift escape.

Without a moment's hesitation, he breaks into a run, charging away from the mocking elevator, away from the lobby. His destination is not down, but up. He barrels into the stairwell, his feet pounding rhythmically on the steps as he ascends toward the roof. His suit jacket is discarded mid-run, his hand deftly untangling the cord from his hidden parachute.

Bursting onto the flat expanse roof, he heads straight for the edge, the open cityscape yawning before him. His toes curl over the precipice, a dizzying fifty-four stories above the ground. Far below, seven tiny specks spill out of the Tora-nomon Hills complex, scattering like ants across the street toward a cluster of waiting motorcycles.

Peter surveys his surroundings quickly. The Mitsubishi is parked on the adjacent side street. Yūki and her yakuza entourage begin to peel out, their bikes growling against the Tokyo nightscape.

The cool air nips at him, the city lights below a glittering embroidery of life. The vertiginous height does nothing to stifle his resolve. He draws in a lungful of crisp air, the taste of the impending chase fueling his determination, and, with one last glance over the vast city, he pushes himself off the edge.

The wind tears at him, stinging his eyes as he hurtles toward the sprawling cityscape below, his fingers working to control his trajectory, his heart thrumming in his chest, the adrenaline a potent cocktail in his veins.

A moment that stretches into a lifetime passes before he yanks the cord of the parachute. The sudden, violent pull of the expanding chute jerks him upward, arresting his plum-met. The city, once an abstract blur, sharpens into focus, a giant grid of lights and buildings.

With calculated precision, Peter manipulates the parachute cords, directing himself toward the awaiting Mitsubishi Evo. He battles the wind, the parachute pitching dangerously, but his focus remains unwavering, his gaze locked on the glinting black body of the car.

The ground surges toward him. He braces, and with a final taut pull on the cords, he cushions his descent, executing a tuck and roll upon impact. His parachute wilts behind him, and he hastily unclips the harness, abandoning the chute in the middle of the street as he bolts toward the Evo.

The car purrs to life at his approach, the engine a low rumble of anticipation, like thunder in a storm. He vaults into the driver's seat, the roar of the engine filling the entire street as he stamps on the gas and seizes the stick. He doesn't spare a glance back at the looming silhouette of Toranomon Hills. He only has eyes for what lies ahead.

Nightfall is still fresh, and the hunt has only just begun.

———

A DEEP GROWL rumbles out from within the city, a primal sound that heralds the arrival of a predator. Yūki and the others immediately glance at the mirrors of their Honda Firebirds, spotting the Mitsubishi Evo coming up on them fast.

Inside the car, Peter grips the wheel, his knuckles white against the black leather. His gaze is hard, jaw clenched.

The motorbikes weave through the traffic, their riders leaning into every curve with practiced ease. Peter's eyes flick from one bike to the next, tracing their paths, looking for the one which holds Yūki Yokashina. His foot presses down on the gas pedal, the Evo responding with a surge of power, his heart throbbing in time with the engine's rhythm.

The Tokyo streets blur past him as he accelerates, the neon signs and city lights smearing into streaks of color. He swings the car around a tight corner, tires squealing against the asphalt, the smell of burned rubber filling the air as he rounds a garbage truck. He grinds his teeth, feeling the car skid for a moment before regaining traction. The bikes, agile and nimble, dart in and out of the narrow lanes, but Peter doesn't let them out of his sight. He pushes the Evo to its limits, threading through the bustling city streets, dodging between the slower vehicles. His eyes flicker to the GPS mounted on his dashboard, tracing the route ahead. The motorbikes split up, each taking a different path in a bid to lose him. Peter's lips curl into a determined grimace. He chooses the one holding Yūki and goes after it.

The bike darts down an alley, and Peter follows, the Evo's engine howling like a beast in the tight space. Yūki dares a look over her shoulder, her eyes betraying a spark of fear as Peter throttles the Evo, its bumper looming danger-ously close to the bike's quivering rear tire. She jerks the handlebars in a last-ditch swerve, but Peter anticipates it, his car screaming in protest as he wrenches it into a matching turn.

The Honda darts erratically, its rider stealing another fleeting look back at Peter—only this time, her lips curl into a smile that freezes his blood. She whips her gaze back to the alley, and with a final burst of speed, she guns it across a narrow intersecting road.

Her next tactic is a risky one: She swerves into a passage on the opposing side, a claustrophobic alley barely wide enough for two pedestrians to scrape past one another. Peter, so zeroed in on his prey, misreads the alley's narrow throat—

The Evo slams into the corners of both sides with a thunderous, metallic shriek. The world inside the vehicle detonates into uproar. Impact sends shockwaves through the car's frame, rattling Peter's bones. The airbag explodes in his face like a white-hot flashbang. The engine gasps, then wheezes into silence, a shroud of smoke billowing from beneath the crumpled hood, choking the air.

Peter shakes off the daze, and when his vision clears, he finds the alley hauntingly empty—Yūki has evaporated. His heart drops, frustration searing his veins. He smashes a fist against the steering wheel, then sucks in a sharp, steadying breath.

The Evo is ruined, its once sleek hood crumpled and twisted grotesquely against the unfeeling brick wall. With no more injury than a bruised ego, Peter steps from the wreckage, the deserted backstreet looming around him.

Retrieving his cell phone, he punches in a number with practiced ease. "I need a pick-up," he states, his tone steely, resolute. "And another car."

Akechi's voice crackles over the line. "Where's Haiko Shusaku?"

"Dead."

"And Yūki?"

Peter sighs, a lone sound in the alleyway. "Alive and well."

"So you failed, then, Azrael-san?"

"It would appear so." His voice is icy, inflexible, the tone of a man whose hunt is far from over.

FIFTEEN

SHINOSHIMA

LATE LAST NIGHT, AROUND NINE, AN OMINOUS HISS began to permeate from the ventilation grid above Michael's head. In an instant, the confined cell became flooded with a thick white fog that clawed its way into his lungs. An intoxicating struggle ensued until the world spun and darkness dragged him down into sleep.

Now consciousness is creeping back, the kid's head a leaden weight threatening to topple from his neck as he labors to sit upright on the prison cot. He peers through the drowsiness shrouding his vision, surveying the all-too-familiar surroundings.

Nothing has altered in the room. But then, it isn't the room that has been transformed. The change has occurred with him.

A cold, alien pressure is clamped around his neck. He tentatively traces it with his fingers, discovering a metallic vise-like apparatus. Gathering his strength, he heaves himself to his feet and stares into the vast mirror of the panels. His reflection bears a shocking revelation: a metallic collar fastened around his neck.

The panels begin to shake in their frame—*chink*. Someone is leaving the next room, coming around to the cell. The door slides open, and there standing with her hands on her hips is Mayu.

She tilts her head to the side and smiles manically, the dimples showing on her cheeks.

He doesn't find them so cute anymore.

"You like your necklace?" she asks.

Michael goes to rush at her, but no sooner is he halfway across the cell than she has pressed a button on some type of fob, and Michael is reeling from the most intense electric shock he's ever experienced. The ground rushes up at him as he stumbles onto it, the prongs of the shock-collar stabbing into his neck, sending electricity surging through him. It is as if a thousand needles are piercing his skin all at once. His body involuntarily convulses, the shock overwhelming his senses. A taste of metal invades his mouth, his vision blurs, and a deafening, piercing buzz fills his ears.

As quickly as it came, the shock subsides, leaving him gasping for breath, heart pounding away in his chest like a jackhammer. The room spins around, and he reaches out from the floor, desperate for something to hold on to.

Mayu comes over him and leans down with the remote in her hand. "From now on, Michael-san," she says menacingly, "you stay in your cage. Okay?"

SIXTEEN

OSAKA

Locating a tattooist in Osaka to fill the void left by the one felled in the skirmish with the Australian mercenaries had been a task of patience for Yūki. It wasn't just any tattooist she sought, but one skilled in the ancient art of *tebori*. This method, devoid of electronic convenience, employs a hand-carved bamboo handle with a cluster of needles attached, each puncture manually executed by the artist. A laborious task demanding exceptional skill, it typically spans multiple sessions as the artist painstakingly etches the design onto the skin. And it hurts—a fact that entices Yūki more than it deters her.

She lies supine in the parlor, her creamy, alabaster skin bare under the harsh glare of the lamps. The artist toils in silent concentration, his tool rhythmically pecking at her flesh. It is an intricate artwork of torment that he paints, a fiery panorama of hell that sprawls across her torso. The ten kings of hell, garbed in somber black and sitting on horse-back, overlook a chaotic sea of sinners writhing in a fero-cious storm of flames.

Two of the sinners have been fully rendered: a faceless man entranced by his own reflection in the hand mirror he holds up, and a gluttonous figure feasting on his own entrails, chopsticks ferrying the viscera from stomach to mouth. The artist now etches a third: a eunuch, limbs contorted grotesquely, tormented by hell's wardens with monstrous bull and horse heads as they hold his amputated appendages aloft as though on the verge of throwing them to the flames.

Each meticulous detail is a chilling testament to the grotesque torments of a searing hell—Yūki's living Hell Screen. There's space for more, including a spot by her navel reserved for the final addition: Koji Tanaka. Perhaps there will even be room for Azrael to suffer alongside them.

Sweat drips from the artist's brow, swabbed away inter-mittently by a crumpled handkerchief he keeps in the pocket of his *jinbei*. His mind wanders back to the wonder of her skin. Decades of inking yakuza brutes had never introduced him to such a canvas. But it isn't her allure that unsettles him. No, it is her stoicism.

The absence of even a whimper as he navigates the sensi-tive stretch from her breasts to her belly is unnerving. He knows only too well the pain that it causes. It runs from the tip of the toes to the core of the head. A sharp, stabbing pain. However, this woman, this beautiful woman, is stag-geringly strong, even compared to the hardest of men. She hasn't emitted a single moan since he started three hours ago, not one.

To steady himself, he finds solace in conversation.

"As we tattoo," he begins, his voice punctuating the rhythmic pricks of his tool, "we hold the skin taut with the left thumb, laying ink with each incision. We pros cherish the sound it makes. *Tohibiki,* we call it—'distant echo.' To others, the sound is chilling. But to us, it is music."

Yūki listens, her only response an occasional smile.

"A large work like this also takes patience," the old man goes on. "Because of the ink in the tattoo, you will feel twice as cold in winter and must wear cotton-padded clothes. It doesn't mean, though, that it cools you down in summer. No such luck. No, carrying a tattoo means a lifetime of patience."

Yūki has to smile at this. Patience, after all, is her greatest virtue. She has waited fifteen years for this. Fifteen years to inch closer to Tanaka, etching one damned soul at a time into her flesh.

SEVENTEEN

TOKYO

Haiko Shusaku's lifeless, broken body was discovered at the base of the towering Toranomon Hills not long after all hell had broken loose, the grim aftermath of a fatal plunge from the heights of his own luxurious penthouse balcony. The unforgiving impact had left him unrecognizable, obscuring any telltale signs of the rumored mutilation that had occurred prior to his fall.

Only when an unassuming package arrived at one of Tanaka-Corp's sprawling corporate buildings did the chilling reality come to light. Opening the latest medical container from Yūki Yokashina had led to a gruesome reveal of what had been taken from Haiko Shusaku before his death, and it cast a disturbing shadow over an already gruesome scene.

Beneath the glow of a neon sign, Peter sits at a bustling street market, steam rising from a plate of freshly cooked gyoza. The savory aroma of the dumplings mingles with the scent of exhaust fumes, and the cacophony of vendors hawking their wares fills his ears, the energy of Tokyo's nightlife enveloping him.

Without invitation, a man slides into the seat next to him. Turning sideways, Peter rolls his eyes at the sight of Akechi Akiyama. The latter tosses a dismissive glance at Peter's plate before addressing him.

"Your failure hasn't gone unnoticed, Azrael-san," he remarks.

Peter continues chewing, his gaze fixed on a steaming dumpling pinched between his chopsticks. "I'll do better next time," he retorts, his tone casual, as though discussing the weather.

Akechi shifts his body, his eyes narrowing. "And there's another matter. A day ago, your son was caught outside of his cell."

Peter's blood goes cold.

"What was he doing?" he asks, trying to sound surprised.

"That's what we would like to know."

"Well, where did he go? I mean, he's on an island. It's not like he's gonna swim away from it."

"We don't know where he went. He'd disabled the cameras."

"How did he escape?"

"He downloaded a Trojan horse virus which took over the island's security systems."

"Where was he caught?"

Akechi's eyes pierce. "Look," he says, his voice as cold as a winter wind, "whatever he was up to, it doesn't matter.

There will be no escape for him from Shinoshima except Yūki's death. Is this understood?"

A wave of relief floods over Peter. They clearly only think the kid was trying to escape. He must have gotten rid of the camera before they caught him.

"You need to maintain better control over your house, Azrael-san," Akechi says.

"I'll let him know," Peter replies curtly.

Without missing a beat, Akechi then delves into the next assignment. Pulling out his phone, he flicks to a picture and slides it across the table. The picture is of a small, rodent-looking man with splashes of gray in his black hair. In the picture, he is being escorted out of court by a police officer, the two manacled together by their wrists.

"Kato Myomoto," Akechi begins, his voice dripping with disdain. "Currently serving a life sentence in Fuchu Prison for orchestrating the gruesome murder of his wife and her lover."

Peter's chopsticks pause mid-air. He snaps his gaze to Akechi, his brow furrowed. "And just how am I supposed to get close to a man locked behind bars?" he inquires, incredulity etching into his tone.

Akechi Akiyama merely smirks, tapping the phone with a single, gnarled finger. "Don't worry, Azrael-san. It is all arranged."

"What is 'all arranged'?" Peter counters, his patience thinning as rapidly as the dissipating steam from his now cold gyoza.

EIGHTEEN

FUCHU PRISON, OUTSKIRTS OF TOKYO

A MERE TEN HOURS LATER, PETER FINDS HIMSELF manacled in the back of a prison van, being driven through the giant gate of Fuchu Prison. The voice of Akechi Akiyama echoes in his mind: "Only the warden knows your true identity."

Peter is ushered out of the van and into a rain-drenched courtyard. There, he is handed over to the prison staff. The men who had transported him undo his shackles, and the prison guards instruct him in Japanese to walk the yellow line.

Peter looks down. Three lines lie painted on the wet ground: red, blue, and yellow. With a forceful prod of a baton to his back, he begins walking the yellow line toward the prison building.

He is led through open doors into a tiled room, where a man with beady eyes hidden beyond thick glasses awaits him sitting behind a desk. The room is permeated by the sharp, acrid stench of human sweat.

The man at the desk barks at Peter to undress. He does as he's told, his possessions swiftly confiscated and stowed in a box.

As Peter removes his clothing, the man at the desk drones out the foreword of the prison rulebook: "From today you are incarcerated in Fuchu Prison," he says in Japanese, not even bothering to ask Peter if he wants it translated into English. He just goes on and on: "Here, more than two thousand prisoners serve their time, and must live together. That is why order and discipline must reign, and it is therefore unthinkable that everyone behave as they wish. It is in that spirit that the rules, more numerous than in normal life, have been designed..."

Once the speech is finished, Peter is handed the prison rule book and directed to the blue line, which leads him into a shower room.

After an invasive search, a hasty delousing process, and being sprayed down with a hose, Peter is hurried along the blue line to a changing room. Given no time to linger, he dresses in his prison uniform: a grey *monpe*, a loose-fitting jumpsuit cinched at the waist with a drawstring.

Akechi's words flitter back to him: "You will be housed close to Kato. On the same landing, very close to his cell. All your work groups, recreation time, feeding, has been arranged for the same time as Kato. Stay close to him. Watch him."

In his slightly undersized monpe, Peter is escorted through the bowels of the prison, the oppressive scent of sweat growing stronger with every step along the yellow line.

To his surprise, the prison is eerily quiet, a stark contrast to the chaotic din he has experienced in other countries' prisons—being that this isn't the first time he's been placed inside one to reach a target.

Peter's mind buzzes with Akechi's predictions of Yūki's infiltration plans. "She will want to kill him personally," he said, "so it won't be one of the prisoners who go for Kato. She'll manage to find a way into the place."

"And how in the hell is she going to sneak herself into a prison?"

"The same way you have. By bribing someone."

Peter makes his way along a balcony. The other prisoners —many of them sporting yakuza tattoos—hang around their cells, staring threateningly at the *gaijin* as he passes.

"The place is full of yakuza," Akechi had told him. "Different factions. Some of them could be working with Yūki."

His journey ends at a cell. His cellmate, a shirtless man with a plump, tattooed torso, sits on a straw mat inside. He eyes Peter through narrowed slits. As the cellmate raises himself to his full height, his fists curled up at his sides, Peter can't shake Akechi's warning: "Kato is housed in the most dangerous wing of the prison. You will be the only foreigner there. It will place a huge target on your back. You will have to protect yourself."

As the cell door shuts behind him, Peter feels the weight of his situation. He is trapped in the lion's den, with danger lurking in every corner. The last words he remembers from Akechi ring in his ears: "Good Luck, Azrael-san. You are going to need it."

NINETEEN

FUCHU PRISON

Next morning, the door is unbolted, and a harsh command slices through the stale air of Peter's cell: "*Heya kara dero!*"

Get out of the cell!

Peter unfolds himself from the thin mattress and begins rolling it up. The guards bark at his cellmate too, but the man doesn't stir, sprawled out on his mat like a discarded doll.

"Oi!" they shout in Japanese. "*Beddo kara dero!*"

Get out of bed!

The guards tell Peter to step aside and then enter the cell. Upon closer inspection, they discover the other man unconscious, his face a battlefield of bruises and cuts, the aftermath of a brutal beating that occurred sometime around three a.m. when he tried to jump Peter in his sleep. The *jumper* quickly became the *jumpee*.

Peter offers a casual shrug when the guards ask him what happened.

"Maybe he had a nightmare," he says, his voice thick with feigned concern.

Leaving the cell, Peter is told to follow a green line along the landing. It leads him to the cacophony of a mess hall. The harsh clang of metal on metal explodes in the air as the prisoners attack their meals with animalistic urgency. Everywhere, signs warn not to talk, so the only sounds in there are the scraping of cutlery and the wet slurping of a thousand masticating mouths.

As he stands in line, Peter's gaze sweeps over the room, finally resting on Yūki Yokashina's next target: Kato Myamoto. The rat-like man is an island in a sea of chaos. He sits in a far corner, flanked by his entourage. His bodyguard, a mountain of a man with long, scraggly hair like a caveman, looms over them all, eyes as cold and calculating as a predator's. The man is clearly the top of the food chain at Fuchu Prison.

It is as Peter takes a seat with his food that his beaten cellmate appears in the mess hall, shambling like a specter, his loyal gang trailing in his wake. The second the cellmate spots him, he points. Then he and his three amigos come sauntering over, their yakuza tattoos a tapestry of intimidation across their flesh.

They move toward Peter with calculated menace. Each step is a drumbeat in the oppressive silence, the room's murmur dying down as they approach—all eyes on the men, and then the *gaijin*.

Peter doesn't have to look up from his food to know that they are approaching. The sudden drop in sound, the purposeful shuffling of their feet, and the sharp scent of menace give them away.

His cellmate, his face a mosaic of bruises and cuts from the previous night's beating, comes to a halt before Peter's table.

"Thought you'd get away with it, *gaijin*?" he sneers. His voice sounds much louder than it is in the tense quiet, eyes burning with promised retribution. The three fellow yakuza flanking him fix Peter with cold stares, their hands twitching, ready to spring into action.

Peter breathes out slowly through his nose and places his spoon down beside the bowl of ramen. He slowly lifts his eyes to meet the threat head-on, his gaze steady, a wry smile playing on his lips, the fear buried beneath layers of resilience, his posture radiating defiance. "I'm just enjoying my breakfast," he says, his voice even, as if discussing the weather.

The tension in the air thickens, the other prisoners casting nervous glances in their direction. The yakuza thugs close in, their shadows falling over Peter like a dark omen.

But right at the moment they are coming around the table, and Peter is picking his spoon up, and not for eating, the harsh bark of a guard's command cuts through the air like a katana. Two of them, truncheons in hand, approach with brisk, authoritative strides. "Enough! Back to your tables," one orders, his gaze flitting between Peter and the quartet.

"Go on!" the other guard snaps. "Back off!"

They glare at the yakuza men, hands clutching their batons, their message clear: Disperse, or face the consequences.

The cellmate holds Peter's stare for a moment longer before turning away, his departing glance promising that this is far from over. The three fellow yakuza follow him, leaving behind a heavy silence, the quiet before a storm.

Peter exhales and lets go of the spoon, the full weight of the encounter settling over him, knowing that he will have to beat those men into bloody pulps before his time here is finished.

"You shouldn't provoke them," an old voice says.

Peter turns to find an elderly man standing stooped next to him. His face is a parchment of time, each wrinkle etched with tales of hardship. "You shouldn't provoke them," he says again, repeating his advice, his voice like the sound of gravel underfoot.

"And maybe they shouldn't provoke *me*," Peter retorts.

The old man smiles. Bending his old bones into position, he takes a seat next to Peter. He must be at least seventy, the remains of his hair completely white. There is hardly anything to him, either, his bony chest sticking out of his vest, the faded green of his tattoos showing under a nest of gray hairs.

Peter slides the remnants of his ramen toward the old man. Gratefully, the man takes it up. He then crushes some bread into the tepid broth with gnarled and trembling fingers.

Casting a sidelong glance at Kato, Peter asks, "What's his story?"

The old man looks up from the ramen and the soaking bread and squints at Kato, appraising him. "Oh, him," he finally says. "He's loaded. See that gorilla next to him? He's on a payroll of over two million yen a month that goes to some elderly mother in Kyoto—who would have thought a beast like that even had a mother, right? Anyway, it's easy money for playing the guard dog."

"That's almost fifty grand in US," Peter observes.

"And worth every cent if it means breathing another day," the old man grunts, focusing on his meal. "But it's not just the muscle he pays; the yakuza and the guards get a share too. Having a man like him in here... it's like winning the lottery for some."

Just then, a guard saunters toward Kato's table, bearing a tray laden with an array of dishes that is a veritable feast compared to the meager servings doled out to the rest of the prisoners.

"Huh," the old man complains. "Even in here, money makes you a different species."

———

UNDER THE RELENTLESS glare of the midday sun, Peter finds himself out in the yard. The ground beneath his feet is a dry, hardened dirt that swallows the heat, and the oppressive presence of the gun towers loom over the prisoners like gargoyles perched high above.

"Do you feel it?" The old man's voice is barely audible over the murmur of the men.

The old guy had followed him out of the mess hall. The two of them now stand close to the wall.

"Feel what?" Peter asks, his eyes scanning the yard.

"The tension," the old man replies, his wet, bloodshot eyes fixed on the distance.

Peter looks around. The yakuza are scattered around the

yard, their bodies poised like coiled springs, their eyes narrowed and focused on one thing: the *gaijin*. A palpable current of anticipation ripples through them, as if they are wolves waiting for the right moment to pounce on the deer.

"The yakuza," the old man begins, his voice a gravelly whisper, "operate like a single organism, bound together by ties stronger than blood. When you join, you swear an oath. Your brethren become more important than your family, than your father, mother, wife, or child. Your only family is the organization."

It is then, as he finishes this final sentence, that the old man lunges, a crudely fashioned shank materializing in his hand as if by magic. Peter is ready. His reflexes kick in. He intercepts the attack, his hand as quick as a striking cobra as it catches the old man's wrist and closes around it. A swift, brutal twist and the old man cries out in pain, the shank falling from his now broken hand.

Peter kicks the blade away, his heart no more than a murmur in his chest. He next tosses the old man away from him. It is at that point that a gunshot shatters the tense silence. It resounds from the nearest gun tower, the sound reverberating off the high walls of the prison. A booming voice on the loudspeakers commands everyone to hit the ground. Without hesitation, Peter drops onto his front, the taste of fear and dust filling his mouth as he presses himself against the hot, coarse dirt.

———

FROM THE GROUND, Peter watches the old man being carted away, his face twisted in pain as he clutched his broken hand. He had managed to get close, nearly convincing Peter of his innocence. But only nearly. Peter had already deduced the old man's intent by the time they had entered the yard, having witnessed his liver-spotted hand playing with the shank in a pocket of his *monpe*. His heart-felt tale of yakuza loyalty had merely been him getting himself geed up for the act.

Probably a lifer, Peter muses as he reenters the prison. *The old man would have gained better conditions, even some respect amongst the other inmates, had he succeeded.*

Who had sent him, though, is the question that really bothers Peter.

His cellmate? Perhaps.

Or maybe it had been Kato Myamoto himself.

As Peter walks along the yellow line of a corridor back to his cell, his mind flicks back to the hours before his arrival at Fuchu, poring over the dossier on Kato that Akechi Akiyama had given him. Two years prior, Kato had been just like the other men marked for death by Yūki Yokashina: a rich and powerful businessman. An intellectual prodigy with an IQ of 180, he had outshone his peers, earning a scholarship to MIT at age sixteen. His meteoric rise continued with the launch of his own tech company at twenty-one, his first code spawning an open-source operating system kernel. It had revolutionized the tech industry, powering everything from smartphones to supercomputers, and made him a billionaire by twenty-five.

Then it had all come crashing down. Not long after he made his fortune, he met his wife, a stunning actress and ex-model. They had quickly become Tokyo's golden couple, but whispers of Kato's possessiveness trailed them.

Ironically, he might have been on to something. His wife, whether pushed into it or not by Kato's jealousy, had fallen in love with a female costar on one of her film sets. The affair had caused a scandal when it had been uncovered by paparazzi: a whole slurry of risqué photographs spread across the tabloid pages of the two women caught in a tender moment on a Philippine beach.

Kato Myamoto had gone supernova. In his jealous madness, his vaunted IQ seemed to plummet, eclipsed by a blinding rage. Instead of hiring a hitman or simply walking away, Kato took matters into his own hands. His hasty, venom-fueled execution of the couple was anything but discreet. Having discovered them in a Tokyo hotel, he had stormed in and shot them both in cold blood.

Police had found him minutes later, cradling his wife's bullet-riddled body in a tragic picture of love and loss, his meteoric rise having ended in a crash landing. Now he was just another inmate in Fuchu, surrounded by predators.

Was he capable of sending the old man at Peter?

Perhaps.

Or perhaps it is someone else, someone that is neither Kato nor his cellmate. Yūki Yokashina? Does she have someone working in here? Surely she does. Otherwise, how is she going to get to Kato Myamoto?

The corridor leading to Peter's cell is silent when he arrives, devoid of its usual litany of loitering men—something that's probably got a lot to do with the guard stationed outside his door.

"The warden wants to speak," he grumbles in English, eyeing Peter with a steely gaze.

Peter nods, allowing the guard to guide him along the

labyrinthine corridors of the prison, their path marked by a solitary red line snaking its way to the heart of the institution —the warden's office.

The warden is an unassuming figure, a small, round man with features so nondescript he could blend into any crowd on Earth. Nevertheless, there's something about him that commands respect, a certain air of authority that is hard to ignore. His face almost entirely obscured by a pair of thick bifocals, he sits hunched behind a massive desk, his brow furrowed in concentration as he goes over a stack of papers.

Peter walks all the way to the end of the red line, which abruptly ends three feet from the desk. The guard then retreats from the room, leaving him alone with the warden.

Without uttering a word, the warden tugs open a drawer on his desk, his hand emerging with a plastic phone card. He extends it toward Peter, who accepts it without hesitation.

"You must establish contact," the warden instructs, his voice as cold and resolute as the prison walls themselves. Peter nods, slipping the card into the pocket of his monpe. The warden returns to his paperwork, his pen scratching rhythmically away at it.

Taking this as his cue to leave, Peter turns to go.

He has just reached the door when the warden's voice, now tinged with a hint of warning, halts him in his tracks.

"And a word of caution, Peter-san," he begins. Peter turns to face him, his hand still resting on the doorknob.

"It has come to my attention," the warden continues, his gaze never leaving the papers in front of him, "that several plots to murder you are already in motion. I would advise you to tread very carefully from now on. Next time, they may not send an old man."

THE TELEPHONES ARE LINED up against a grimy wall on the ground floor of the prison wing, a row of dull, beige life-lines in a sea of concrete gray. Peter chooses the last one, the handset cool and heavy in his hand. Around him, the wing is almost quiet, but the hostile glares of the other inmates are almost deafening in their silent threats.

Peter slips the phone card into the slot and dials the number. After several rings, a familiar voice answers.

"Hey, Peter."

"Hey, Mikey. How you holding up?"

"Oh, just great. They got me rigged up to a shock collar now."

Peter winces. "Yeah, I heard you got caught trying to escape. Was it bad?"

"Got my ass kicked by a cosplay enthusiast."

"A what?"

"Mayu."

"The chick they used in the honey trap?"

"Yeah. Turns out she's here on the island running security."

"Ouch. How does your ego feel?"

"Bruised. But then, not as bruised as my body."

"That bad?"

"I won't be giving her a chance next time."

Peter grins at his son's cockiness. "Well, I guess you heard. You're not the only one in a cell anymore."

"Yeah, I did. But at least you haven't got a shock collar around your neck."

"Nope. But I did almost get shanked by the world's oldest yakuza earlier."

"They sent an old man after you?"

"Yeah."

"Underestimation of the year," Michael quips. "Where is he now?"

"The infirmary."

"Figures. Anyway"—Michael's tone changes—"I better get to the point. Tanaka's people have discovered something while wiretapping the cell phones of Kato Myamoto's associates."

"What?"

"They found out that he's planning to escape. He's been in text conversation with some girlfriend he met through an inmate program. She's apparently waiting for him on the outside."

"Any details on how it's going to happen?"

"Not how, but when. Tomorrow."

Peter almost chokes. "Tomorrow?!"

"Yep. So you have to stay close to him."

It is then, as Peter surveys the room, that a sinking feeling hits his stomach. The two guards who were there only a few moments ago have vanished. Peter glances around; the common area of the wing is quietly emptying out, many of the prisoners skulking off to their cells, leaving only a dozen shirtless men behind, their black eyes fixed on Peter, the yakuza tattoos crawling over their skins promising dark things.

"Mikey," Peter says, a note of finality in his voice, "I gotta go."

He puts the phone down. The twelve men fan out in

front of him like a pack of wolves, their eyes gleaming with hate and anticipation. His cellmate and his four pals from earlier are among them, hostility radiating off them like heat from a furnace.

The first punch comes without warning, a clumsy haymaker. Peter deftly sidesteps it, using the man's momentum against him in a move straight out of aikido, shoving him in the back as he comes staggering past and sending him sprawling into one of the telephones.

The rest of the men pile in. Peter must move away from the wall, get into the open. A meaty fist slams into his jaw as he tries to maneuver his way into more open space. He staggers back, the world spinning momentarily as shockwaves of pain radiate through his face. He quickly regains his footing, ducking as another punch is thrown his way.

He stoops low as another haymaker swings high overhead and tackles its sender in the midriff, pushing him back and using him as a battering ram against the others, knocking them out the way. The men are too frenzied, too grouped together. Peter pushes the guy through the crowd, breaking it up, before smashing him into a solid concrete wall with a slap of bare skin and a sharp expulsion of wind.

Peter lets go and steps back, landing a swift jab to the man's stomach. He grunts and doubles over, but his companions are quick to take his place. They come at Peter from all sides, their fists raining down on him in a brutal rhythm. But he is more in the open now. He can use the space available to spread the fight out.

The next man lunges for him, aiming a poorly executed kick at Peter's midsection. With the agility of a skilled Muay Thai fighter, Peter catches the foot, yanking it upwards and unbalancing the man before delivering a sharp elbow strike to his exposed flank. The man screams out like a slaughtered pig as his ribs fracture, collapsing in a heap.

Peter is warmed up; he has his feet now. He's in the game. He moves as if he's in a dance, his body twisting and turning to dodge the onslaught, his limbs flowing through the forms of kung fu, his movements fluid and controlled. He dodges and weaves, ducks and spins, his hands and feet lashing out in a flurry of well-placed strikes. The men are relentless, charging at him with reckless abandon, their punches wild, their kicks erratic. They lack finesse, but their sheer number and brute strength pose a significant threat. Being so vastly outnumbered, it is inevitable that blows will manage to break through his defenses, bruising his ribs, splitting his lip. Pain blooms across his body, but it is a distant thing, a faint buzz in the back of his mind: pushed all the way to the far corners.

With a sudden burst of energy, he launches himself at his attackers. His fist connects with a jaw, a stomach, a throat. He kicks, punches, and head-butts, each movement precise and calculated. Drawing from the aggressive techniques of Krav Maga, Peter targets vulnerable areas—throats, groins, knees—rendering each attacker incapacitated in quick succession.

The men are strong, seasoned fighters, but Peter is faster, smarter. He weaves through their attacks, landing his own with deadly precision. One by one, they fall, groaning and clutching their injuries.

Finally, the wing falls relatively silent. The only sound that remains is the pained wheezing groans of the defeated men. Peter stands amidst them, his chest heaving with exertion. Blood trickles from a cut on his lip, and his body screams with pain. But he is standing. He has won.

He looks up, his gaze meeting the eyes of the other prisoners who had watched the fight from the balcony. They stare back, a newfound respect gleaming in their eyes for the *gaijin*. Peter has proven himself. He is a force to be reckoned with, a fact that won't be forgotten anytime soon.

TWENTY

SHINOSHIMA

IN THE STERILE CONFINES OF HIS CELL, MICHAEL hunches over the computer, the cold glare of the screen reflecting off his eyes. The shock collar around his neck itches, a constant reminder of his confinement. Every now and then, his hand rises unconsciously to scratch at it.

The schematic plans of Fuchu Prison fill the computer screen, the kid trying to find some way out of there that Kato Myamoto may be taking tomorrow. As for his own chances of escape, his internet access has been limited to the tasks assigned by his captors. YouTube, Instagram, and Facebook are all off limits. There will be no cyber prison-breaks, no hidden back doors to slip through. And by the looks of things, no escaping down to the labs of B-35. The camera he hid persistently worries him.

But then something happens. An unexpected message pops up in the corner of the screen from "K." His heart skips a beat as he reads it. *I found your camera. Don't worry, it's safe.*

The internal computer systems of the island have a messaging service, so that the people working there can communicate within Shinoshima without linking to the outside Internet. Tanaka's people tend to use it when communicating with Michael. It's easier because the program it uses can translate accurately between languages— meaning that they don't necessarily need to get an English speaker to communicate with him.

The words leap off the screen, searing into his mind. He is about to type a reply when his fingers freeze over the keyboard. What if this is some trick? Maybe Tanaka's people know about the camera but haven't been able to find it. Using this as a ruse to smoke him out.

So Michael replies: *What camera?*

K: *The one you hid on top of the ventilation.*

His heart freezes. He goes to type before again stopping himself. What if they've discovered the camera and now want to find out who his contact is on the island? This could still be a ruse.

So he types: *Don't have a clue what you're talking about. Who is this?*

K: *The same person who left it for you on B-35 inside the arm of a hazmat. The same person who has been compromised by you getting yourself caught.*

Michael stares at the message, his fingers hovering over the keys. Should he trust it?

M: *Still have no idea who this is.*

K: *This could go on forever, so I'm just gonna get to the*

point: Tonight at 3 the security systems on your floor will go offline. Your cell will become unlocked.

Michael's attention is caught. He types.

M: *Doesn't matter. They've been gassing me at 9 every night.*

K: *How long can you hold your breath?*

M: *I don't know. Two and a half minutes at a push.*

K: *Good. The gas is only released for 30 seconds. Two minutes should be enough time for it to clear long enough for you to breathe again without losing consciousness. Tonight, I need you to hold your breath.*

As he cautiously engages in the digital back-and-forth, Michael's mind races with possibilities. The promise of escape, so tantalizingly close, sends a thrill of adrenaline coursing through his veins. His heart hammers in his chest, his fingers shaking as they fly across the keyboard. He casts a wary glance at the glass panel to his left, the guards on the other side oblivious to the life-altering conversation unfolding just meters away.

M: *What about the guys in the room next door?*

K: *Ever since they've been gassing you, they haven't occupied the room after 9:30. They just watch you on the camera. But the camera will be on a loop tonight. You'll be free for as long as you need.*

M: *For as long as I need to do what?*

TWENTY-ONE

FUCHU PRISON

Cold, hard bricks press into Peter's back, an unwelcome reminder of his new reality. After discovering the twelve injured men, they'd dragged him off the wing and chucked him in a windowless *hogobo* ("protection" cell). Essentially, it's a stark white box, its bright strip lighting casting harsh shadows and making sleep impossible. The chill of the floor seeps through his thin prison uniform, making his bruised flesh ache underneath. Occasionally, he dabs at the fresh blood trickling from the corner of his split mouth with the back of a hand.

Eyes closed, he waits.

It is now the next morning: the day of Kato Myamoto's supposed escape.

The scrape of locks jolts Peter from his thoughts. The cell door creaks open, revealing the warden's small figure in the doorway. He nods at the guard with him, steps inside, and the heavy door thuds shut behind him.

Peter wastes no time. "You know he's planning on escaping?"

His voice bounces off the cold walls.

The warden's thin lips curl into a knowing grin. "Of course I do. Our mutual friend is paying me a high price to look the other way; something that won't do my career any favors. I am doing my part. However"—his gaze sweeps over Peter, taking in the bruised and battered man before him—"you, Peter-san, are not doing your part so well." He gestures dismissively at the stark cell. "My guards want you locked in here for the next six months."

"Then isn't it lucky I have you," Peter retorts, the corners of his mouth twitching with the hint of a smirk.

The warden's gaze hardens. "Yes. And now you need to stay out of trouble, concentrate on the job in hand. Another incident and I won't be able to get you out of here again. Now get ready for work."

"Work?" Peter repeats, his brows furrowing.

"Yes," the warden affirms, a note of finality in his voice. "Today you will be working in the laundromat. Kato's escape will happen there. So get yourself together. Your shift starts in twenty minutes."

———

A GIANT PRISON laundromat gradually fills with men, the prisoners forming rows along the white lines that cover the floor, everything orchestrated to the final detail.

There are twenty minutes of exercise at the beginning of

the shift. At their front, a guard with a bullhorn commands them to perform jumping jacks, stretches, and a whole host of other exercises. Once this is finished, the men are assigned stations, and they go off to them.

Peter is assigned to one of the large folding machines. Soon, everything is switched on, and the laundromat hums into life, an orchestra of mechanical churns and whirls. Washing machines and dryers, dozens of them, roar in tandem, their noise punctuated by the thudding precision of the folding machines, a roaring chorus of industrial white noise.

Peter begins feeding sheets into the machine, his eyes darting around the room in search of Kato Myamoto. The air is heavy with the scent of industrial-strength detergent and bleach, mingled with a faint undercurrent of stale sweat and grime. Everything is saturated with humidity, the moisture clinging to the walls and windows, the air thick in Peter's lungs, and soon his clothing clings to him.

He finally spots Kato and his mountain of a bodyguard in a far corner. The two men are exchanging hushed words. Then Kato nods. The bodyguard approaches one of the massive dryer drums, glances furtively around, and heaves the heavy metal door open.

Pretending to be absorbed in his work, Peter covertly observes the unfolding scene, watching the two men check to see if the guards are looking, then wasting no time, Kato clambering into the darkness of the dryer before the body-guard follows suit. The door is then closed from the inside, leaving no trace of their escape.

Realizing the time is now, Peter abandons his cart of linen and strides toward the dryer. Reaching it, he swings open the metal door and climbs inside. Slipping into the dryer's hollowed interior is like stepping into another world. The men are nowhere to be seen. But Peter is sure he knows where they've gone.

A large section at the back of the huge drum has been cut away to create a space big enough for a man, the cut-away piece standing to the side. Squeezing through, Peter finds himself in a gap running between the back of the machine and the wall. Gazing along the length of the cavity, he spots the giant figure of the bodyguard as he drops down a sewer hatch.

Sidestepping along, the gap not wide enough for his shoulders, Peter creeps his way to the open manhole. It leads to a dimly lit sewer tunnel. The nauseating stench of waste hits him like a physical blow the second he steps down into it. Steeling himself, Peter begins to navigate the slippery tunnel, the sound of distant splashing echoing through the sewer. Water sloshing around his ankles, he moves with calculated precision, trying to match the pace of Kato and his bodyguard while staying undetected.

As he makes his way deeper into the guts of the sewer system, Peter knows he has to remain vigilant. His senses on high alert, every fiber of his being is tuned into the hot and sticky environment around him. With each passing moment, his determination only hardens.

The tunnel begins to bend, the way ahead unseeable. There is a sudden, pungent odor of sweat and aggression that fills the tunnel as Peter rounds it—and comes face to face with Kato's bodyguard.

The colossus of a man looms in the dim light, blocking the path like a monstrous gatekeeper. His beady eyes glow with malicious intent as he cracks his knuckles, a grim smile spreading across his immovable face.

Peter takes a deep, steadying breath. He knew this fight was inevitable. He is smaller, lighter, and at first glance, physically inferior. But Peter has something the bodyguard doesn't have: a lethal combination of martial arts training and years of experience.

The first punch comes at Peter like a wrecking ball, raw power that could easily shatter the bones of his face. Peter sidesteps, narrowly avoiding the blow, and retaliates with a sharp jab to the bodyguard's ribs. His fist meets a brick wall of muscle, the impact barely phasing the larger man.

The bodyguard laughs, a low, rumbling sound that reverberates off the sewer walls. He launches himself at Peter, those giant fists flying at him. Peter blocks and dodges as best he can in the tight space of the sewer, but the bodyguard's reach and power are overwhelming. A brutal punch lands on Peter's jaw, snapping his head back. His vision blurs, and his body screams in protest.

But Peter isn't beaten, not yet. He taps into his reservoir of strength, drawing from his training. Mother and Magda didn't teach him to give in to larger opponents; they taught him how to beat them into smaller ones. He blocks a wild punch, redirects the bodyguard's momentum, and lands a precise elbow strike on his opponent's temple.

The bodyguard staggers, disoriented for the first time. Peter doesn't waste the opportunity. He darts forward, delivering a flurry of punches and kicks, each one hitting its mark.

Still, the bodyguard is resilient. He roars, shrugging off the blows, and launches himself at Peter again. In the frenzy, he manages to land a powerful blow to Peter's midsection. The air is forced from his lungs, a sharp pain radiating through him. Peter falls to his knees, gasping for breath. The bodyguard sneers, comes over him, and raises his fist for the finishing blow.

But Peter has one last trick up his sleeve. As the fist comes crashing down, he rolls sideways, evading the punch. He surges upward, using all his remaining strength to drive his own fist into the bodyguard's throat. The impact is immediate; the bodyguard chokes, his eyes bulging. Peter follows with a swift, brutal jab to the solar plexus, causing the bodyguard to double over.

With a final, desperate burst of energy, Peter whips around the back of the bodyguard and wraps an arm around the thick neck, applying pressure. The bodyguard thrashes, but Peter holds on, locking his hands at the back of the guy's wide neck, squeezing until the thrashing gradually slows, then stops. Finally, the bodyguard's massive body slumps, then collapses lifeless onto the wet ground of the sewer.

Peter releases him, panting heavily. But there is no time to rest. He has to keep moving. Kato Myamoto is still ahead.

———

RAIN POURS down from the heavens in sheets, pelting Fuchu in a flood that turns the grimy city streets into a dreary watercolor. A manhole cover pops in the middle of a deserted road, and emerging from the sewer, Kato Myamoto takes a moment to savor the cool touch of the rain on his face.

"Whoo!" he cries out, relishing the chilly welcome of

freedom before suddenly becoming aware that he is now officially a fugitive of the law.

He snaps his gaze along the stretch of street. About a hundred yards away, at the end, is the tall wall of Fuchu Prison. A guard tower stands proud like a sentinel in the middle of it, and when a burst of lightning erupts behind it, Kato can make out the silhouettes of the guards inside.

A sudden feeling of being vulnerable, of being out in the open, comes over Kato. He turns his back to the prison and goes in the opposite direction. It's then that he spots the red taillights of a car farther along.

This must be his ride.

Reaching the waiting car, he slips inside. There is a single occupant in the driver's seat: a woman with a blank expression, her eyes veiled by sunglasses, something that contrasts starkly with the bleak weather.

"Hey, baby," Kato says as he gets in, shutting the door behind him.

He reaches his face across the car, pursing his lips. The woman grimaces.

"No kiss?" he asks.

"Where's Hiroshi?"

"I'm not sure. He told me not to wait. The guy you told me about, the hitman. He followed us into the sewer. Hiroshi stayed behind to stop him coming."

"Then we need to leave."

With a swift, practiced movement, she engages the gear, and the car rolls forward, swiftly vacating the vicinity.

Peter isn't far behind. He emerges from the sewer just in time to see the taillights disappearing around a corner. Without hesitation, he bolts toward a parked Honda moped on the side of the road, jumps on it, and rips the ignition paneling off. He tugs out the wiring, finds the two he needs, and brings the moped to life. Its engine then gurgles beneath him as he surges into the soaking streets.

The traffic becomes thicker, the sedan somewhere farther up, the relentless rain hammering down on the city with a ferocity that makes visibility near impossible. The slick asphalt becomes treacherous as he maneuvers through a maze of cars, the world around him a cacophonous blend of honking horns and the roar of the storm.

He catches a glimpse of the sedan ahead, but it's quickly swallowed by traffic. Fear gnaws at him as it vanishes amid the muddled dance of vehicles, threatening to get away from him.

In a daring act of desperation, Peter spots a pedestrian at the edge of the sidewalk engrossed in his mobile phone, oblivious to the high-stakes chase unfolding around him. Without slowing down, Peter reaches out, snatches the phone from the guy's hand, and dials Michael's number as he speeds away, the pedestrian's cries lost in the rain's hissing tumult.

"Michael," Peter shouts into the stolen phone, "I need you to trace a car."

"What's the plate?"

"I don't know. I haven't gotten close enough yet. I need you to access..."

A burst of horn as Peter is almost taken out by a truck lurching out from a side street, the driver not looking. In a sharp movement, Peter maneuvers the bike one-handed across the lanes to escape being wiped out.

"I need you," he begins again once he's out of danger, "to find it on CCTV."

"In Fuchu?"

"Yes. In Fuchu." Peter scans the street names up on the posts. "Okay. I'm on Keio-dori. Close to the library," he adds as he passes the building.

"Give me a second... Okay. I'm in. What does the car look like?"

"It's a black Mazda3."

It takes Michael several seconds, but soon he comes back. "Okay. I've got them," the kid says. "I've also got you. You're about two blocks behind. They're still on Keio-dori. Just keep going straight."

Guided by Michael, Peter is able to stay with the sedan, even if it does stretch another two blocks farther ahead. Then, with the kid leading him through the labyrinthine streets, Peter is finally pointed toward a desolate stretch of industrial land that sits beside the Tama River. He arrives mere minutes after the Mazda, finding himself at a section of riverbank covered in weeds and the rusted remains of shipping containers. The rain has transformed the terrain into a sodden mud-field, a harsh landscape under the storm's assault.

The sedan is parked beside the road. As well as three Honda Firebird motorcycles.

Kato is nowhere to be seen.

Abandoning the moped by the roadside, Peter advances, each step calculated, his senses on high alert.

About fifty meters farther along through a mass of salt grass and rusted metal, standing close to the flowing brown waters of the Tama, is Kato Myamoto, the newly freed convict. He stands defiant against the tempest, the rain soaking him to the bone, his hair matted against his forehead.

Before him stands Yūki Yokashina, her haunting figure illuminated by the sporadic flashes of lightning. Her jet-black hair, drenched and clinging to her, seems to absorb the scarce light, her eyes as dark and merciless as the sky above.

Kato looks confused.

The woman opposite is not who he thought she was. He thought her name was Ann, a woman he met through the prison love letters scheme, who promised him in phone calls that she would help him escape. She kept that promise, it has to be said. But when they arrived at this odd location and these three yakuza brutes started calling her Yūki, he became confused—and then it dawned on him.

"*Tanaka's bitch,*" he had hissed.

Now he is cornered on the bank of the river like a rat.

Yūki stands there in the torrent, glaring at him, her brother, Tatsuo Yokashina, at her side, his reputation as the formidable leader of the Bosozoku yakuza clan adding a palpable layer of tension to the scene.

Creeping up on them, Peter places himself at the edge of one of the containers, observing them from his concealed position. Instinct urges him to intervene, yet the gravity of the situation demands patience.

"You recognize me now, Kato?" Yūki shouts over the rain.

"Yes. I thought you were dead."

"Maybe I am. Maybe this is a ghost exacting her revenge on you."

"It was you who killed the others, wasn't it? Ishi, Kujira, and Haiko."

"Yes. And now it is your turn."

Yūki turns to one of the men. He brings over a sheathed katana. There is a deafening crack of thunder as she unsheathes the blade, pulls it out, and slices through the torrent of rainfall, the drops splashing off it before settling the blade into an upright position extended from her hand.

She nods, a signal to another of her men to bring forward a second katana in its sheath.

"Both these blades," Yūki says in a chilling tone, "are my pride and joy. They are equal."

The yakuza brings the blade over to Kato and holds it out. The fugitive doesn't know what to do. He glances at the sheathed katana, then back at Yūki.

"Take it," she says. "It is your only hope of walking away from this river alive."

Kato takes the sheath with a trembling hand. He slips the blade out of it and throws the mahogany case onto the dirt ground.

Yūki Yokashina, her dark eyes gleaming in the scarce light, holds the weapon with an expert's grace. Kato Myamoto, on the other hand, holds the katana with both hands in a way that suggests he may as well be holding a mop.

"You used to beat your wife," Yūki says.

Kato says nothing. Just meets her gaze, his own blade reflecting the storm above, the tension between them crackling like static, their lethal dance about to begin.

"You murdered her and her lover. Murdered two innocent people in cold blood."

"They weren't innocent. The same as you weren't."

"And are you innocent, Kato Myamoto? Are you and your fellow men innocent for what you did to me?"

Kato remains reticent.

"I think it will be fitting," Yūki goes on, "that you will meet your end at the hands of a woman."

Yūki moves. Kato isn't completely unskilled with the katana. He took lessons as a boy in fencing. He believes himself more than a match for this "woman." Their bodies become a whirlwind of steel and flesh, their blades meeting in sparks. Yūki draws him in, letting him think he can defeat her. Each of her moves becomes a study in letting his ego expand before she lays the deadly blow, the duo performing a lethal ballet amid the downpour.

In the background, Tatsuo and the others stand watching when one of them cries out, "He's here!"

Tatsuo and the other yakuza turn to him. He's pointing a finger at Peter's position. They whip their guns out, and the air is torn apart by the savage roar of gunfire, the members of the Bosozoku yakuza clan opening fire on Peter's position. Bullets rip through the sheet of rain, ricocheting off the shipping container as Peter disappears into the maze of rusting containers, the bullets a deadly chorus resonating all around him.

Unarmed and outnumbered, he must become a shadow weaving through the rusty labyrinth. His movements swift and decisive, he uses the containers as both shield and weapon, using the environment to his advantage. The yakuza come after him, spreading out and trying to surround him, but there are more than enough nooks to hide in.

Peter uses his impressive hearing to find the nearest man as the guy creeps along. He's just around the corner of the next container, his boots making sloshing sounds in the mud as he creeps up. Tucking himself into an edge, his back to the rusted metal, Peter waits for him. The guy's pistol makes a sock-puppet appearance first, then the rest of him.

Peter explodes from the corner, his movements so swift they are barely perceptible amid the storm. Before the guy can even cry out, Peter has disarmed him and jabbed him in the stomach, sending him down onto his knees, and as lightning illuminates the wet air and thunder bursts in their ears, smashes him in the face with the guy's own pistol, sending him crashing straight into unconsciousness.

One down, two to—

Bullets whip through the rain, forcing Peter to dive for cover and striking the rusted, skeletal remains of the shipping containers, their reverberating clanks echoing throughout the barren space.

With every passing moment, the duel between Kato and Yūki intensifies. Kato, face contorted in rage, launches himself at Yūki, his blade desperately seeking her life. But she is a tempest, her movements fluid and lethal, her katana a silver blur in the rain. It meets each of Kato's strikes with unwavering resolve, the sharp clash of steel mirroring the distant gunshots.

Their swords collide again, steel scraping against steel. As he strains against her, Kato senses this woman toying with him. A permanent half-smile plays across her lips. As they stand face to face, their swords pressed together, his back foot digging into the ground for leverage, he tries to push her off, something he should easily achieve with his superior weight. But there is some demon in this woman that possesses her to fight far beyond her natural physique. It is she who pushes Kato away, sending her opponent reeling. His katana flails wildly, his footing almost lost.

As he regains his balance, fear runs up Kato. Real fear. And for the first time, he sees his own death reflecting from Yūki's eyes.

Meanwhile, across the yard, the gunmen have lost sight of Peter in the labyrinth of containers. One of the men wanders aimlessly down a gap. On the other side of the next container, Peter is clambering up it like a spider. The rain beating off him, he creeps in a low position to the edge; he spots the man inching his way along, oblivious to his presence. He doesn't want to use the pistol he stole off the last man—the gunshot will alert the other man looking for him. He waits for the target to come beneath him and jumps. Before the guy can cry out, Peter has neutralized his pistol, placed a hand over his mouth, and dragged him to the shadows, where he breaks his neck.

Two down. One to go.

At the same time, Yūki decides enough is enough. She's done playing with Kato. It is time to end this and strike the final blow. With a flurry of her katana, she pushes his sword to the side, opens up a gap, and brings her blade down on his wrist with such force that it cuts the hand off in a clean slice.

Kato screams into the rain, the katana dropping to the muddy ground, along with the hand. He falls to his knees, grabbing hold of the stump at the end of his right arm, his face contorted into a grimace of pure pain.

His swollen eyes look up at Yūki as she comes toward

him, holding the katana down by her side. She stops a few feet from him, her eyes as cold and dead as hell itself.

"You are a blind fool," she tells him. "Blinded by your envy. Like the others, you think you deserve more than you are. But you are nothing. Just blind to the way things really are."

And with that, she makes a quick movement, the katana stabbing through the air—once, twice—its end poking out Kato's eyes.

He screams once more, the blind man howling up at the black sky, the blood washing down his face from his mutilated sockets.

Yūki lets him have his pain for a moment, then, with another swift movement of the sword, she takes his head off.

In the containers and the mud, Peter finds himself face to face with Tatsuo Yokashina, the leader of the Bosozoku. The two of them are trapped on the edges of opposing containers in the narrow maze, their eyes locked on each other.

The night erupts in a symphony of gunfire as they unleash a hailstorm of bullets, each seeking to eliminate the other. Peter peels from his edge, spinning around to the other side of the container. Tatsuo does the same, and before they know it, both men are facing each other from opposite corners. That's when Peter's pistol clicks empty. Tatsuo's isn't far behind, the deafening sounds of their battle replaced by an eerie patter of thrumming rain.

Both men throw down their empty guns like discarded stones and step out of cover, their eyes locked across the alley. With a roar, Tatsuo charges at Peter, and the two men come crashing together like speeding freight trains. In

Akechi's intel, it had been written that, like his sister Yūki, Tatsuo Yokashina had been trained by their father in the art of martial arts. He shows it now, performing several well-executed combinations. He sends a jab out with a quick, straight movement aimed at Peter's face. It is a quick and snappy punch that serves to create distance between them as Peter leans back to avoid it: a clear setup for further attacks.

As Tatsuo retracts the jab, he pushes off his rear leg explosively, transitioning to a Muay Thai flying knee. He drives his hips forward, bringing the rear leg up and extending the lead leg for a powerful knee strike, aimed at Peter's head.

Peter snakes his body and parries the knee away with the palms of his hands. He does well to match Tatsuo's every move, their grunts and cries punctuating the blistering rainstorm. Tatsuo may have the upper hand in speed, but Peter owns him on physical presence: his reach is better, his blows heavier. For all the hits Tatsuo lands on Peter, it is the ones that he himself lands on Tatsuo that cause the most pain.

At one point, he intercepts a gyaku-zuki reverse punch, parrying it away, and as Tatsuo attempts to bring his lead leg around and sweep Peter's feet, Peter gets in a devastating liver shot using a chudan tsuki middle punch. It causes Tatsuo to sprawl onto the cold, muddy ground.

Peter looms over him. Tatsuo goes to get back up, but Peter doesn't let him. His fists rain down on the yakuza leader like the relentless storm around them, and then—

A gunshot bursts through the thunder and the storm, the metal container sparking as a bullet hits it inches above Peter's head. He turns to find Yūki Yokashina standing at the end of the passage, her smoking gun aimed at him.

Peter gets off of Tatsuo and steps back. He quickly takes in his surroundings, realizing he's only ten yards away from the river, the oily waters of the Tama flowing past in the background.

Yūki speaks, her voice cutting through the patting rain like grumbling thunder.

"Once again you are too late, Azrael-san," she says.

As imperceptibly as he can, Peter begins stepping backwards, toward the Tama.

"How do you know who I am?" he asks.

She merely smiles at him and asks a question of her own: "Did Tanaka tell you why I want my revenge?"

Peter shakes his head. "No," he says. "He didn't."

The smile widens. "Then he still doesn't trust his underlings with the truth. Same old Tanaka."

She raises the gun and Peter makes a run for it. Two gunshots come in rapid succession. His body stiffens as he feels them both, one skimming the flesh of his right flank just above the hip, the other lodging itself in his shoulder, the shockwave propelling him toward the sanctuary of the Tama.

He reaches its edge and, with a pained grunt, plunges into the dark depths of the swollen river. Water erupts around him as more shots ring out, the bullets creating violent geysers around him.

Yūki rushes to the edge, the gun pointed at the water as the rain cuts its murky surface up, watching frantically for any sign of him coming up for air.

"There!" Tatsuo shouts from beside her.

He's pointing downriver. She follows the gesture.

A passing garbage barge trundles down the Tama, and there, swimming toward it, is Azrael: master assassin.

As she aims her pistol once more, police sirens begin to make themselves known above the sounds of the weather.

"Come on," Tatsuo says. "We have to go."

With one last despairing look at the barge disappearing around a bend in the river, Yūki cries out in frustration, then joins her brother in escaping the carnage, leaving the dead behind—including the headless remains of the recently escaped prisoner Kato Myamoto.

TWENTY-TWO

SHINOSHIMA

THE ICY HISS OF GAS INFILTRATING HIS CELL IS A chilling serenade to the imminent danger it represents. Michael lies on his bare cot, his breath held captive in his lungs as he clings to consciousness. The gas winds its way around him, wispy tendrils attempting to coax him into slumber. His lungs scream for release, each second stretching into an agonizing eternity as he denies his body the oxygen it demands.

After an endless minute, the shrill whistle of the gas ceases. Now he must wait another two until it clears. His fingers tighten around the rough blanket, knuckles bleached bone-white from the strain. He counts the excruciating seconds down, the blood filling his ears, feeling each beat of his heart in them, his body begging for release, for the sweet rush of oxygen.

Two minutes end. He waits, a few moments more, until

he is sure the gas is cleared, before he lets out a silent sigh, taking in shallow, rapid breaths so as not to pull in too much of the remains of the sedative fog. Straining his ears, he listens for the telltale sounds of the guard in the adjoining room. The clinking of the glass panels resonates in the silence, the shift in air pressure signaling his watcher's departure. His heart murmurs in his chest as he waits to be sure.

Emboldened, Michael slides off the cot, his bare feet recoiling from the cold kiss of the concrete floor, and approaches the door of his cell. It opens, gliding to the side with a soft hiss.

The corridor beyond is a cold, stark stretch of concrete, punctuated by the rigid uniformity of steel doors. The harsh overhead strip lights bathe the entire length in an unforgiving, sterile glow.

Each step he takes is a dance with danger, Michael all too aware of the shock collar around his neck. He wonders if everyone inside the facility has a fob for it like Mayu.

Tonight, he has a new place to go. F-11. It's on the other side of the facility and a lot more busy. Michael has to be a phantom, a ghost in the machine. Along the way, he has to constantly slip past patrolling guards, ducking into the safety of the shadows whenever footsteps resonate ominously in the distance, his heart fluttering in his chest, the adrenaline in his veins urging him on with purpose.

After what feels like ages, he finally arrives at F-11.

A gargantuan underground warehouse sprawls before him, teeming with the organized chaos of crates, forklifts, and men in uniform. At the far end, a monorail train is being unloaded of its cargo. The steel song of metal on metal resonates in the vast space.

Having snuck in through a corner, Michael stays within the cover of things, gliding behind a tall stack of wooden crates. His eyes scan the warehouse, mapping out a path in his mind.

Navigating his way through the maze of boxes, shipping containers and racking, his senses on high alert, he makes it to the spot he's been aiming for. Nestled in a hidden corner, almost camouflaged against the cold concrete, is the GoPro camera K had stashed there for him. He retrieves it from a cavity in a wall, the tiny device feeling surprisingly weighty in his palm—heavy with the gravity of its purpose. He powers it up, the small screen flickering to life, ready to document the secrets of this underground hell.

Michael retreats to a strategic vantage point. Ensconced behind a tower of wood crates, he finds an unobstructed view of the sprawling warehouse floor. His attention is immediately drawn to the monorail train. A rail-mounted gantry crane runs along its length, unloading it of shipping containers. One is lifted and set aside, away from the typical cargo. It appears to gain more attention than any of the other things pulled off the back of the train. This is proven when a set of doors open on the far side of the room and out step three men dressed in lab coats.

These, Michael thinks, must work down in B-35.

They approach the container right at the moment armed guards crack its doors open. The second he sees what is inside, a chill slithers down Michael's spine, his stomach turning at the sight.

People. Men, women, children—each one blinking into the harsh light of the warehouse as they are led out. It is sickening, their gaunt faces etched in confusion and fear, children clutching onto the hands of adults, their eyes wide and teary, their clothes worn and dirty. A testament to their arduous journey in the metal confines of the container.

Michael steadies his trembling hands, aiming the camera at the scene unfolding below.

The people are corralled like livestock by the armed men, their guns a menacing reminder of the power dynamics at play. The ones in the sterile white lab coats bustle around them with digital tablets, taking down details and photographing them with an efficiency that is eerily cold.

As each person is processed, a shock collar is fastened around their neck, the metallic device a stark contrast against their skin. The people flinch as the collars snap into place.

His focus locked onto the captives, Michael doesn't hear the soft pad of footsteps behind him, the scuff of boots against concrete muffled by the industrial din of the warehouse. The noise and movement is an effective screen for a predator stalking its prey.

It is only when a shadow falls over him that Michael senses the presence of another. But by now it is too late.

He turns, his heart lurching in his chest as he finds himself face to face with one of the guards. A gasp of surprise is smothered by a gloved hand clamping down over his mouth, the grip iron-tight. Panic flares within the kid, a primal instinct that has him thrashing against his assailant. The GoPro slips from his grip, clattering to the concrete floor and skittering out of sight.

And then he sees it. A small, black device in the guard's free hand—a fob. Recognition hits Michael like a punch to the gut. The shock collar around his neck suddenly feels heavier. A jolt of terror seizes him, making him redouble his efforts to free himself.

But it is too late. The guard presses the fob, a malicious grin splitting his face. Instantly, a cruel blast of electricity arcs through Michael. Pain sears through him, his body convulsing against the relentless current. He can hear his own scream, muffled and distorted, as his vision tunnels, the warehouse spinning into a disorienting blur.

His struggles gradually weaken, his consciousness slipping away under the onslaught of the shock collar. His last thought, before darkness claims him, is a desperate prayer that the images he's captured will somehow find their way to the outside world, that justice can be served upon these people.

TWENTY-THREE

TOKYO

Peter sits on an aluminum table while Hirako the vet sits on a stool behind him, his squinting eyes studying the wound to Peter's shoulder while removing pieces of the shattered bullet with medical tweezers. The gash on his flank is already sewn up and bandaged.

In the background, a dog whines in its cage, a sure sign that this isn't a hospital but a twenty-four-hour veterinary surgery.

The outside buzzer sounds, pulling Hirako's attention toward the door. He doesn't say anything, merely gets up and leaves the room. Peter thinks he knows who it is, and when the vet returns, it is confirmed when he sees the bald head of Akechi Akiyama accompanying him, his fingers gripping his cane, the duck's bill slipping between his fingers.

The reticent Hirako returns to the stool and continues

with his work. Akechi retrieves another stool from a corner, brings it over, and takes a seat. His brow furrows, lips tight as if biting back an unfavorable comment.

"So she didn't kill you, then," he says dryly, his immovable eyes staring at Peter. "That is a shame."

Peter remains silent, only wincing when Hirako's tweezers dig into his flesh.

"You are running out of chances, Azrael-san," Akechi goes on.

Peter has had enough of this man and his master. In a snappish tone, he says, "Just tell me who the next target is."

Akechi breathes out. Then, "Gladly. The next target is a man by the name of Kenji Kiobi. He is the last before Tanaka-shachou, so this could be your final chance."

The look on Akechi's face tells Peter all he needs to know about what it could cost him if he misses it.

"Who is Kenji Kiobi?" he asks.

"He is the son of a billionaire industrialist. He attended school with Tanaka and has several investments in Tanaka-Corp, being one of its major shareholders."

"So he's just another megalomaniac like all the others, then?"

"Not quite," Akechi replies. "Kiobi-san is extremely rich but has never really worked in his life."

"Trust fund kid?"

"Yes. Kenji comes from one of the most prestigious families in the whole of Japan. The youngest of four sons, he found himself a little left behind. While his brothers went into the family company, Kenji preferred to spend his days traveling around in his yacht and doing... well, not much."

"Not much," Peter repeats in a sardonic tone. "So where is this lazy playboy currently doing not much?"

"You are in luck. He is on his yacht, anchored just off of Tokyo Bay, at the entrance point. However," Akechi adds in a sinister undertone, "Tanaka-shachou has decided to play more hands."

Peter narrows his eyes. "Does that mean what I think it does?"

"And what is that, Azrael-san?"

"That he's sending in more assassins."

"It does," Akechi replies with a nod of his egg-shaped head. "After your recent failures, he is hedging his bets."

"Shouldn't surprise me," Peter mutters, glancing at the buzzing fluorescent light overhead as it flickers. "And who are these 'others'?"

"They are professionals," Akechi replies. "Highly skilled, like yourself. You should consider them competition."

"Competition, huh?" Peter flexes his shoulder, grimacing as the pain radiates down his arm. "And you don't think that might get a little... messy? Too many chefs spoiling the broth, and all that?"

"Indeed, it could. However, Tanaka-shachou believes that this approach will... speed up the process." Akechi shrugs, the movement small but eloquent. "It seems he is growing impatient."

"And here I was, thinking he was the patient type," Peter responds dryly, his gaze flicking over to the door. An idea begins to form in his mind, a risky one, but perhaps it's time to switch things up. "Well, Akiyama-san," he adds, "if there's nothing else..."

Akechi stands, his face still wearing that disapproving mask. "Just one more thing, Azrael-san," he says in a cold tone. "Do not fail again."

And with that, he walks out of the room, leaving Peter with Hirako and their canine audience.

TWENTY-FOUR

SHINOSHIMA

THE WORLD FADES BACK INTO EXISTENCE AROUND
Michael. A rock band of pain plays heavy metal in his skull,
and his shoulders ache from the awkward position he finds
himself in. He forces his eyelids open, revealing a featureless,
grim room, the hard cement floor and bare concrete walls
dimly lit by a solitary, hanging lightbulb. Its sallow light casts
a pool of pale yellow around him.

He glances down and sees his body bound by thick
leather clasps, securing him to a chair as though he were
some psychotic in need of containment. He pulls against the
bonds, muscles straining. They hold firm.

Footsteps reverberate outside the room, the cruel staccato of polished boots on concrete. The door slides open,
and a figure steps into the circle of light.

It is the guard who incapacitated him—a thickset man
with a face carved from granite, the cold stones of his eyes

glinting in the dim light. His thick lips split into a smirk upon observing that Michael's awake.

He speaks in Japanese, not caring that the kid can't understand a single word of it. "Waking up, are we?" he asks in a voice as rough as gravel, the sweet taste of satisfaction evident in his tone.

Michael swallows, wincing at the dryness in his throat, and attempts to put on a defiant front. "I have no idea what you just said, but I'll tell you this: I ever get the chance, I'm gonna shove my foot so far up your ass, it's gonna waggle out of your mouth like a tongue."

The guard chuckles at this, shaking his head as if amused by a child's innocent bravado. "We'll see, won't we?" he says in his native language.

He holds up the fob and rests his thumb on the button. Michael braces himself.

But before he gets to press it and send Michael into paroxysms of agony, the staccato tap of a lighter, eerier footfall breaks the tension in the room.

A new player enters the grim game—Mayu. She steps through the door, a wicked grin dancing on her lips, the dimples showing. Her hair is bubble gum pink today, her eyes painted in black gothic tears that stretch down her cheeks. The collar around Michael's neck seems to hum at her presence.

The guard straightens with her arrival.

"The party's just getting started, I see," Mayu chimes in with an air of detached amusement. Her voice is soft and melodic, but there is an undertone of something else that Michael can't quite place.

She comes right up to him, taking his chin in her cold hand.

"A delightful evening, isn't it?" she purrs, her voice weaving an unsettling melody.

Michael's stomach clenches at the underlying menace.

Mayu steps back from the prisoner, letting go of his face.

"What was he doing?" she asks her colleague in Japanese.

"I found him with this," the guard replies, taking the tiny GoPro from his pocket and handing it to her.

Mayu looks over the camera, then at Michael, narrowing her eyes fiercely.

"And where was he?" she asks.

"F-11."

"You know where he got it from?"

"I was about to ask him," the guard replies, holding up the fob to her. She smiles.

The thought of another jolt of electricity tearing through him sends a shiver of dread down Michael's spine.

Speaking in English, Mayu, her burning eyes on the prisoner, asks, "Who gave you this?"

Michael smirks a little. "I brought it with me."

"You're lying."

"No I'm not. I won't tell you where I was carrying it, but it was with me."

Mayu looks at the guard. His mouth widens into a cruel smile. He presses the button.

A sudden, devastating jolt of electricity tears through Michael. His body convulses violently against the bindings, agony snaking its way through every nerve. He grinds his teeth together, his gasps morphing into a raw, visceral howl.

When it stops, it is like everything is being drained out of him. It takes a while to get his breath and his vision back. The guard wears a huge smirk. Mayu bites her lip.

Why is she biting her lip? Michael can't help asking himself.

"Where did you get it?" Mayu says the second his eyes focus on the camera in her hand.

"Br-br... I, eh, brought... it," Michael stammers breathlessly.

Mayu rushes up to him, grabs his hair roughly, lifts his hanging head, whispers, "Just tell us. Tell us who gave it to you. Tell us about K."

His heart drops. *They know about K.*

"Tell us or he'll kill you," she goes on in a soft tone. "Word just came through that your father has failed again. They've called in other people. Your life isn't worth so much to them anymore. Tell us or he will kill you, Michael Black."

Michael's eyes are narrowed. The way she speaks to him, it's almost friendly. *Good cop, bad cop?*

"I-I brought... it."

She almost looks sorry for him, an expression of pity on her face.

"Don't be a hero," she breathes. "Not this time. Just tell us what you know about K."

Eyes locked on to Mayu, Michael replies, "I brought it."

His world throbs and judders, his vision begins to blur, his breath comes in gasps. He is certain he sees Mayu look away. As for the guard, he watches eagerly. The glint in his eyes, his unwavering smirk, are a haunting echo of Michael's torment.

Then, just as the pain becomes unbearable, just as he is about to black out, something changes. A sudden action from Mayu catches his eye. She moves with startling speed, her hand darting out, and before the guard can react, she has snatched the fob from his hand.

The collar goes dead, the cessation of pain abrupt, almost shocking, like a violent storm suddenly hushing. Michael's agonized mind struggles to make sense of the sudden shift.

"Playtime's over," Mayu hisses, her former melodious tone now hard and cold.

The guard, frozen in shock, doesn't have time to react. Mayu spins, her leg swinging in a swift arc, connecting solidly with his kneecap. A sickening crack fills the room, followed by the guard's howl of pain as he crumples. Another swinging kick, a roundhouse, smashes him in the face with such fury that he is knocked into unconsciousness.

Mayu turns her attention back to Michael. She takes a key from her pocket and comes to him, her nimble fingers disabling the collar with a swift turn of it.

As the collar clicks open, Mayu lifts it from him and tosses it aside before moving to remove his bonds. She unbuckles the leather straps that confine him to the chair, gradually freeing his body.

"Apologies for all the messing around," she murmurs as she unfastens the ones holding his legs. "But it was the only way to make it convincing. You getting spotted the other day meant that I had to deal with things myself."

The straps undone, Michael staggers to his feet with Mayu's assistance. She then stands back, and their eyes meet across the stale air as she holds a hand out to him.

"K," she says.

TWENTY-FIVE

OSAKA

Returning to the tattoo parlor, Yūki lies beneath the stark overhead lights once more, her skin bared and ready for the next installment of her Hell Screen. The tattooist prepares his tools, the bamboo handle of the tebori instrument steady in his experienced hands. The anticipation of pain heightens her senses, and she meets his gaze with a stoic calm that had unnerved him during their previous sessions.

"I'm ready," she murmurs, her voice a whisper against the background hum of the busy streets surrounding the tattoo parlor. "You can stop staring and begin."

In acknowledgment, the artist dips the needles into the ink, the pitch-black liquid glistening as it clings to the pointed ends. He then turns his attention to her skin, to the empty space near her navel that has been reserved for the fourth addition: Kato Myamoto.

The tattooist's hand begins its rhythmic dance, the needle-tipped bamboo handle moving over her skin in a painstakingly slow progression. The pain is immediate, sharp, and searing, yet Yūki remains still and silent. Her stoicism is nothing short of remarkable. Every etch, every stroke, she bears without a sound.

As the tattooist works away, he begins to render Myamoto's figure amidst the sea of flames, his body writhing and twisting in the inferno. He digs deeper into the fleshy canvas, carving out two hollow sockets where Myamoto's eyes should be. The effect is disturbingly realistic—a man blinded to his own misdeeds, forever trapped in a fiery abyss of torment.

The artist, lost in his work, doesn't notice the hours passing. His sole focus is the design, the hellish scene unfolding beneath his skilled hands. When he finally steps back, sweat beaded on his forehead, he allows himself a moment to admire his art.

Yūki, too, examines the newest addition to her Hell Screen, her fingers lightly tracing the fresh ink. A small smile curls the corners of her mouth as she looks upon the depiction of Myamoto, his eyes nothing but bloody sockets, his body consumed by the infernal flames. It is a fitting addition to her living testament of revenge.

"*Arigatō*," she says to the artist, her voice filled with a chilling satisfaction. The artist, for his part, simply nods, acutely aware of the gravity of the scene he has just etched onto her skin.

TWENTY-SIX

SHINOSHIMA

"You know," Michael remarks as they sneak along the dimly lit passageways of the facility, the sound of their footsteps swallowed by the concrete walls, "your English is a lot better than it was back in Hokkaido."

"That was just an act," Mayu replies.

"I get that now. But it's much better than most Japanese."

"My English teacher was very good."

"Where did you go to school?"

Mayu sighs, a note of frustration lacing her voice. "It doesn't matter," she says. "Just keep quiet till we're back at your cell."

They cautiously navigate the maze-like structure. The threatening hum of silence envelops them as they approach the familiar door of the cell. The metallic screech of it sliding to the side resonates eerily as Mayu ushers him in before shutting them both inside the cold, sterile confines.

"This needs to go back on," she declares, her voice resolute yet laced with regret as she holds up the metal shock collar.

"Great," he grumbles, a note of bitterness evident in his voice.

His body tenses as she steps closer, recalling the ass-whupping she gave him not so long ago. Yet she's surprisingly gentle as she secures the collar around his neck.

"I am sorry," she whispers, her voice barely audible as she steps back, a hint of genuine remorse in her eyes.

They take seats on the edge of his narrow cot, their reflections staring back at them from the panels. Their combined silence is a heavy blanket in the room, only serving to amplify the racing thoughts in Michael's mind. He doesn't understand why they've returned to this cell.

"Why are we back here?" he asks.

Mayu turns toward him, her stoic façade crumbling as genuine sadness shows in her expression. "Because there really is no escape from Shinoshima, and it'll be much better for you if you're here when they find us."

"But you? You're K, the CIA's contact. They'll kill you."

"No they won't. But they might kill you. That's why I have to be here. To protect you."

"Mayu, I don't understand."

"You soon will," she replies with deadly certainly.

Before he can process her cryptic assertion, the harsh glare of the emergency lights paints the world a disturbing red hue, and the blaring of alarms shatters the tense silence.

"They've found Masahiro," she breathes, her voice barely audible above the cacophony. "It won't be long now."

"And we're just gonna wait here for them?"

"It's all we have. The only other option is to survive up top on the island. That's suicide."

"But if they find out you're working for the CIA..."

She holds a hand up to him as clanging footsteps reverberate in the hallway, sending a cold shiver running through them both. The glass panels clank in their holding. He can hear the murmur of voices seeping in through the ventilation, their words laced with alarm. As the cell door slides open, two imposing figures armed with pistols step inside, their hostile presence almost filling up the entirety of the cramped space. More men crowd the corridor outside.

Mayu rises from the cot, her icy demeanor contrasting with the fear coursing through Michael's veins. The intruders halt a few steps away from her, wariness evident in their stance. She must hold some sway in this place.

"We found Masahiro," one of them says. "He says you attacked him."

"Masahiro was going to kill the prisoner. If he dies, his father will stop hunting Yūki Yokashina and start hunting us instead."

"Who cares about Azrael? Tanaka-shachou has lost patience with him. He has hired others to kill the woman."

"But with his son dead, Azrael will come for us. We are already tied in knots by Yokashina and her yakuza. Let's not add another enemy to our growing list."

"You had no right to attack Masahiro. We've seen the—"

"Shut up!" she interjects, her words exploding throughout the cell.

Michael watches from the sidelines with a fearful curiosity, not understanding one word they say. Mayu stands firm, unbowed and unbroken. Her outburst hangs heavy in the room, her unwavering resolve the only barrier against the impending storm.

"Now leave this cell," she says through grinding teeth, "or my father will find out."

The mention of her "father" has an effect on the men.

The first man nods and turns to his colleague. The second nods as well. They depart, not lowering their pistols until they are back in the corridor with the others, leaving Mayu and Michael alone in the cell. As the door closes behind them, Mayu lets out a soft sigh. Michael looks at her, confusion etched across his face.

"Mayu," he starts, "I don't..."

"I am Koji Tanaka's daughter," she interrupts, not meeting his gaze. "Okay?" Turning to face him, she adds, "I'm his daughter. Now, please. Just stay in this cell. Help your dad. Get off this island before it's too late."

TWENTY-SEVEN

THE TOKYO BAY ENTRANCE POINT

JUST SOUTH OF THE MIURA PENINSULA AND BOSO
Peninsula, in the vast expanse where the boundless Pacific
Ocean meets the edge of land, is the Tokyo Bay Entrance
Point.

As the sun dips below the horizon, casting hues of gold
and crimson upon the waters, Kenji Kiobi reclines on the
deck of his sumptuous super yacht. The man, a playboy to
the core, sprawls with ease and entitlement, a thin white
robe barely clinging to his shoulders. Open at the chest, it
reveals a physique honed by the best personal trainers money
can buy. His eyes are half-lidded as he lounges lazily, basking
in the dying light and the attention of a bevy of beautiful
women.

They drape themselves around him, their sequined
bikinis sparkling under the gentle fall of twilight. A flute of
effervescent champagne, kept at the perfect temperature by

the cool ocean breeze, never leaves Kenji's perfectly manicured hand, and attentive staff members, as discreet as they
are impeccably dressed, flit around the deck like silent
specters. One refills Kenji's champagne flute from a silver
tray, another offers a platter of delicacies from around the
world. All the while, Kenji reclines on his sun lounger, a king
holding court as a dark-haired beauty delicately feeds him a
succulent strawberry, laughter sparkling in her eyes as he
teases her with playful bites.

Everything on this super yacht screams luxury from the
shimmering mosaic swimming pool, to the decadent spread
of food, to the women draped around the place. Yet beneath
the façade of decadence and hedonism, a sinister undercurrent stirs. All around the yacht, and unseen by the unwitting
playboy and his party, a trio of lethal predator groups watch
from the shadows.

On the horizon, half hidden by the encroaching gloom,
several stealthy vessels dot the calm waters. Within are cold-
eyed killers, their bodies coiled with anticipation as they
observe the spectacle on the yacht through field glasses.

Inside a black combat rubber raiding craft (CRRC), a
four-man group of Israeli Defence Forces (IDF) lie in wait.
Their faces are stern, etched with the indelible mark of
countless covert operations, their bodies tight with anticipation. Their eyes, as sharp as a falcon's, never stray from the
luxurious spectacle of the yacht.

Closer to the shoreline, more pairs of field glasses scan
the floating paradise. A cadre of Republic of Korea Special
Forces (ROK-SF) watch the scene unfold from their own
small boat. Their black, nondescript attire is a stark contrast
to the glamorous colors of the party yacht. They watch with

steady vigilance, their gazes as unyielding as the boat beneath them, their muscles as taut as drum skins.

Unbeknown to the three-man Korean team, nestled within the foliage of a lush grove of trees high above them on clifftops, a sniper from Russia's clandestine SVR perches like a deadly bird of prey. His VSS Vintorez sniper rifle is as much a part of him as his own limbs, the cold metal against his shoulder providing a stark reminder of his grim mission. His eye clamped to the weapon's telescopic lens, the crosshairs dance over the unsuspecting revelers. Yet, they never come to rest on the playboy's content face or the exposed skin of his female entourage. Because the real target has yet to show herself.

As the evening descends into night, a deadly paradox unfolds. Beneath the laughter, the music, and the popping of champagne corks, a dangerous stillness resides. Each operative, from the shore to the ocean, from the ground to the trees, waits with bated breath for the appearance of their target: Yūki Yokashina.

TWENTY-EIGHT

OSAKA

Peter isn't anywhere near Tokyo Bay. No. Instead, he's two hundred and fifty miles away, doing his best to melt into his surroundings, a phantom observer harking back to his prime surveillance days in the CIA. A pair of Oakleys conceal the flicker of his eyes, while a baseball cap cloaks his face in shadow. Distance keeps him veiled from his target.

Unlike his rivals, Peter's focus isn't on Kenji Kiobi, or even Tokyo, for that matter. Instead, his attention is riveted on Tenma, a traditional neighborhood nestled in the heart of Osaka's old town. Amid the winding streets and alleyways, he's become a temporary resident, renting an apartment with a choice vantage point.

From his balcony, the tang of matcha tea clings to his taste buds as he sips it from a china cup, while his ears pick up the symphony of urban life: the faint murmur of a conversation happening on one of the other balconies, the chirping of birds, the distant rumble of traffic. Yet his eyes are drawn to none of that.

Just a story below on the opposite side of a narrow passage, another balcony hangs off the side of a five-story wooden and stone building, a graceful tribute to the timeless architecture of Osaka. Delicate wooden latticework criss-crosses the windows, and a detailed tilework adds an intricate flourish to the rooftop.

From the seclusion of beaded curtains, an old man emerges onto the balcony, tapping a thin cane before him. He pauses at a flower box, deftly shifting the cane to hang from his elbow, and finds a small watering can by touch. His hands, aged and precise, nurture the plants—pruning a dwarf cherry blossom and a Japanese maple with careful attention.

Peter savors the bitter tang of the green tea, feigning interest in the newspaper unfurled before him. Meanwhile, the old man's fingers—nimble and practiced—explore the foliage like sentient tendrils, seeking out errant sprouts. Every subtlety, every tick, each habitual gesture, etches itself into Peter's keen observer's mind—cogs in the intricate mechanism of a life lived in shadows. For this is no ordinary elder: this is Takashi "The Gun" Yokashina—the blind ex-yakuza hitman, the patriarch of Yūki and Tatsuo Yokashina.

As the sun falls over Osaka, basking the narrow streets of Tenma in velvety shadow, the old man recedes into the beaded curtain's embrace, vanishing from Peter's sight. A minute lapses—an eternity in the espionage game—before Yokashina reemerges at the bottom of the apartment block wearing a casual black montsuki jacket, a traditional upper garment worn by Japanese males. He wears it over more contemporary attire, using it as a thin coat. As he walks off down the alley, Peter spots something. Taking up the entire back of the montsuki jacket is a drawing: a large, ogre-like creature with a fierce expression in its wide eyes, twisted horns flowing from its head, and sharp teeth dripping with blood.

Peter knows enough about Japanese folklore to know that the creature on Takashi's back is an "Oni." Oni are "Yokai" (monsters, ghosts, demons) that are commonly portrayed as malicious beings who seek to punish perceived wrongs or injustices. Often they are enforcers of karmic justice.

Takashi spills out onto the street, his cane tapping in rhythmic staccato as he navigates the dimmed maze of Tenma with a certainty you wouldn't expect to see in someone with no sight.

The second Takashi is out of sight, Peter descends from the vantage of the balcony, leaving the apartment, and blends into the tangle of life that fills Tenma's narrow streets, just as the old man is turning left.

As Peter follows behind, the falling sun paints the world a warm gold, and the air begins to hum with life. Called forth by dusk's call, the locals spill from their quant little residencies, their chatter and laughter seasoning the evening air.

The two enter the tight arteries of market stalls— vegetable vendors displaying their colorful wares, rows of hanging ducks, humble noodle shacks cradling a handful of customers, their slurping and contented sighs mixing with the exotic clash of scents that tugs at Peter's senses.

Up ahead, the old man navigates the sensory landscape with a practiced grace, his cane a reliable guide amid the bustling cacophony of Osaka's streets. Though his target may be blind, Peter stays as far back as he would from a man with sight, fearful that the wily ex-hitman may sense him some other way. Sightless but not helpless, Takashi Yokashina exudes an aura that commands Peter's respect, compelling him to maintain a cautious distance.

The old man halts at the stalls as if guided by an invisible map, his hand caressing the produce, his nose drinking in the freshness. His heightened senses are a testament to his resilience and adaptability.

As Peter trails behind, his phone rattles in his pocket.

"What?"

"Why aren't you at Tokyo Bay like the others?" the voice of Akechi Akiyama snaps.

"Because," Peter replies in a hushed tone, trying to keep his voice well below the sounds of the market as Takashi ducks into a small tea shop, "I'm sick of waiting for Yūki to make her move. I think it's about time I made one myself."

"Where are you?"

"Watching someone."

"Who?"

"Goodbye, Akechi-san." Peter puts the phone down and continues to watch.

The blind ex-hitman emerges from the shop front carrying a box of tea under one arm, his stick at the end of his other arm, tapping away at the rough paving stones. Peter continues to track him, staying as far back as he can. After all, Takashi proves that even without sight, he may be able to sense him if Peter gets too close. As he passes a stall of crockery, one of the traders backs into the shelves from the other side and into a stack of donburi bowls. As the tower of dishes tips over, as quick as lightning, Takashi reaches forward with a hand and stops the bowls from falling and shattering on the ground, pushing them back into their former upright position.

Peter is amazed. Takashi must have felt the air move, quiver ever so slightly. It's the only way it can be explained.

Then comes further proof of the strong nature of the old man's remaining senses.

Takashi leads him across a road into a thin alley that moves between the backs of opposing tall apartment blocks. As Peter enters, a group of children come running out of one of the houses and stream past, their loud, chirping voices filling the void of the passage. Then, as quickly as they had come, they are gone, and the two men are alone, nothing but the garbage cans and the alley, the smells of cooking coming from the open windows above them. The back passage leads them deeper into the haphazard confluence of buildings, where the different structures of old and new Osaka meet and merge as unpredictably as river currents. Peter can't figure out what the old man wants here. Maybe a shortcut.

On a corner of the passage, Takashi stops to pet a street cat that is sitting atop a garbage can. The cat arcs its back to receive the touch, the old man cooing to it in unheard words. Peter stays back, watching from an alcove about twenty meters away, making sure to remain hidden.

The old man is on the move again. He disappears around the corner of the alley.

Peter leaves the nook, heads to the corner, and turns it—finding the passage empty. He's confused. There is at least another fifty meters of alley. Where could the old man have gone? He quickly finds out.

Peter takes a step forward. Something moves to his left, bursting from a recess. There follows a short scuffle, and the next, the sharp point of a knife is being pressed to Peter's stomach and he is face to face with Takashi Yokashina.

"*Naze watashi o otte iru n desu ka?*" he asks in a rough voice.

"Do you speak English?" Peter asks.

A snarl bends Takashi's lips. Like he's annoyed. Then, "Why are you following me?"

"I'd like to speak with you, Takashi-san."

"What about?"

"Your daughter."

The knife is pressed farther into Peter's guts.

In a cool voice, Peter says, "Be careful, Takashi-san. For I am not the only one with a weapon pointed on me."

Only then does Takashi appear to sense it. He instinctively looks down. He doesn't see it, obviously, but knows for sure that Peter is holding a pistol no more than an inch from his own stomach. It would most definitely beat the knife to the punch. Or at least do a lot more damage should it become a tie.

"The last man," Takashi says just as coldly, "who pointed a gun at me found himself dead not long afterwards."

"I mean you no direct harm, Takashi-san. I only mean to point it at you for my own protection."

"Mmmm," the blind man muses.

He puts the knife away, returning it to his belt and covering it over with the montsuki jacket. At the same time,

Peter retracts the pistol, returning the FN 509 back to its underarm holster, tucked away beneath his steel-blue blazer.

The two men step back from each other. Peter studies the blind man as Takashi simply stands there staring directly at Peter's chest; essentially staring straight ahead, his faded, useless eyes seeing nothing. He appears to be thinking, the wrinkles of his brow creased slightly. If Peter is studying him, then Takashi is most definitely doing the same back: weighing up where to go from here.

"What do you want with my daughter?" he asks, his gruff voice echoing up the walls of the tall alleyway.

"I've been sent to kill her."

In a flash, Takashi's hand is on the hilt of his knife.

"Please, Takashi-san," Peter says, his hands held up in submission, even if the old man can't physically see them. "I only mean to talk with you. Ask some questions."

"So that you can use the answers to kill my own flesh?"

Peter, eyes fixed to the hand and the hilt, replies slowly, "I don't know yet."

"What do you mean you don't know? An assassin always knows."

"Look, can we go somewhere else? A more casual setting. Your apartment, perhaps?"

The clouded eyes narrow, the corner of one twitching. He breathes in, then out, then, "Okay." Holding an elbow out to Peter, he adds, "You can guide us back to my apartment. It'll be quicker like that. After all, you know the way. You've been following me since I left it."

Seated on the old man's modest balcony, they indulge in the delicate ceremony of tea. Takashi's sightless eyes look nowhere and everywhere as he measures the precise distance to the cups with practiced grace. The scalding liquid fills the porcelain to the brim, nary a splash staining the meticulously clean saucer. An almost mirror image of each other, both cups brim with the same level of amber fluid.

"How long since you lost your sight?" Peter asks.

"Ten years."

"Your other senses have compensated impressively."

Takashi shrugs lightly. "I'm simply performing the actions I'd mastered while I still had my sight. Seems my body doesn't require eyes for certain tasks, just a sense of timing."

After Takashi distributes the tea, the two men settle into a comfortable silence. The rhythmic hum of Osaka's daily life ascends to their perch—the lively chatter of locals, sporadic car horns, and the tantalizing aroma of food being prepared.

"So what do you wish to know about my daughter?" Takashi finally breaks the silence.

Peter cuts to the chase. "What really happened between Yūki and Tanaka?"

The weight of his question lingers in the still air. Takashi's stoic façade barely wavers, but the sight of an unexpected tear gathering in the corner of his eye belies his emotional turmoil. "I'm not the one who has any right to tell you that." His voice maintains a firm edge, even as he quickly wipes away the telltale tear. "As a father, I should have protected her... but I failed."

Peter decides not to push further. Instead, he proceeds to his main point.

"I want to set up a meeting with Yūki," he says.

Suspicion creeps into Takashi's blind gaze. "For an ambush?"

Peter shakes his head emphatically. "No, I merely want to talk."

"About what?" Takashi counters, his hands unerringly finding his teacup and guiding it to his lips.

"That's a conversation for Yūki and me. All I can assure you is that I bear no ill intentions. This would be a parley. I have a proposition. If she agrees, well and good; if not, we part ways and revert to our previous standoff. I only request five minutes of her time, Takashi-san."

Sighing, Takashi carefully places his cup on the table, turning to face Peter. "Place your hands on the table," he says.

Peter eyes him warily. "Why?"

"You question my request yet expect me to trust you?"

With a reluctant movement, Peter extends his hands, placing them palm-down on the weathered table, the coarse texture pressing into his skin.

Takashi's worn hands rest atop his, their warmth surprisingly vital, akin to separate entities teeming with life. His blank stare is unnerving, prompting a suspicion that his sightless eyes are not just observing Peter but penetrating deep within. Takashi mutters something under his breath as he sizes Peter up.

Finally, he nods, withdraws his hands, and reclines, resuming his tea. "Very well," he concedes. "I will instruct you on where to find her. Where the two of you can meet."

"And where would that be?"

"Yūki partakes in two rituals after each retribution. First, she completes another section of her intricate tattoo. Second, she embarks on a pilgrimage to a temple or shrine. It just so happens that tomorrow morning, she will be at the Kiyomizudera Temple in Kyoto, not far from here. This secluded sanctuary, atop a natural hot spring, is where she will immerse herself in the waters. It is her way of cleansing and seeking spiritual absolution for the souls she has ushered into the afterlife."

TWENTY-NINE

KYOTO

THE FOLLOWING MORNING FINDS PETER IN A DINGY hotel room in Kyoto's inner city, facing his reflection in a cracked mirror. He deftly wraps bandaging around his abdomen—not to tend to any new injuries, the bullet wounds from before remaining the only mementos of his mission so far—but to conceal something tucked in the small of his back. The binding keeps it hidden and secure.

His cell phone rings, breaking the silence.

"Hey, Mikey," Peter answers. "Are you okay?"

"Not particularly," comes the reply. "They've decided to attach me to the bed with a length of chain and to monitor me every twenty minutes. But that's not why I called."

"I didn't think this was a social chat."

"No, it's not. They're demanding that you return to Tokyo. They want you with the others in Tokyo Bay."

"Well," Peter murmurs, his gaze fixed on the stained mirror, "I'm preoccupied at the moment."

"Well, they want me to tell you that if you're not back in Tokyo by six this evening, they'll sever one of my fingers for every hour you're late. You need to contact them as soon as you arrive."

"Has Kenji Kiobi moved?"

"No. He's still at the same location, surrounded by three groups of assassins."

"Then what's the rush? If the bait's still set and the trap's still positioned at Tokyo Bay Entrance Point, I don't see the issue with me going my own way."

"Regardless," Michael retorts, his voice laced with sarcasm, "if you could at least promise to be back in Tokyo by six, I would highly appreciate ending the day with all my fingers and toes intact."

———

KIYOMIZUDERA TEMPLE SITS atop a long road of stone steps. At the bottom, a woman is sweeping the front of her little house when Peter arrives. He asks her for directions to the temple, and she points the way before leaving him with a resounding warning.

"You should be careful up there," she says a little tongue-in-cheek. "My grandma used to tell me that the place is possessed by lonely spirits."

Peter climbs to the top.

Kiyomizudera Temple is an impressive wooden structure that sits atop the wooded hillsides of eastern Kyoto. The temple complex is characterized by its large wooden terrace known as the "Kiyomizu Stage," which juts out from the main hall. The stage is supported by tall wooden pillars and offers panoramic views of the surrounding city and lush greenery.

The hot springs are farther along.

The temple grounds are adorned with beautiful gardens, stone pagodas, and smaller shrine structures. Peter walks through the serene wooded area, coming alongside a flowing stream, and then he is emerging from the trees at the edge of a natural hot spring bubbling and steaming.

There are small wooden huts for changing. Peter removes everything but his underwear, only the bandaging to his shoulder and abdomen covering his torso. He steps to the edge of the water, a layer of steam over the top of it like a mist. As he steps in, he doesn't see anyone else, but as he lowers his body into the warm, almost hot, water, he spots the silhouette of someone sitting on the other side, obscured by the steam.

Peter takes a position not far from this person, so that the both of them are directly opposite each other, about four meters between them.

Yūki's eyes narrow the second she recognizes her fellow bather. Underneath the water, her hand moves to the sheathed wakizashi she is hiding between her legs. Her fingers wrap around the handle, her thighs holding the mahogany sheath tight. She pulls it a few millimeters from the scabbard and keeps it there.

At the same time, Peter sits with the water up to his neck, a hand inconspicuously reaching around to the small of his back, where the handle of a kogatana knife pokes out from the bandaging he spent all morning wrapping around himself to hold it there, as well as hide it.

"Do you know who I am?" he asks.

She replies in a cold voice, "The man stupid enough to follow Kato out of prison. I'm also sure you are the fool who followed us from Shusaku's. But most of all," she adds bitterly, "you are the one stupid enough to take up Tanaka's job offer."

Her fingers grip tightly around the handle of the wakizashi.

"I asked you here for parley," he says.

"I know. My father informed me. Is that why you're gripping on to that kogatana knife strapped to your back?"

Peter grins. "Yes. It's also the same reason you're holding that wakizashi under the water."

The grin is reciprocated.

Both assassins loosen their grips around their weapons. But don't let go. Not yet.

"That's some tattoo you've got there," Peter mentions. "It's not complete yet, is it?"

Yūki looks down at her naked torso, at the flames running along her breasts, the screaming faces caught within, the men she is sending to hell.

"No," she says, looking up. "There's just two more, and then it's complete. So if you've come here to stop me finishing it, you'd better act now."

"I told your father I only wanted to talk. My knife is for protection. I knew that you would bring your own. I also knew that these hills would be surrounded with yakuza. I spotted several loitering around the trees on my walk here from the temple. They tried to stay hidden, but the signs of them are everywhere."

Yūki glances for a split second at the trees to his left. There is discreet movement in them.

Her eyes back on Peter, she says, "So what have you come to talk to me about?"

"I want you to end your revenge. Go home. Be at peace. Allow me to deal with Tanaka."

Her eyes pierce. "Is this a trick?"

"No trick. But I do want to play one. You see..."

Peter explains his predicament. The CIA mission. Getting Michael into Shinoshima. The contact. The chemical weapons. Taking the job as a ruse to get them access to the island.

"But I need your help," he adds at the end. "I need to get access to Tanaka, and the only way I can do that is either with your assistance or with your head."

She doesn't say anything for a few seconds. Merely stares coldly at him. Then she says, "Tanaka has your son, does he not?"

"Yes."

"And he will kill him if you fail?"

"Yes."

"Then I would say that the only way you can get access to Tanaka is with my head."

At that moment she stands, her whole naked glory there before him. She takes a robe that is folded at the side of the hot spring and places it over her shoulders. As far as she is concerned, the meeting is over; she has nothing more to say. But as she steps out of the spring, ready to join her brother and the rest of the yakuza surrounding them, Peter says something that stops the blood in her veins:

"Your daughter is alive, Yūki Yokashina."

She whips around to him, and when her gaze is facing him, for the first time, she reveals genuine emotion.

"He's keeping her on the island," Peter adds.

THIRTY

SHINOSHIMA

KOJI TANAKA'S PRIVATE APARTMENT IS A HARMONY of natural and modern materials. Gleaming walls of brushed concrete are offset by warm bamboo and finely crafted hinoki wood. Delicate Japanese paper screens, shoji, subtly partition the vast space, lending a sense of intimacy and discretion without sacrificing the spaciousness of the bunker.

Mayu runs her hands along the surfaces as she makes her way through it. In the heart of the space is the living area, defined by an elegant, low-lying leather couch and a hinoki wood coffee table. The walls here are adorned with a blend of ancient and modern Japanese art—traditional ink wash paintings share the space with abstract canvases inspired by the post-war Gutai movement.

The dining area is equally striking. A large wooden slab table made from polished zelkova sits on a handwoven tatami mat, surrounded by hand-carved floor cushions. Overhead, a modern chandelier emits a soft, warm glow that reflects off the minimalist tableware set out for a meal.

In the kitchen, Mayu stands at the sink, staring out of a wide window. At first glance, it appears to be a simple wooden frame showcasing an idyllic vista. But on closer inspection, it is actually no more than a piece of modern technology—a digital screen, seamless and nearly indistinguishable from the real thing.

A view of Mount Fuji is on it, as though the kitchen were looking out on the famous mountain—and not fifty feet below the surface of the Earth. The mountain is beautifully replicated, every detail digitally rendered. Its peak, pristine white and gleaming with morning frost, pierces the sky, its noble form reflected in the calm waters of nearby Lake Kawaguchi. You can almost feel the crisp chill in the air, the tranquil atmosphere of the high altitude perfectly conveyed.

"Hello, Mayu," a familiar voice says from the doorway.

Without turning around, she replies, "Hello, Father."

"You always did like that view," he adds.

She closes her eyes. "And you promised you'd take me to it one day."

He says nothing, just stands there in his gray cashmere cardigan, hands dug into his pockets, his eyes giving nothing away, no emotion, no hint of humanity.

"You rescued the killer's son," he finally says.

At last, Mayu turns to him from the fake view.

"Masahiro could have killed him," she says.

"Then you should have stopped it another way. You shouldn't have attacked him like that."

She doesn't mention the fact that her main priority was to get the camera somewhere safe.

"He wouldn't stop," she says. "He kept—"

"Silence!" Tanaka shouts, losing his earlier cool.

Mayu clenches her eyelids shut and grits her teeth. Anger rises up in her like bile.

"You are my daughter," he goes on in a calmer tone. "People expect a certain standard. I allowed you to join the security staff so that you could get your teeth into things."

The eyelids flick open. "Only because I've spent most of my life locked up in here. Because I want to live."

"It is safer here," Tanaka growls. "We have enemies."

"*You* have enemies," she corrects.

"And my enemies will use *you* to get at me. So in the meantime, it is safer for us here."

"Because of this yakuza woman coming after you?"

"Yes."

"Because she thinks you ruined her life?"

"Yes. But soon she will be gone."

"And then I'll get to leave this place? Go to a real college. Not just a bunch of university professors paid to teach me here."

A twitch runs up his face as he says, "We will see."

Mayu senses the hesitation in his voice. "I'm never going to leave this place, am I?"

"Was Hokkaido not enough?"

"How could it be enough? I was watched every step of the way."

"But you got to experience a little of life, didn't you? Got to see how people live out there. See them struggle from one day to the next. Living together like a herd. Waiting for the day they're loaded into a trailer and driven to the slaughterhouse."

In the heart of the pristine kitchen, they stand across from one another, their eyes locked, the surfaces around them gleaming under soft, artificial sunlight. Mayu's fingers trace the edge of the countertop as she grounds herself before delving into a conversation that is sure to start an argument.

"Dad," she begins, her voice quivering slightly. "I want to really see the world, the real world, not just Hokkaido... and I want to know more... about Mom."

Tanaka flinches at her words. He turns to the digital window displaying the crisp view of Mount Fuji, its digital cherry blossoms blooming in an eternal spring, the serenity of the scene a stark contrast to the emotional storm brewing inside him. "Mayu," he begins, his voice strained. "It's not as simple as you think."

"But it is, Dad! It's as simple as telling me about her. I have only fleeting memories... her smile, her laugh. I want more than that." Mayu's voice is insistent.

Tanaka's face grows stern, a wall built to keep the past at bay. "Mayu, I've told you everything you need to know. Your mother was a beautiful, caring woman. She loved you, and her memory should remain untainted."

"But I need more than a memory, Dad! I need to know who she was. I need to know why I am trapped here, why you refuse to talk about her!" Mayu's voice rises with frustration.

The room falls into silence. Tanaka is still, his face a mask of stoicism that does little to hide the pain etched in his gray eyes.

Suddenly, Mayu's patience snaps. Her pent-up anger and frustration explodes in a single, heart-wrenching cry.

"Where is my mother?!" she bawls, her voice resounding with a mixture of desperation and fury. It is a plea, a demand, and a challenge all at once, shaking the tranquility of Tanaka's underground sanctuary to its very core. The silence that follows is almost deafening, a testament to the depth of her question and the world of answers it demands.

Tanaka looks straight at her, his fists curled at his sides, the usually stoical tycoon doing his damnedest to keep his emotions in check. "I have loved only three things in my entire life," he begins, his voice breaking. "Power. Something I will readily admit to loving fiercely. You. The only person in the world today besides myself that I truly care about. And your mother. Who was the first human I ever came into contact with that I genuinely loved."

"But who was she? All I have is a single photograph. You have *none*! If you loved her so much, why don't you have any of her photos around?"

"Because it is too painful to be reminded of her, of the loss. To be reminded of the one thing I want more than anything else, but the one thing I can never have."

"Because she is dead?"

He looks away when he says, "Yes. Because she is no longer here."

Mayu lets out a long and withered sigh. A burning frustration ebbs and flows inside of her. Perhaps it is that which makes her say what she says next.

"Maybe you're being punished," she declares in a voice dripping with malice.

Tanaka looks up, fixing her with his stare. "Punished for what?" he asks indignantly.

"For the things you do. Maybe Mommy was taken because you're being punished for all the people you've hurt. All the things that are done here on this island."

Tanaka is shaking. No one would ever dare talk to him like this. No one ever has.

His vision becomes bathed in imaginary flames.

When his voice finally returns to him, it is as though he is summoning a demon spirit. In a low growl, he tells her, "You think there is a God that goes around punishing people? You believe in yokai? In spirits? Karma is what you make it. There is no universal justice except our own. Those people who we bring here are taken from the worst places on earth. They live in squalor with no use to society, nothing but a minus. They beg, or they live in refugee camps, or they simply clutter the earth with need, sucking up resources and giving nothing back. The only use any of them will ever have is the data they supply from the experiments we run here at Shinoshima."

Mayu stares at him through wet, tear-drenched eyes.

"Who are you to make those types of decisions?" she puts to him in a whisper.

"Who am I?" Flames ignite behind his gray eyes. "I," he says sternly, "am the type of man who drags mankind forwards without fear of invisible forces or some stale moralism that no longer fits. It is men like me who give humanity its future. Men like me are the only reason civilization wasn't swept away by disease and famine centuries ago."

"And it is men like you," she retorts, her voice stronger

now, "who always seem to be the ones who drag the rest of us into hell in the name of *your* progress."

It is then that his eyes narrow to mere slits in his face. "Now I am sure," he growls.

"Sure of what?"

"Sure that you are the leak on the island."

Her eyes widen as a cruel grin works its way up his face.

"I'm right, aren't I?" he says. "That my own daughter is the reason my name is regularly mentioned in intelligence circles, including the CIA."

The next part fills her with horror.

"The reason," he adds coldly, "you recommended Azrael and his brat. The reason the brat is running around my home with *this*."

For the first time, Tanaka removes his hand from his pocket. He raises a closed fist, and when it opens, there is a small GoPro in it. The same one that she hid in her room. The one with Michael's pictures on it.

At this exact moment, two men emerge from behind Tanaka and enter the room: Jin and another. It is Jin who has the syringe in his hand, some clear, menacing liquid dripping from the end of its needle as they cautiously approach.

"The tide is turning, my girl," Tanaka says as they grab ahold of her. "Your betrayal has only speeded up inevitability."

THIRTY-ONE

TOKYO

THE JAPANESE COUNTRYSIDE BLURS OUTSIDE THE window as the bullet train speeds from Kyoto to Tokyo. Within the humming cabin, Peter withdraws a nondescript burner phone purchased from a local 7-Eleven back in Kyoto, and dials a memorized number.

"It's me," he states the instant the call connects.

"Hello, me," comes the gruff voice of Ben Knight. "I thought we agreed to cease all communication until your son procured more substantial evidence than just a bunch of laboratory pictures."

"I'm confident he's on it. But this isn't about that," Peter responds, glancing warily at his fellow passengers. He keeps his voice low, tinged with an urgency that brooks no argument. "I need you to get something for me."

"What?" Knight's single-word question hangs heavy with suspicion.

Over the course of the next minute, Peter outlines his request in hushed tones. He describes the unique item he needs, detailing the necessary steps for sourcing it—and then for working on it.

When he is finished, the line falls silent.

"That's a hell of an ask," Knight eventually murmurs, his voice thick with disquiet. "It breaches at least six US laws, violates an amendment of the Bill of Rights, and infringes upon several more Constitutional clauses."

"Can you do it, though?" Peter's tone is resolute, leaving no room for dissent. "I mean, you and I both know that constitutional law was never really a problem for the CIA before. Not when they're on foreign soil."

Knight hesitates, his breathing loud in Peter's ear, filling the silence. Then he affirms, "Okay. But there's no way I can procure it in the US. It'll have to be abroad."

"That works better. It will make the second part more plausible if it originates from Asia."

"The second part," Knight repeats, the strain in his voice betraying his unease. "Locating someone to fulfill this 'second part' is going to be a challenge."

"But there are professionals who do that sort of work, aren't there?"

"Yes, but not to this extreme. And certainly not as drastically."

"It's the only way, Ben."

Knight pauses. "Are you certain?"

"Without a doubt."

Ben Knight exhales audibly. "Then I'll get it for you," he commits, the line falling silent as the gravity of their conversation reverberates inside the speeding bullet train.

A TORRENT of rain soaks the world when Peter disembarks at Tokyo. The city bustles with energy despite the downpour, the colorful streaks of neon lights reflecting off the glistening streets and skyscrapers.

As he navigates the chaotic sidewalk, a sleek, black car pulls up alongside him, its presence immediately commanding his attention. Two intimidating men step out the front, their demeanor as ominous as the outlines of concealed pistols beneath their tailored suit jackets.

One of the men opens the back door, revealing Akechi Akiyama seated comfortably in the depths of the vehicle. The other man comes in close so Peter can smell the ramen on his breath as the guy breathes into the rain.

"Get in," Akechi demands. The instruction is unnecessary as the two men flanking the car subtly move their hands inside their suit jackets in an unspoken threat.

Complying, Peter slides into the vehicle, settling beside Akechi. As soon as he is inside, the men return to their positions in the front, the car jolting forward into the early evening traffic.

"Where have you been?" Akechi asks, his tone laced with an edge of irritation.

"Working," Peter responds nonchalantly.

"Where?"

"Kyoto."

Akechi's eyes narrow as the corner of his mouth twitches. "And what is in Kyoto?"

"A beautiful shrine built over a hot spring. You should visit sometime."

Akechi stares at him incredulously. "While your son is in danger, you choose to indulge in sightseeing?"

Peter remains silent, curious to see if Akechi is truly naïve enough to believe that is true.

Ignoring the silence, Akechi continues, "You should be monitoring Kenji Kiobi. Like the others."

As the car's windows are peppered with rain, Peter casually replies, "Who says I'm not heading there right now?"

"Then let us take you there ourselves," Akechi proposes, retrieving his phone from his pocket. "And while we're driving, let me show you this."

After a few quick taps, he hands the device over to Peter, a video queued up on the screen.

Peter winces as the disturbing footage begins to play. Michael is suspended by chains from a ceiling beam, his body bearing a painful tattoo of bruises. His hands are bound behind his back, and a long chain suspends him by them from a ceiling beam that runs across the concrete cell so that his body is stretched out, with all his weight on his twisted arms. The torture method is called strappado. The person's body weight places tension on their arms, causing extreme discomfort and sometimes dislocation or injury to the shoulders. Historically, it has been used as a method of extracting confessions or exerting physical pain during interrogations. It was prevalent during certain periods of history, particularly in the context of judicial or military settings. The Spanish Inquisition loved it.

A man stands to the side holding a cattle prod. After a few seconds of footage, he begins jabbing it into Michael's flesh so that he writhes on the end of the chain, screaming out. The pain in his shoulders must be excruciating.

The sight of his son, bound and tortured, stirs a rush of anger within Peter. One he does his utmost to hide.

"Why are you showing me this?" Peter manages to grind out between clenched teeth.

"To refocus your priorities and remind you of your obligations," Akechi replies, his tone icy. "Because your son's unfortunate circumstances have revealed a security issue within Shinoshima."

Akechi's words send Peter's heart hammering against his chest.

"It seems we have an informant among us," he reveals, his tone growing increasingly severe. "And it appears that's not the only betrayal." He pivots his gaze to Peter, his face as impassive as a mask. "Just an hour ago, our informants reported seeing you in the vicinity of the Kiyomizudera Temple."

Peter opens his mouth to counter, but Akechi cuts him off.

"Let me finish," he interjects. "At the same time, our scouts identified several individuals associated with Yūki Yokashina in the same area. Associates of her brother's Bosozoku gang. Do you believe this to be mere coincidence?"

Stunned into silence, Peter can only stare at Akechi, the pulse in his temple throbbing visibly.

"Now, Azrael-san," Akechi continues relentlessly, "would you care to explain your activities in Kyoto?"

Peter's mind races for the right response. Lies. "I was tailing her father in Osaka. Through him, I discovered she frequently visits the temple. But I was too late. By the time I made it to the hot springs, they were gone. Hence my return to Tokyo. It's more prudent to be near Kenji Kiobi from now on. I took a gamble. I failed."

Akechi scrutinizes Peter with piercing intensity. Finally, he speaks. "Regardless of your reasons, their relevance is negligible. The future remains unchanged. From this point forward, Azrael-san, your options have narrowed considerably. You must abandon any thoughts of an alliance with Yūki Yokashina. Your primary concern now should be the well-being of your son. If you fail in eliminating Yūki, his life will be the cost. It's as simple as that."

The rest of the journey is marked by an oppressive silence. The car leaves the city behind, veering along the coast toward the tip of the Miura Peninsula, a point that overlooks the expansive mouth of Tokyo Bay. It takes them about an hour to reach it, and that's when things take another turn.

As they round a curve along the coastline, the men inside the car involuntarily stiffen, their gazes locked on a point in the distance.

A plume of smoke unfurls from the water's surface, snaking up into the darkening evening sky. As they move closer, the scene unfolds further. The bay is ablaze; various vessels, including a distant yacht, are consumed in a furious dance of flames.

Emergency vehicles swarm the parking lots adjacent to the coast, their flashing lights piercing the flames and smoke as rescue boats and helicopters spring into action.

"Seems like your other teams have been hit," Peter observes, his voice barely above a whisper. "And hit hard."

Nearing the harbor, they spy a figure stumbling down the cliffside toward the road. He clutches a rifle bag and moves with a frantic, panicky energy. As he lurches onto the road, Akechi's car grinds to a halt mere feet from him.

Upon seeing the car's occupants, the man's fear-stricken eyes widen.

Akechi steps out. "What happened?" he demands.

"They ambushed us," he replies in heavily accented English.

Peter takes him for Russian.

"Ambush?" Akechi repeats.

"Yes. Your woman and her comrades. It was madness. The rest of my crew is dead. Most of the others too."

"And Yūki Yokashina?"

He shakes his head, his eyes going blank. It is as though Akechi just asked about the devil himself.

"She's vanished," the Russian says. "But so has the decoy."

Akechi's brow furrows in confusion. "Decoy?! What decoy? What do you mean?"

"The man on the boat wasn't Kiobi," the Russian replies. "It was a stand-in hired to live it up on the yacht for a week. Unfortunately for him, your woman vented her frustration when she realized it wasn't Kiobi. The guy's now at the bottom of the bay, a bullet in his skull."

Akechi's face hardens. "Then where is Kenji Kiobi?"

———

IN THE CROWDED hubbub of Takeshiba Ferry Terminal, Tokyo, a man in heavy disguise waits at a counter with three large men. The traveler, looking nothing like his usual self, his stylish attire replaced by what he would term peasant's clothing, is none other than Kenji Kiobi, the man who was supposed to be on that yacht. Or at least at the bottom of the ocean with a bullet in his skull.

Instead, he is buying a ticket for the night ferry to Hachijō-jima island; a lush, volcanic island that is part of the Izu Island chain south of Tokyo. There, he will be staying in a small, desolate cottage belonging to the three formidable men he will be traveling with.

The Hidari brothers—Benma, Tenma, and Kuruma—are in the employ of Kenji's father and are first-class security experts. Their uncanny ability to sniff out danger is what prompted Kenji Kiobi to leave the decoy on the yacht and go with them to their remote island hideaway, and not to use any of his usual transport. None of his boats, none of his cars, certainly not his private jet.

Rather, they will be taking the nine-hour night ferry to Hachijō-jima. Then, once they have him at the safe house under watch, the brothers will begin their hunt for Yūki Yokashina and her gang.

While the Hidaris get the tickets at a booth, Kenji stands to the side, nervously watching all the people, gripping his body with his fingers. Even behind the huge shades, the fake beard, and the baseball cap, he feels dreadfully exposed.

"Hey!"

He turns to look. One of the brothers, Tenma, he thinks, is standing there holding out a ticket.

"Keep your eyes open," he says. "I could have been anyone. Now here's your ticket."

The much larger man hands it to him, and the four of them are on their way. The ferry departs in half an hour, so they join the bustle that trudges to the entry gate, passing a large window on the way that looks out onto the harbor wall. When the ferry comes into view, a shockwave of dread ripples through Kenji Kiobi.

It's a battered relic of a bygone era, its small, rust-encrusted hull rocking with every lap of the ocean against it. Its deck is a patchwork of hastily welded repairs, and the railings are missing in places. The paint, once a bright sea blue, is now faded and peeling, revealing the corroded metal beneath. It is a vessel that inspires not confidence, but fear—a diminutive, dilapidated shell bobbing uncertainly at the edge of the quay.

"We're going on that?" Kenji croaks, pointing in disbelief at the unseaworthy-looking ferry bobbing in the water.

"Uh-huh," Benma responds nonchalantly, the mere grunt rattling Kenji further.

"No way," he retorts, his voice filled with incredulous horror.

All three sets of eyes pierce him.

"You're joking, right?" Benma snaps.

"No, I'm not. I don't think it makes sense to run from one killer"—his voice goes up as he gestures the ferry outside the window—"only to get on board another. I mean, look at it."

Karuma, the eldest Hidari brother, quashes his protest. With swift authority, he grabs ahold of him, hauling Kenji close.

"You listen to me," Karuma growls into his face.

The playboy isn't used to being treated this way. He goes completely limp in Karuma's grip, the elder Hidari brother practically holding him up.

"You listen," he goes on. "I told your father. It isn't just

Yūki we need to avoid. It is Tanaka's spies. They are every-where. They will be watching every house, car, boat, plane you own or rent. They will be watching those that belong to your family, to your friends. We must use transport that isn't being watched. This is it. Now, nod your head if you agree."

Kenji can only swallow, as if swallowing down his objec-tion, and nod, his eyes reflecting a newfound understanding. With no other words exchanged, the group continues their journey toward the inconspicuous safety of Hachijō-jima island.

THIRTY-TWO

TOKYO

"Peter?" Michael's voice is a threadbare echo down the line, filled with palpable anxiety that seems to resonate through the speaker of the phone.

Peter stands by the window of another nondescript hotel room, eyes tracing the transition of Tokyo from the harsh light of day to the seductive allure of night, neon hues splashing life into the darkness.

"How you holding up, kid?" he inquires, his tone low, intimate. A mentor assessing his protege.

Michael chuckles, but there's no real humor in it. "They let me down from the chain. So that's something, I suppose."

Peter nods, though the action is lost in the void of their phone call. "You gotta find the silver linings, Mikey."

Another mirthless chuckle. "You can gather this isn't a social call," Michael says, shifting gears.

Peter sighs, turning his back to the mesmerizing view of the city. "I figured as much."

"They found him. Kiobi."

"Where?" Peter's voice sharpens, the question slicing through the tension.

"Tanaka's people ran facial recognition software through every bit of CCTV in and around Tokyo. While they didn't find Kenji Kiobi, they found three men known to work in the security division of his father's company. They were spotted boarding a ferry with another man, whose physical features closely match Kiobi. I'm sending you pictures."

Peter's phone vibrates with the arrival of the images. His fingers glide over the screen, zooming in on the faces. The breath catches in his throat. He knows them.

"The Hidari brothers," Peter says. "Otherwise known as the Gods of Death. Ex-South Korean special forces, now turned assassins. Their reputation precedes them, especially their operations in North Korea. These guys don't mess around."

The cogs in his mind are turning now, running through the possible scenarios and outcomes. But there's little time for that. Michael's voice grounds him back to the present.

"There's a boat waiting for you at the Takeshiba Ferry Terminal. A small speedboat moored up at the adjacent marina. The ferry they're on will reach Hachijō-jima in about six hours. Your task is to intercept it before it reaches there, get onboard, and take Kiobi."

"Understood," Peter affirms, striding out the door. "I'm leaving now."

He goes to put the phone down, but Michael stops him. "They want you to do it their way," he says.

"What does that mean?"

"They want you to kill the Hidaris, take Kenji, and bring him to a place they've got set up in Hokkaido in the middle of the sticks. They want you to keep him out there. What remains of the other teams will be there, too. They want you..."

"I'm gonna stop you there," Peter says as he steps into the elevator, his mind already plotting his next steps. "I do my own thing. You know that."

"They're not gonna allow it." The kid's voice sounds tired. "They want you to grab Kiobi, rendezvous with the others, bring him up to Hokkaido. Wait for Yūki there."

Peter thinks about it. "I'll see what I can do."

He says a quick farewell to Michael as the elevator reaches the bottom. The hotel lobby is a whirlwind of activity as he navigates through it with practiced ease. The night outside envelops him, the city's vibrant pulse thrumming under his feet.

Across the street, he catches sight of one of Akechi's watchers. The man is trying to blend into the urban thrum, but his attempt is clumsy, his finger against his earpiece as he speaks into his comms a dead giveaway.

Peter swiftly changes course, veering into a dimly lit alley. The open back door of a restaurant draws his attention, as does the Toyota van parked nearby, men unloading boxes of fresh vegetables from it. With swift precision, he grabs a box overfilled with daikon radishes, using it to shield his face as he strolls unimpeded through the bustling kitchen into a service corridor, dumping the vegetables down once he's clear.

Adrenaline surges through his veins as he ascends a

stairway and enters a hotel. A corridor stretches out in front of him, numbered doors a blur as he marches toward an emergency exit at the end. The fire alarm is rigged to the door, a potential siren waiting to screech. But he's prepared.

Peter checks behind him. The coast is clear; no one's followed him. He reaches into his pocket and takes his wallet out. In the zip compartment is a small magnet. The alarm's trigger system has a little tab inside the part attached to the door frame that is pushed up by a spring. The magnet in the part attached to the door pulls the tab on the spring downward, thus breaking the electrical connection that supplies power to the alarm system. When the door is opened, the tab springs back up, due to the magnet in the door being moved away, and the alarm goes off. Peter keeps the tab down by sliding the magnet alongside the switch while the door is closed. He spits his gum into his hand and uses it to stick it there, meaning that when he opens the door, the alarm stays silent.

Peter steps out onto a metallic fire escape. As he descends, he removes his jacket and turns it inside out. Its pattern is completely different on the other side, a tartan pattern as opposed to slate gray. He also takes a folded-up baseball cap from a pocket and shoves it on his head along with a pair of Oakleys—his appearance altered.

Dropping into an alley, he slips back into the city streets, joining a moving field of people. Three blocks away, he spots a 7-Eleven and heads inside. In cash, he pays for a burner phone, puts a couple of thousand yen on it in credit, and makes a call.

"I hear your target wasn't where he was supposed to be," he says the second it is answered, continuing through the crowded streets in the direction of the ferry terminal. "Want to know where he is now?"

There's a second of silence before she responds. "I do."

Peter leans in closer to the phone, his voice dropping low. "Kenji Kiobi is currently on the night ferry to Hachijō-jima. But beware—there are three very dangerous men escorting him."

Her reply is curt, laced with suspicion. "Who?"

"The Gods of Death. South Korean ex-special forces turned assassins. They're brutal, relentless. This won't be an easy task."

There's a pause on the other end, and Peter can almost feel Yūki mulling over this information.

"You seem to know a lot about them," she eventually says.

"I've crossed paths with them before," Peter replies, leaving out the details. "Let's just say they're as brutal as they come."

A prolonged silence fills the line, then: "I'll handle it."

As the call disconnects, Peter finds himself alone on the bustling street, the weight of his task settling heavy on his shoulders.

THIRTY-THREE

THE PACIFIC OCEAN

THE NIGHT IS DEEP, AND THE WATER IS LIKE obsidian. Waves lap threateningly against the hull of the rusting night ferry, the beleaguered vessel making its slow, lumbering journey toward Hachijō-jima. High above, storm clouds gather, their ominous presence like specters on the horizon.

With the weight of inky blackness and the impending storm pressing down on him, Peter sits low in the cockpit of a stealth-black XSR-48 speedboat, its advanced hull design minimizing its acoustic signature as it heads determinately toward the ferry. Credit to Tanaka's people, they certainly can source the best. The XSR is a ghost, skimming across the obsidian sheen of the Pacific with a motor that purrs so quietly it barely whispers above the sighing of the waves.

In the distance, the looming hulk of the ferry rises and falls with the tumultuous ocean. Even from afar, it appears monstrous—a colossal beast of rusted iron, creaking and groaning as though in agony against the building fury of the storm.

Slowing the speedboat down, he applies the LUX-14L night vision monocular to his eyes and holds his gaze on the ferry, scanning along the deck from the stern to the bow. He spots one of the Hidari brothers standing at the front of the ship, his figure outlined by the sporadic flashes of distant lightning.

He has a pair of binoculars. Peter is at least half a mile away. Pushing the throttle forwards, he begins moving across the water, away from the ferry and the spying eyes. He'll have to come around in a loop, making sure to avoid the lookout.

He's sure that Kenji Kiobi and the other two Hidaris will be below deck in their cabin.

Pulling a balaclava over his face, Peter inches the speedboat closer, guided by the hushed hum of the XSR's engine. The chill sea spray lashes his face, but he is oblivious, his concentration unwavering. He maneuvers to the rear of the ferry, staying out of sight of the Hidari at the front.

Each breath Peter takes is measured, precise, the rhythm of his heartbeat steady in his ears. He controls the speedboat with the precision of a surgeon, inching ever closer, ever silently toward the rear of the ferry, a wraith in the night, swallowed by the shadows. As the storm descends, the Pacific begins to convulse, each wave swelling larger, more turbulent than the last. Peter's gaze darts back and forth from the ferry to the frothing sea, timing his approach. Then, using the crest of a wave, the speedboat is thrown upward, aligning with the ferry's lower aft deck.

A mooring cleat sticks out the rear of the rusted hull. He manages to hook a mooring line and secures the speedboat to it. With the waves beginning to churn more violently, Peter takes advantage of the momentary rise, making his move. He leaps, gripping the lowest rung of a rusted metal ladder built into the hull of the ferry. His body swings perilously for a second before he finds his footing and ascends, a ghost disappearing into the belly of the beast.

On deck, he melts into the shadows, an extension of the dark itself. The ship shudders as the storm breaks, rain suddenly thrashing the metal deck in relentless sheets. Every surface is transformed into a slippery hazard. The world becomes all noise and fury—the onslaught of rain, the thunder, the groaning of the ferry—providing the perfect cloak of distraction.

He stalks closer to the bow, a predator hidden in the maelstrom, his senses acutely aware of his surroundings. Each step is a dance with danger, his heart matching the rhythm of the storm, the taste of salt and anticipation heavy on his tongue. His grip tightens around the FN 509 that's concealed within his jacket, his knuckles turning white. The time is nigh, the tension taut as a wire garrote. His heart roars louder in his chest. He is ready, he is close, the hunt at its pinnacle. He has become the storm.

He decides to leave the lone Hidari brother at the front and goes below deck. It is, however, as he stealthily navigates the dimly lit passageways of the ferry, that a sudden vibration from his pocket disrupts Peter's focus. Anticipating a call from Michael, he pulls out his phone only to see Akechi's name flash across the screen. A chill trickles down his spine; he answers, bracing himself.

"You've tipped her off," Akechi's voice snarls. "She's coming. The boy told you to intercept Kenji, take him to Hokkaido with the others, but you've made sure she's coming tonight."

Peter tries to feign confusion. "What are you—"

He's interrupted as the phone quivers against his ear, signaling an incoming message. His blood turns to ice as he opens the picture attachment. Michael is on the screen, sitting on the cot in his cell, black-eyed and bloody-nosed. A man stands over him with a pistol aimed at his head.

"Choose, Azrael." Akechi's voice returns, dripping with menace. "Yūki's life or your son's."

The line cuts abruptly, leaving Peter staring at the haunting image of his son, vulnerable and defenseless. His mind whirls, the gravity of the situation threatening to consume him. But amid the rising tide of fear and desperation, Peter knows he must remain calm. Lives are in the balance, and every decision he makes could be the difference between salvation and annihilation.

He comes to a rapid decision, his plans changing.

Amid the deceptive calm before the storm, he makes his way through the insides of the ferry. He reaches a corridor of cabin doors and his eyes train on the grim image of Karuma Hidari. He stands halfway up the corridor with his arms crossed, his face bearing a mask of icy resolve.

Peter's mind is a whirlwind of thoughts as he approaches. Drawing closer, he addresses the eldest of the brothers. "Karuma Hidari," he begins, a light note of respect lacing his words, "We've not had the pleasure of meeting in person. Though I believe we both know each other. I am Azrael."

Karuma's steel-gray eyes narrow, appraising Peter with a scrutiny born out of countless battles. Azrael makes sure to keep his hands visible and away from his gun. Karuma nods curtly, acknowledging Peter's introduction but keeping his silence, awaiting the point of this.

"I've come to give you a warning," Peter continues, holding Karuma's gaze with an unwavering stare. "You have trouble on your tail in the form of Yūki Yokashina and her Bosozoku gang. They are en route as we speak."

This earns Peter a startled blink from Karuma, his unflappable exterior rippling for a moment. Nevertheless, he quickly regains composure, his face betraying nothing.

Peter doesn't wait for him to process the words. He gets straight to his proposition. "I have a speedboat waiting nearby. I suggest we take Kenji and leave, now, before they arrive."

His words hang in the air, the gravity of his proposal permeating the tense silence. A beat of hesitation passes before Karuma speaks.

"You are working for Koji Tanaka, are you not?" he puts to Peter.

"I am."

Karuma grunts a chuckle. "Then you wish to use my boss's son as bait?"

"It's the only way to preserve his life."

"Yes. Which is why we're taking him somewhere fortified. But now you tell me the woman is coming anyway."

"Please. We don't have time. You need to get Kiobi now so we can leave on the speedboat before they arrive."

The words linger in the tense silence, echoing through the narrow corridor. Karuma holds Peter's gaze, measuring the seriousness of the situation from the intensity in his eyes. "And why should I trust you, Azrael?" he finally asks.

"Because we have a common enemy, and Kenji Kiobi's life hangs in the balance," Peter replies firmly, his resolve resonating through the musty air.

Just as Karuma is about to respond, a voice buzzes in his ear; his brother up on deck speaking from the earpiece of his comms. Karuma's eyes widen. A porthole stands at the end of the corridor. He runs to it and looks out. A fleet of speed-boats slice through the storm-struck sea, rapidly approaching the ferry.

Peter sees it too, his heart sinking. His eyes meet Karuma's, both men's faces reflecting the grim reality. Yūki and her gang have arrived sooner than expected.

They are out of time.

"We need to move!" Peter shouts, breaking into a run toward Kenji's room, the grim reality of their situation washing over them both. The battle is about to begin.

———

THE ATMOSPHERE on the ferry becomes as thick and lethal as a viper's pit, seething with impending doom. Tenma and Karuma Hidari assume a protective stance around Kenji Kiobi, the three of them following Peter through the metallic bowels of the ship. The third brother, Benma, is set to rendezvous with them on deck.

Meanwhile, the deadly specter of Yūki, her brother Tatsuo, and their Bosozoku gang ascend onto the ferry, throwing a mass of grappling hooks up onto it and climbing aboard like a gang of pirates. Their intent is as sharp as the wakizashi blade their matriarch carries under her clothing; every gang member is mentally prepared for the imminent carnage that will surely come next.

Peter, brimming with an iron resolve, leads Kenji and the two Hidari to the top of the stairs onto the open deck, but it is too late. The harsh chill of sea air meets them alongside an unexpected standoff. An ocean of yakuza form a formidable blockade, their steely gazes and lethal Heckler & Koch MP5 machine pistols making it clear that there is no easy way out of this.

Their way forward and their way back blocked, tension hangs like a cloud as the two factions face each other, the two Hidaris instinctively maneuvering Kiobi against a rusted steel wall of the ship, positioning themselves as his human shields.

The deadly ballet finds its prima ballerina in Yūki, her entrance marked by the silent rustling of her clothing and the unwavering coldness of her eyes as she joins her men. Her gaze latches on to Peter, narrowing in realization of his newfound alliance.

"Is there no allegiance you won't betray, Azrael-san?" she questions, her voice a whip in the silent confrontation.

Peter retorts, "He found out about our meeting, about me tipping you off. My son... they're going to kill him. I have twenty-four hours to deliver your head to Tanaka."

Yūki's response is one of seeming indifference. "My condolences," she coolly replies. "But as they say, a dance with the devil only ends when the music stops." Her words resonate with dark intent over the deck, marking the initiation of a deadly waltz that none can escape.

UNSEEN TO THE different parties involved in the standoff, two figures silently emerge from the rolling waves, having docked their own silent vessel on the side of the ferry. With expert precision and practiced movements, they slip undetected onto the lower levels of the massive ferry. Clad in black, faces hidden under shadows and fitted gas masks, they are virtually invisible—lethal apparitions assigned with a single mission: incite chaos.

Members of the elite Israeli special forces, they each carry a rucksack filled with a cocktail of destruction—canisters of highly flammable fuel and sophisticated incendiary devices. Time is of the essence, and they move like shadows through the labyrinthine passageways, unnoticed by the unsuspecting crew and passengers.

In the belly of the ship, the engine room hums with raw power. The duo split, each with their individual targets. One heads for the fuel lines, quickly and deftly attaching multiple small devices along the maze of pipes. The other makes his way to the main engine control panel, carefully connecting a remote-controlled detonator.

Once their respective tasks are complete, they rendezvous back in the shadows of a secluded passage. A quick, silent nod is exchanged—an unspoken confirmation that their tasks are complete. Then, as they slip away from the engine room, one of them presses a button on a small, nondescript remote. The incendiary devices ignite, catching the flammable fuel in an explosive ball of fire and smoke. Almost instantly, the lower levels of the ferry are engulfed in a fierce inferno, flames licking hungrily at everything within their reach.

Within moments, the roaring fire spreads through the insides of the ferry, the flames leaping high and searing everything in their path. Smoke bellows out, choking corridors and filling cabins. The fire alarm shrieks into life, its wailing siren a haunting accompaniment to the approaching mayhem.

The Israeli operatives disappear as silently as they appeared, returning to their boat and leaving behind a blazing inferno. Their mission is a success. The fire, their deadly puppet, is now the master of the dance.

———

ON DECK, the silent standoff breaks like glass. The third Hidari, Benma, makes his long-awaited appearance. A bark of gunshot preludes one of the yakuza going down, a spray of blood shooting from his head. Another gunshot, another dead yakuza, the rest scattering across the deck like frightened birds, finding cover wherever it is available. Then all hell breaks loose. Gunfire erupts across the deck, bullets ricocheting off the metalwork, the ferry plunged into violent disorder.

Tenma and Karuma Hidari herd Kenji Kiobi back to the stairs, taking cover there. Peter finds himself out in the open. He grabs the nearest yakuza, twists him around, and uses him as a human shield, while firing from behind him. He takes out two men with quick headshots—one, two—before the meat-shield is so riddled with bullets the yakuza drops to his knees dead as Peter dives behind the cover of a lifeboat.

It is then that a thunderous, creaking rumble comes from beneath them. Plumes of smoke cough out of the hatchways. Down below, the ferry is engulfed in a raging inferno. The flames race along corridors, devour cabins, and lick at the edges of the deck. It cuts off any route of escape. The spot the speedboat is moored to is now separated by a wall of fire. Panic erupts among the innocent passengers—they begin running from the hatchways, pouring out with the smoke. They run across the deck, oblivious to the gunfight. A crowd heads for the lifeboat Peter hides behind. A member of the ferry crew begins loading it with passengers. Peter steps out from behind it, his gun in his hand.

About twenty yards on the other side of the panicking mob stands Tatsuo Yokashina: leader of the Bosozoku clan, brother of Yūki. His eyes reflect the flames, his jaw taut, the look of death upon him. He holds his pistol up as people run in front of him and ejects the magazine, placing the gun on the ground. Then he begins rolling up his sleeves.

If Peter were as ruthless as Mother had tried to make him, he'd shoot the guy straight in the head right this minute and move on to the rest of the mission. But there are other things to this. A mutual respect. Tatsuo is doing this for his family, and so too is Peter. Neither man has any personal malice toward the other, but what has to be done has to be done.

So Peter places his FN 509 Tactical on the deck and gets ready.

The passengers finally finish boarding the lifeboat, and the crew member turns a crank that lowers it into the water. The flames, now all over the deck, lick away at everything, making the rainy air quiver.

It is only them now.

The two men lunge at each other, making up the distance between them in a few strides. Tatsuo throws a vicious right hook at Peter's head. Peter deflects it with a swift Muay Thai block, the hard edge of his forearm colliding with Tatsuo's fist—and then they're apart, circling each other. The floor beneath them rocks in rhythm with the churning sea, the deck of the ferry awash with madness. The crackling, popping symphony of an all-consuming inferno plays the cacophonous backdrop to the spectacle that is unfolding. At the epicenter stand Peter and Tatsuo, their faces set in determined grimaces, their minds primed for the brutal combat that lies ahead. Peter's eyes bore into Tatsuo's, assessing the lethal potential that dwells within the compact frame of the yakuza soldier. Tatsuo's eyes hold a similar story, both men acknowledging the prowess they find themselves pitted against.

Again, they charge simultaneously, bodies moving in unison like cogs in a violent machine. Peter uses Krav Maga, capitalizing on his agility, throwing a series of swift jabs aimed at Tatsuo's midsection. Tatsuo, having mastered Taekkyeon, adeptly deflects them, his fluid movements a stark contrast to Peter's straightforward attacks.

Despite the fire, the storm and all the lifeboats having been launched, the combatants fight on, the battle transcending into something primal.

On the other side of the ship, the Hidari brothers hold off the yakuza onslaught, the flames having ejected them from the hatchway, and now the four of them are forced to use the seating at the bow section as cover, trapped at the front of the vessel. Amongst the yakuza who push them farther toward the ocean is the clan's matriarch Yūki, her face a mask of icy concentration. Tenma Hidari is hit. He goes down, grabbed by Karuma as he does, the older brother catching his fall and laying him gently down. The bullet has struck him in the chest, and as Karuma kneels over him, Tenma goes to say something but instead coughs up a mouthful of blood, and in a second, his eyes glaze over and he is dead.

Karuma scans the chaos. All he sees are bodies, flames, and rain. At their backs is nothing but raging, stormy sea. In front, a mass of yakuza and their automatic pistols.

Never in his life has the elder Hidari felt so lost. *And for what?* he thinks, glancing back at the cowering Kenji Kiobi. *This worthless wretch?*

───────

ON THE OTHER side of the ferry, separated from the others by a barrier of flames, Peter and Tatsuo fall into a savage dance. They exchange vicious blows, their expertly trained bodies moving fluidly, weaving in and out of the scattered bodies. A capoeira kick from Peter is blocked by Tatsuo's tae-kwon-do low block, only for Tatsuo to counter with a hapkido twist throw. Establishing a solid grip on Peter's arm, he contorts his body in a quick and fluid motion, generating power for the throw. Peter rolls with the momentum, using jiu-jitsu to redirect the force, landing on his feet and launching himself back at Tatsuo with a brutal Krav Maga strike. But Tatsuo manages to parry it and move away.

The two men are locked in a ferocious display of skill and force, their bodies moving with lethal grace, each attack met with a deft counter. Techniques honed with Tatsuo's father's guidance meet their match in Peter's equally polished skills, a fusion of various martial arts. They become mirror images, the brutal dance a tapestry of pain and power.

In a calculated move, Peter lunges for Tatsuo's throat, but his attack is intercepted, Tatsuo's hand shooting out to clasp Peter's wrist in an iron grip. A swift roundhouse to Peter's flank sends him sprawling, but he bounces back immediately, barely concealing the wince as pain shoots through him.

Impatience begins to creep into the fight. Peter moves with explosive intensity, launching punches and kicks, each one a potential fight-ender. Tatsuo, on the other hand, moves like a ghost, a testament to his father's training, avoiding attacks with elegant evasion maneuvers.

And all this among a fire.

The heat from the encroaching flames begins to lick their skin, their sweat mixing with the acrid smoke that cloaks them. Their movements become languid, the struggle to breathe over the smoke and the exhaustion setting in. A spinning heel kick from Tatsuo has Peter reeling, but he is far from beaten.

———

AT THE BOW, the flames dance wildly around the players. Karuma Hidari stands there, his gun spent, his chest heaving. Crouched behind him, practically curled into a ball, is Kenji Kiobi.

Karuma is now the last remaining Hidari. Benma lies at

his feet, a bullet hole in his neck, a growing pool of blood spreading from his lifeless body along the rusty metal deck.

Opposite is Yūki and her remaining yakuza, all of them cast in a volatile glow by the blazing fire. She steps forward, locking eyes with Karuma Hidari, their fates now intertwined.

Karuma tosses his spent pistol away, plucks his karambit knife from his hip, and flicks the hooked blade out. Yūki smiles, holsters her pistol, and unsheathes the wakizashi from her hip. The steel blade radiates light as it is drawn out. With the blaze casting an eerie glow that illuminates their figures, they begin to circle.

"You'd die for him?" Yūki says, her voice piercing the sounds of the fire and the storm.

"I am a man of honor," Karuma replies. "As were my brothers. When the Hidaris take on a job, they see it until the end."

"Even if the job is protecting a worthless worm like your boss's brat?"

Kenji Kiobi, paralyzed by fear, remains huddled in a trembling ball behind Karuma, his terrified eyes fixed on the intense struggle playing out before him.

"We gave our word," Karuma says.

"Then so be it," Yūki snarls as a burst of lightning illuminates the rain and the flames.

She flies at him. Their clash reverberates through the raging storm, a melody of crashing steel, thunder, and crackling fire. Each strike is met with the other's deft parries, their movements effortless and calculated. Sparks erupt with every collision, casting fleeting light upon their fierce struggle.

PETER FINALLY FINDS HIS GAP. Using his knowledge of Brazilian jiu-jitsu, he shoots forward, taking his opponent by surprise, and wraps his legs around Tatsuo's waist, his arm sliding up and around Tatsuo's throat in a classic rear-naked choke. Tatsuo doesn't yield; he twists and writhes, a bucking bronco unwilling to be tamed.

Peter holds on, feeling his own consciousness fraying around the edges as Tatsuo's elbow finds his ribs repeatedly. The pain is searing, but the thought of Michael, trapped, alone and facing imminent death should he fail, fills Peter with a renewed burst of determination. He tightens his grip, feeling Tatsuo's struggles slowly diminish. Finally, the yakuza's movements stop, his body collapsing onto the hot metal deck beneath them.

Struggling for air and nursing a battered body, Peter disentangles himself from the unconscious Tatsuo, the relentless blaze creeping closer, illuminating the victor and the vanquished in a flickering glow.

The scent of charred destruction hangs in Peter's nostrils as he grabs the fallen man and shoves him over his shoulder. Except he doesn't get to be the good Samaritan. No, instead he gets to hear the snap of a distant gunshot; gets to feel the bullet burrow into Tatsuo's lower back as he drapes from Peter.

Dropping Tatsuo, Peter dives along the deck, using the rising flames along the edges to hide from the Israeli sniper hidden somewhere on the waves, ready to eliminate anyone who gets off this ferry alive. The deck is a hellscape of roaring flames, billowing smoke, and crumbling wreckage. Amid the chaos, Peter sprints with all his might, his heart thumping in his chest, the scorching heat on his back as the relentless pursuit of the Israeli sniper closes in. Bullets whizz past him, tearing through the air, each gunshot powering his adrenaline-fueled sprint.

With every step, he can feel the metal deck groaning beneath his feet, threatening to give way under the weight of the inferno. His lungs burn, desperate for oxygen in the thick smoke-filled air. But he pushes on, his survival instincts driving him forward. The Israeli sniper's shots continue, the sound of the distant crack reverberating through the mayhem.

Finally, reaching an edge of the deck where the flames aren't so strong, Peter leaps into the air, his body soaring for a brief moment before crashing into the cold, unforgiving water below. The impact sends shockwaves through his body, but he fights against the pain, battling the powerful current as he struggles back to the surface.

As his head bursts from the ocean's watery veil, gasping for air, he glances back at the fiery wreckage of the ferry. He then twists around in the water. The Israeli sniper stands at the edge of his craft, the optics of his rifle's scope reflecting the burning ferry, his eyes scanning the waves. His partner stands beside him, wearing a pair of field glasses. Both men appear to be busily looking for Peter, his rivals wanting to take him out of the game. The sniper's gaze reaches Peter, and their eyes meet for a split second, a silent acknowledgment of the deadly game they are playing, and then the sniper places his rifle back to his shoulder.

With a burst of energy, Peter dives beneath the surface, disappearing into the murky depths of the ocean. The muffled sounds of gunshot above slowly fade, replaced by the soothing quiet of the water enveloping him.

———

YŪKI'S EYES blaze with determination as she unleashes a rapid flurry of strikes, her wakizashi whistling through the smoke-filled air. Karuma fights back with skillful evasions and precise counterattacks. The intensity of their battle is heightened with each passing moment, their movements a blur of deadly grace.

In a desperate surge of adrenaline, Karuma lunges forward, his karambit slashing through the suffocating heat. Yūki, fueled by a mix of fury and sorrow, evades his attack with lightning speed, her body moving as if guided by unseen forces. With a swift motion of the short sword, she seizes the opportunity and disarms him, flicking the karambit from his hand as she cuts it across the palm, sending the knife spiraling into the fiery abyss.

Karuma's defenses are shattered, his vulnerability laid bare. Yūki seizes the moment, her wakizashi finding its mark with chilling accuracy. The blade pierces straight through his chest, tearing into his heart. A guttural gasp escapes Karuma's lips as searing pain courses through his body. He stumbles backward, his strength fading like the dying embers of the burning ship. Falling down, he places both hands on his rapidly bleeding chest, the blood pumping through his fingers with the last beats of his broken heart, until it stops, and the lifeless hands fall away.

As the flames roar and crackle around them, Yūki stands over the fallen Hidari, her breath ragged, her own heart pounding. Sweat mixes with tears, cascading down her soot-stained face. The weight of her vengeance and the sorrow of her losses bear down upon her, threatening to consume her spirit.

Silent witnesses, the yakuza gang members stand in reverence, their eyes fixed on their leader. The fiery frenzy that engulfs the ferry seems to pale in comparison to the storm raging within Yūki's soul.

In that harrowing moment, as the burning vessel teeters on the precipice of destruction, Yūki's resolve hardens. She knows her journey for justice is far from over, and the flames that lick at her heels only fuel her determination.

Her attention fixes on Kenji Kiobi.

Standing over him, her wakizashi glistens with Karuma's blood. Kenji, cowering before her, is a pathetic sight. His normally arrogant eyes, wide with fear, are unable to detach from the sight of his slain bodyguards. The playboy persona has evaporated, revealing a terrified child beneath the veneer of wealth and power.

"All your life," Yūki's voice cuts through the roar of flames and rain, "you've basked in a luxury you have never earned. You've played at being a man while the real work was always done by others."

Behind her, one of her men advances, heaving a heavy rucksack that is filled with rocks. Kenji's eyes follow the man, a new fear dawning as the yakuza comes over him and picks him up by the scruff. The rucksack is forced onto Kenji's shoulders, its weight causing him to stagger on his weak, trembling legs. A chain is then looped around him, locking the crushing burden in place.

"You've never carried your own weight, Kenji Kiobi."

Yūki's voice is as cold as the ocean that churns around the burning ferry. "It's time for you to understand what it means to bear a burden."

Her men drag him to the railings, the inferno at their backs.

"No, please," Kenji begs as they force him up onto the railing.

Yūki says nothing. She merely smiles. Then, with a forceful shove, she sends him over and plunging into the dark, furious waves below. The chain and the rucksack take effect immediately, dragging him down into the black depths. Kenji claws desperately at the water, his frantic struggles becoming smaller and smaller as the surface slips farther and farther out of reach. His privileged existence has not prepared him for this. Like Sisyphus, he is left to carry his long overdue burden, sinking farther into the cold, sightless abyss.

Above him, Yūki watches as Kenji Kiobi disappears beneath the rough waves, his futile struggles ceasing as darkness claims him.

"We need to leave," one of her yakuza whispers in her ear.

Yūki takes her eyes off the water and scans her surroundings.

The ferry is now a floating hell.

"Where's Tatsuo?" she asks.

Her companion is on the cusp of answering when a bullet tears through the side of his head, and she is forced to dive for cover. The shot came from the waves: from the Israeli sniper.

THE SEA RAGES AROUND PETER, a wild, untamed beast that matches the fury of his own heart. With powerful, determined strokes, he cleaves the dark water, the ferry's burning wreckage above the surface a looming, grim reminder of the anarchy he has narrowly escaped. Ahead lies the small craft, where the Israeli sniper and his partner wait, both of them scanning the water for any sign of him.

Each stroke is a battle against the current, a testament to his resolve, his mind focused on one goal: reaching those two men on their boat. Time is a luxury he can't afford, his window of opportunity rapidly closing, his breath struggling in his lungs. Adrenaline surges through his veins, sharpening his senses, honing his awareness, a raw, primitive instinct taking over.

Meanwhile, on the floating craft, the Israeli sniper and his companion comb the waves, their eyes scanning the water for any sign of movement. The light from the fire casts this part of the water in shadow, making it harder to spot things. They know Peter lurks beneath the surface, a determined predator evading his hunters, but the burning ferry commands their attention, a menacing silhouette against the dark waters. After all, their real target, Yūki Yokashina is still aboard, possibly executing her escape while they are distracted by Azrael.

As Peter draws closer, his heart rattles in his chest and his lungs burn, begging for air. With each passing moment, the stakes rise. His heart becomes frantic, his lungs gasping for precious air. His approach must be timed perfectly, his presence concealed as much as possible beneath the water's choppy surface. The distance to his target shrinks with every stroke, the intense situation escalating with every frenzied heartbeat.

The Israeli sniper and his partner exchange glances, a silent understanding passing between them. Their fingers tighten around their weapons, their bodies tensed, ready to engage the impending threat.

Abruptly, a splash fractures the silence as Peter surfaces, just meters behind the boat, before disappearing back under. The men whip around, scanning the barren water for the source of the disturbance. Taking advantage of their confusion, Peter uses his ebbing strength to swim stealthily underneath their craft. The moment of truth arrives as he surfaces on the other side of the boat, hands gripping the edge, their backs to him.

Without hesitation, Peter hoists himself up, using every fiber of his being to pull his body onto the boat. As the men spin around, he thrusts his M9 bayonet into the sniper's chest, while his free hand fends off the second man. By the time his adversary reaches for his pistol, Peter wrenches the knife free and slashes it across the man's throat, grabbing the wrist with the gun, pushing it down as the guy sprays blood everywhere.

Two errant shots explode from the dying man's pistol, puncturing the inflatable craft. Peter can only grumble as the boat begins to deflate rapidly beneath his feet, sinking slowly into the icy water.

His swim isn't over yet.

———

BENEATH THE BLACKENED SHROUD of the night sky, the blazing ferry contrasts dramatically, a monstrous torch bobbing on the unforgiving ocean. The panicked screams of the last fleeing passengers, those who missed the lifeboats, explodes as they abandon the fiery death trap and plunge into the watery depths below, fleeing the firestorm behind them.

Amid this chaotic inferno, a tragedy of a different kind is taking shape. Yūki holds her younger brother Tatsuo in her arms, having found him on the other side of the ferry. His breath is ragged, the life in his eyes dimming.

Tears fall from Yūki as she stares down at her baby brother.

"I'm so sorry, Tatsuo," she says.

"It is... okay," he splutters. "I may not get to see the end... but I am sure you will get there... on your own."

Tatsuo's life, marked by his undying loyalty to his sister and his gang, has been extinguished as swiftly as it was lived, his heart gradually silenced by the brutal sniper's bullet. Yūki's hardened façade crumbles, her eyes wide with a rare terror as she watches her brother's life ebb away, the fire's ghastly glow dancing on their faces, illuminating their last shared moment.

Amid the ruin, Yūki's anguished cry suddenly pierces the air as her brother's lifeless body falls from her arms, his vacant eyes mirroring the dreadful scene unfolding. Her lament is quickly drowned out by the escalating flames and frantic cries of the drowning passengers.

Kissing Tatsuo on the forehead, she stands up, promises him revenge, then takes a run and jumps off the edge of the vessel.

THIRTY-FOUR

SOMEWHERE IN THE PACIFIC OCEAN

IN THE END, THE FERRY EXPLODED, THE FIRE reaching the fuel tanks, flaming pieces of it thrown into the water. That had signaled the final death knoll of the vessel, and it hadn't been long before the last vestige of the Tokyo to Hachijō-jima night ferry had disappeared beneath the rolling waves.

In the tumultuous aftermath, Peter clings to a fragment of the passenger ship, a piece of wall attached to a small buoyancy compartment complete with accompanying port-hole. The cold waves churn around him, the storm clouds having moved on, the night now clear. His limbs scream from exertion and the icy grip of the ocean, but he holds fast, focusing on each labored breath.

He senses something moving in the water beneath him.

Without warning, a shape rises from the dark ocean: Yūki Yokashina, her face a mask of bitter determination despite the visible signs of exhaustion. In her hand is her wakizashi, the edge glinting ominously under the pale moonlight. She lunges at him, and Peter is barely able to evade the deadly strike, kinking his body and parrying the wrist, the chill of the blade passing precariously close to the flesh of his abdomen.

Despite his weariness, years of training and experience click into place. As Yūki prepares for another strike, Peter kicks at her, the force of his action amplified by the water surrounding them. The surprise assault forces her to loosen her already weak grip on the wakizashi, and with a swift maneuver, Peter manages to disarm her, ripping the sword from her fingers and letting it drop through the water into oblivion.

He seizes her by the arm, pulling her toward him. A battle of strength and will ensues as Yūki thrashes and claws at him, but the cold and the exhaustion from the fight on the ferry soon overwhelm her, her struggles reduced to very little.

Sensing her imminent unconsciousness, Peter draws her closer, securing her to the floating wreckage with his belt, tying her wrists to a mooring ring. Sure that she is stable, he holds on to the buoyant debris and starts to kick, using the remains of his ebbing strength and aiming for the shadowy outline of an island in the distance.

———

THE HARSH OCEAN spits them out on the fringes of a small, desolate islet made of rock and sand, a few Japanese cedar trees poking up out of it. Peter, his strength waning, drags the unconscious Yūki from the icy surf onto the sand, their bodies sodden and heavy. With a fading, final burst of determination, he hauls her onto his shoulder and carries them both toward the mouth of a cave carved into the island's rock face.

Inside the relative shelter, he hastily collects what dry kindling and driftwood he can find, sparking a small fire with the Everstryke Pro survival lighter he pulls from a strap-on thigh wallet secured to his right leg. The fire's feeble glow soon casts dancing shadows on the cave walls, the crackling flames and the crash of waves the only sounds in the oppressive silence. The heat is a welcome comfort, but the cold is an unforgiving predator, creeping ever closer despite the fire.

The lingering dampness from their clothes is a chilling menace, their body temperatures perilously close to hypothermia. Peter knows what he has to do. Gently, almost reverently, he strips the unconscious Yūki of her soaked clothing before doing the same for himself. It is a matter of survival, not of dignity or respect. They need to share body heat to stave off the cold, to keep death at bay.

As he draws Yūki's bare form against his own, she suddenly stirs, her eyes flickering open. Her disorientation quickly morphs into panic, her body writhing against his in desperate protest. His wearied muscles strain against her struggle, his low hushes barely audible over her frantic gasps.

"Listen to me, Yūki Yokashina," he implores, his whisper barely carrying over the crackling fire. "We are fighting the cold, nothing more. We need to maintain our body heat, or we will freeze."

The resistance in her body gradually ebbs, her panic-stricken gaze searching his, looking for deception. Finding none, she relaxes against him, her trembling body accepting the shared warmth.

It is then, as they lie side by side on the smooth rocks, the fire flickering away, that Peter says, his voice a raw whisper against the backdrop of the waves, "You know, since this began, I've wanted to ask you one question more than any other."

She doesn't say anything, and he takes this as a sign to go on.

"What did Koji Tanaka do to you to deserve all this bloodshed?"

Gradually, Yūki comes to some inner decision and decides to speak, the shadows along the cave walls becoming a silent audience as she unravels her tortured past. Her voice, quiet yet unyielding, weaves a tale that seems to draw the very warmth from the room, replaced instead by the icy touch of betrayal and suffering.

"Our relationship began as a professional one," she says. "I was Koji's bodyguard; he was my boss. For the first months, we shared barely a syllable. But then one day, I saved his life from a group of robbers and for the first time, I saw the real Tanaka, saw him weakened and frightened, without his power, without his bravado. There was something real about him then. Something that was unmistakably human. See, afterwards when we were getting away from the scene of the attack, though Koji was still shaking, he spoke to me in a natural manner, holding my hand in the back of the car, telling me, confessing that he hadn't been so frightened since he was a boy. He told me a story of being bitten by a pit viper when he was a child. How he was expected to die, and how during the days he spent in hospital in a fever, he had dreamed of going to hell. As he told me this story, I couldn't help seeing him as human for the first time, as a man and not some megalomaniac control freak. Over the coming weeks and months, I found myself falling in love with Koji Tanaka. I became his confidant, the only one who got to see the real Tanaka behind all the bravado. It made me feel special."

Yūki paints a picture of a time when love, vibrant and promising, had blossomed between her and Tanaka. They were young, their futures entwined, filled with the promise of a lifetime together. Peter has to admit he's surprised. He never thought that the two would have ever been in love. He thought only hate could exist in a man like Koji Tanaka.

"Then," she continues, her voice becoming dark, "I got pregnant. It made me start looking at things in a different light. As I nurtured this life growing within me, I started to find a motherhood growing alongside it. Being raised by a man like Takashi Yokashina, the man they call the Gun, isn't an easy thing. I guess I have always been cursed by violence. My mother was killed in front of me when I was an infant, and though I don't remember it, I remember the bloody revenge my father and I went on in the aftermath. I remember each of the men we pushed into the grave. When I began this transition into motherhood, there seemed like there was this great shift in identity. I was a mother now. A protector. Warmth and light. Not a hired gun enveloped in darkness. I started to look at the world around me. The world of Koji Tanaka. And not just that, but *he* changed when I became pregnant."

His love, she tells Peter, metamorphosed into a possessive, confining entity, gradually encaging her within a gilded prison, his grip on her life tightening until she felt the need to flee.

"It was like," she says, her voice quivering like the flickering flames of their fire, "I had become his property on account of his offspring being inside of me."

Pregnant and frightened, she had taken flight on their wedding day, the very day they were supposed to become one, abandoning him at the altar. Carrying his child in her womb, she ran, seeking a new life, a new identity.

And she found it. At first.

Far from the oppressive control of Tanaka, she discovered peace and love anew amid the quiet seclusion of Hokkaido. There, she built a life with another man not far from Sapporo, a sweet man, the exact opposite of Koji Tanaka, who didn't care that she was carrying another man's child. She married him and gave birth to a daughter she named Mayu, placing her new husband on the birth certificate as the father, and for a while, she got to taste the sweetness of contentment, of peace.

But just as life seemed to be becoming beautifully ordinary, tragedy struck. A car accident stole her new husband and daughter, smashing her world into grief-stricken shards. When Peter asks, "Did you ever suspect Tanaka was behind it?" her reply is straightforward yet loaded. "I didn't. No."

"So you always thought it was unrelated?"

"Yes. I never even suspected it until you told me Mayu is alive. It makes sense now. That he would kill Ryu and take her. Have enough power to make it look like an accident."

"So if it isn't for that reason you're going after him, then why?"

Her response is chilling, the words tumbling from her lips, a disturbing testament of her suffering. See, Tanaka wasn't finished there. He hated Yūki for leaving him on their wedding day, abandoning him in front of all their friends and family. No person had ever said no to him before, no one had ever left him feeling so powerless. Taking her daughter and killing her husband wasn't enough. A year after the accident, Tanaka's men descended on her lonely house and abducted Yūki, taking her back to the island. To him.

Her voice is barely a murmur as she continues, describing a monstrous version of Tanaka. A man who boasted of her insignificance, of her replaceability.

"He claimed," she whispers, "that I meant nothing to him. And, as proof, he would show me just how worthless I was. He claimed that I had been the envy of all his friends; that each of them had wanted to possess me as he had. He said that it was time to show me my true worth as nothing more than a whore."

She takes in a withered, sobbing breath before recommencing with the next part.

"He had me drugged, then locked in a room. That's when the true horror began. One by one, his friends came to visit, my body nothing more than material to feed their depraved appetites. Koji wanted to hollow me out. To destroy me. For a whole week, they visited me in my underground cell, had their way while I was too weak to defend myself. I can still recall every detail of that time. Every vivid sensation seared into my memory, each moment meticulously remembered. The order of the men, their smells, their touch—everything a haunting reminder of those terrible days I lay helpless, my body handed over to one disgusting bastard after another."

Peter's realization comes with a sharp intake of breath. "That's the order you're killing them in, isn't it?" he says. "The order they raped you. That's why Tanaka knows who is next."

"Yes. And now," she says, a fresh bitterness infecting her tone, "he knows that *he* is next. That *his* time has come."

———

THREE HOURS LATER, dawn breaks. The mutter of helicopters and naval rescue vessels punctures the quiet outside the cave. Everyone is out searching for survivors of the disaster, but none of them are close enough to the island yet to bother Peter.

Having dried next to the fire, their clothing has been placed over Yūki as she remains sleeping. Peter watches her. It is probably the most peaceful rest she's had since her quest for revenge began. Seeing her so tranquil, he can't help feeling melancholy for what comes next. He checks his Casio G-Shock Frogman wristwatch. It is almost time.

Strapped to his right thigh, a waterproof thigh holster wallet holds the tools of his grim task. He has decided that he will do this as nicely as possible. From the beginning, there was always a chance that it would go this way. So he's made sure to come prepared for such an eventuality, and to make sure that it goes as smoothly as possible. She doesn't deserve to suffer.

Slowly, he unzips the wallet. He retrieves a small plastic vial and a sterile syringe from inside. As she continues to sleep, he unwraps the syringe, attaches the needle, pierces the vial's lid, and draws up the clear liquid inside.

Creeping toward her, his shadow engulfs her tranquil, sleeping form. A part of her shoulder shows, displaying a demon with smoke billowing from his nostrils. The monster holds a pitchfork, on the end of which is the body of a sinner.

Peter lowers himself next to her, the needle hovering mere inches from her arm. But then he hesitates—a fatal error. Her eyes flutter open, widening in alarm at the sight of the syringe. But Peter is swift. He stabs the needle into her, his thumb driving the plunger all the way down. Her resistance is minimal as the liquid courses through her veins, reaches her brain, and renders her unconscious.

Retreating from her, Peter finds himself at a loss, managing only a soft apology.

"I had no choice," he whispers.

This is true. The choice was her or Michael—a choice that could only ever go one way.

THIRTY-FIVE

SHINOSHIMA

THE SETTING SUN IS ANGRY. IT BURNS WRATHFULLY on the horizon, painting the East China Sea with fiery hues. Peter grips the throttle of the speedboat, his knuckles white against the smooth black handle. His glowing mind surges in time to the engine's roar, the force of its rhythm reverberating through his bones. Ahead of him looms Tanaka's island fortress, an imposing silhouette against the fiery sky.

The hell that he has lived these past weeks rests heavily upon his withered soul, and he hopes that today will mark its end.

A cold wind whips at his face. He tastes the sharp tang of salt on his lips. Narrowing his eyes, he tries to discern the details of the island as he speeds toward it. The buildings begin to come into detail, silhouetted by the sun. The little harbor with its quay, the rectangular office block where the overground staff reside, the monorail, all of those little edifices indications of the much larger citadel built beneath, a stark contrast to the wild, crashing sea and untamed jungle surrounding it.

Beside him, on the seat, an aluminum organ transport container, a little bigger than a human head, sits ominously. A package ready for delivery.

Peter tears his gaze away from the fortress to glance at it. He feels a shiver creep up him, not from the cool ocean spray, but from the knowledge of what lies inside the container.

In his pocket, his phone comes alive. He picks it out and answers.

"Azrael-san," the harsh voice of Akechi Akiyama hisses. "We see you on our systems now. About a mile away. You have Tanaka-shashou's package?"

"I do," he answers coolly.

"Then we will see you soon."

Peter's fingers tighten around the throttle. He skims across a wave, the boat momentarily airborne before crashing back onto the water, drenching him with spray. The fortress looms closer, its concrete edifices like soulless sentinels watching his approach.

There is no turning back. Peter, with the container at his side, speeds toward the fortress, ready to get this over with and get his son back.

————

AKECHI AKIYAMA and four of his subordinates are waiting as Peter steps off the speedboat onto a jetty. Without a word, they search him meticulously for weapons, their hands skimming over his body in a practiced rhythm, searching for hidden blades, firearms. They come up empty-handed. Peter is alone, save for the grim package he carries.

"Where is my son?" he demands immediately as Akechi steps forward.

"He is well," Akechi replies calmly, his eyes never leaving Peter's. "Since the news of Yūki's untimely departure reached us here at Shinoshima, no harm has come to him. He awaits you in his cell, eager for liberation. Now may we inspect the package?"

At Akechi's command, one of his men takes the container from Peter. Beneath a gazebo, a small table has been prepared, offering shade. The man places the container on the table and then withdraws, leaving Akechi alone with it. He unclips the clasps of the aluminum box, flips the lid open, and for a moment, he falls silent, his gaze locked on the woman's face within.

She stares back up at him, eyes closed, an expression of peaceful resignation on her face. "She really was as beautiful as they say," Akechi muses aloud, a note of genuine regret in his voice. "Such a shame."

With a sigh, he closes the case. "Okay," he declares, facing his men once more. "The package has arrived. Now we must deliver it to the boss."

They guide Peter up the jetty and onto the quay. The group then moves toward a waiting monorail carriage that will transport them into the heart of the island. Peter cradles the package in his arms. After all, it is his burden to bear, his delivery to make.

———

With an eerie silence lingering in the air, the monorail descends into the depths of the underground fortress. The unsettling hush seems to bounce off the austere walls of the transport car, amplifying the tension in the atmosphere.

They step off at the familiar platform, and the same routine as before ensues—scanning for weapons and ushering him through steel-reinforced automatic doors. Again, a golf cart awaits them, and they continue their journey, trundling through the vast complex. The destination? The same auditorium as before. But this time, a twist: he's led through a side door into an anteroom adjoining Tanaka's private quarters, the same room Tanaka had occupied with his bodyguard before.

Nevertheless, entrance into the megalomaniac's realm isn't quick. Peter finds himself trapped in the room with Akechi Akiyama and his duck-headed cane, the two forced to endure several tests before being allowed admittance. The hours creep by with painstaking slowness, marked by a procession of PCR and POC tests that they must wait for the results of. Each moment is fraught with trepidation—a thing as simple as a common cold could tip the scales and unravel Peter's carefully laid plans.

No need to worry, though. After an agonizing three-hour wait, Peter is relieved of the suspense—he's clean. The green light is given. Literally. And he and Akechi find themselves stationed before a formidable door, waiting for the overhead indicator to signal access. When it blinks green, the door swings open with an automated whir, revealing the sanctuary within.

Crossing the threshold, Peter is immediately captivated

by the surprising harmony of the apartment, of the merger between industrial and organic elements. Robust walls of brushed concrete shine under the gentle lighting, their starkness mitigated by the presence of warm bamboo furniture and the sophisticated charm of hinoki wood paneling. They pass a hanging garden, a tranquil sanctuary enveloped in green, adorned with evergreen azaleas and bonsai maples, their foliage rustling in the breeze of the ventilation system. Wisteria and morning glories spill from hanging pots, their tendrils reaching for the concrete ground below.

Moving on, they stroll beside traditional shoji screens that punctuate the cavernous space, injecting an element of privacy without encroaching upon the apartment's grandeur.

Akechi beckons him onward, leading him into a designated living area, characterized by an understated leather couch and a hinoki wood coffee table. The surrounding walls are decorated with a tasteful mix of traditional and modern Japanese art. A modern chandelier radiates a gentle glow, casting tantalizing shadows across the minimalist furniture below.

Akechi comes to a stop and gestures for Peter to do the same, to take up a position beside him. They're not left waiting long. The arrival of two men disrupts the tranquility of the room, the pair entering from the opposite side. Koji Tanaka, an imposing figure with an unrestrained mane of silver hair, strides forward, followed closely by his compact bodyguard, Jin. Clad in an olive-green samue, his white hair glows softly under the bunker's lighting.

The bodyguard exudes an aura of tranquility and deadly skill. His arms tucked neatly behind his back, he maintains a dignified poise. The contemplative expression on his serene face reveals a life steeped in the disciplined study of hand-to-hand combat, a detail not lost on Peter.

Without a single word of preamble, Peter presents the medical container. "Your package."

Koji Tanaka pauses, eyes narrowing as they sweep over the delivery. Instead of receiving it, he steps back, his expression hardening. It's as if Peter himself is tainted, unfit to occupy the same space.

Jin steps forward. As part of his duties, he receives the aluminum container instead of his master. With practiced care, he places it on a nearby bamboo table, asserting a quiet authority. Tanaka assumes his position at the table, taking a seat along the nearby sofa, his gaze fixed on the box, a silent anticipation hanging in the air.

Despite the comprehensive disinfection process carried out in the anteroom, Jin follows his own rigorous protocol. He meticulously sanitizes the package once again, his movements measured and precise, highlighting his unyielding commitment to Tanaka's safety. The bunker's air thickens with tension as the moment of truth approaches, casting long shadows of uncertainty over them all as they brace for the revelation of the container's contents.

Tanaka begins to unseal it, his fingers flipping the clasps. He slowly lifts the top, and when he has, his gaze becomes ensnared by the sight within. There before everyone present, his hardened visage falters, an uncharacteristic flicker permeating his features as his countenance stretches into shock. A glimmer in his eyes heralds the cascade of tears that soon stream down the weathered contours of his face. His body shudders with each suppressed sob, the usually indomitable figure now visibly shaken. Abruptly, the silence shatters as the restrained sorrow bursts forth in a gut-wrenching howl, transforming the hardened billionaire into a man bereft, weeping unabashedly like a lost child. Words tumble from his lips in a torrent of remorse and pleas, each syllable bearing the weight of his profound regret.

"I'm sorry," he chokes, his words distorted by his sobs. "I'm so sorry," he implores the lifeless face within the box, each apology a desperate plea for forgiveness.

This, Peter thinks as he watches, *must be the defenseless child Yūki mentioned in the cave.*

Tanaka's gaze lingers on the closed eyes, a painful reminder of the life that once inhabited the face he knew so well. The look she bears feels like an indictment.

"Her eyes...," he stammers, his voice barely above a whisper. "They're closed. Jin..." He pauses, turning to his diminutive bodyguard, who has stood by, stoic and silent, throughout the unfolding scene. His command is desperate, his voice trembling. "Open her eyes, Jin. I need to see them."

The request hangs in the air, a poignant reminder of the tangible reality of his loss, its echoes reverberating through the somber silence that follows.

Jin approaches the grim spectacle, his face a picture of resolute calm. With a surprising tenderness, the bodyguard reaches out, gently prying open the sealed eyelids of the decapitated head. The eyes that are revealed are vacant, lifeless—a chilling sight that sends an uncomfortable chill through the room.

Tanaka leans in, his gaze boring into the newly exposed eyes. A moment of tense silence stretches out, each tick of the clock punctuating the anticipation in the room.

Suddenly, he pulls back, a frown creasing his brow. The word leaves his lips in a whisper, yet it resonates through the room like a gunshot. "No." His gaze snaps up to meet Peter's, accusation simmering in his eyes. "It's not her," he hisses.

The room goes deadly quiet. All eyes swivel to Peter, the undercurrent of suspicion and confusion becoming palpable. The air tightens around him, the weight of the room's collective gaze pressing down. For a moment, all is still—a snapshot of suspicion, harbinger of an impending storm.

"No, it's not," Peter affirms, his voice steady. "The head in that box was purchased on the black market two days ago by a CIA operative. I'm assured that the woman who owned it passed away naturally. I don't know her name. What I do know is that it took a skilled plastic surgeon and a makeup artist an entire day to modify her appearance to resemble Yūki Yokashina. Obviously, it didn't work with the eyes."

The memory swims back to Peter vividly, as clear as the cool Pacific waters that surrounded them this morning. He was in the damp, shadowy mouth of the cave, the soft, sporadic drip of water resonating in the hollow space. Before him was Yūki, unconscious. He had known her temper, her fiery spirit, and he had doubted her willingness to listen to his plan, let alone agree to it. He needed her calm, neutral, and somewhere she couldn't just walk away from him. The only way he could ensure that was by putting her to sleep, at least temporarily.

In the dim glow of the cave, Peter had hefted her limp body into his arms, making his way out to a waiting speedboat, a small vessel piloted by a CIA operative who knew no more than he was to pick up a man and a woman.

Nothing about anyone being unconscious. But he knew not to ask questions. So while Peter sat with the sleeping Yūki, the operative drove them out to sea, the boat cutting through the water effortlessly, racing toward a predetermined rendezvous point in the vast expanse of the Pacific Ocean.

There, a submarine waited, the *USS Tang*, its dark form a silent, menacing silhouette against the azure waters. Then, later on, aboard the sub, amid the hum of machinery, Peter had explained his plan to a slowly waking Yūki.

The scheme was audacious, borderline lunacy, but it was their only shot. A ploy designed to deceive Koji Tanaka: to get Peter access to his apartment.

As she had sobered up from the sedative, Yūki had listened, her initial fury ebbing into grudging acceptance. It was a dangerous plan, one that would demand a price. But if it meant reclaiming her daughter, she was ready to pay. In the end, she had nodded, her agreement silent but resolute. They had a plan, and it was time to set it into motion.

Tanaka's eyes go red, the veins in his temples throbbing. He is pointing a finger at Peter. "Where is she?!" he spits.

"Alive and well—and somewhere on this island."

Just as the words leave Peter's mouth, the lights abruptly die out, replaced by the eerie glow of emergency lighting, bathing everything in a threatening red hue. All the digital window screens, made to look like windows and skylights, go dark.

Peter is the only one wearing a smile.

"That would be her now," he declares casually.

"Your son is dead!" Tanaka roars.

Akechi instinctively brings a hand up to his earpiece,

prepared to give the command to end Peter's son. However, nothing but static fills his ear.

"They've hit you with a cyber-attack," Peter says with a smirk as the realization dawns on the others. "Your communications won't work anymore."

The notion is met with furrowed brows.

"Oh, I forgot to mention," Peter continues, the smirk never leaving his face, "it's not just Yūki and the Bosozoku that's here. See, your daughter managed to get those photos sent out a day ago. It means the United States Government on behalf of the United Nations got the arrest warrant about an hour before I arrived. By now, a large section of the US Navy is hovering just off the coastline of Shinoshima, your government having granted them permission to enter Japanese waters. The power outage is their doing. They've hacked your systems remotely."

"Kill him!" Tanaka bellows.

In one swift motion, Jin draws a pistol from his belt. Peter reacts in kind, seizing Akechi Akiyama and pulling him into the line of fire. As Jin aims at Peter, Tanaka shouts, "Shoot!"

Akechi's eyes widen in disbelief as the gun fires three times, the bullets ending Akechi Akiyama's life, turning him into a dead weight. Peter releases him, but he's not fast enough to evade the next two bullets as they strike his flank. He almost loses his footing but manages to dive for the doorway, crashing onto the wooden floor of a hallway, grimacing with the pain of his fresh wounds as he scrambles to his feet and bolts deeper into the apartment.

Pressing himself into an alcove, he pulls his shirt up, removes the two smoldering slugs that have become wedged in the thin sheet of ultra-high molecular weight polyethylene he's wearing over his torso. He throws the spent rounds down, the hot lead burning his fingers.

Through a shoji screen, he spots the creeping shadow of Jin and his pistol. Peter must move, use the tight confines of the apartment to his advantage. Play a game of hide and seek until his opponent is disarmed, and they can begin the dance of death.

———

AN ICY CHILL creeps into the state-of-the-art bunker as its advanced security systems fail, plunging the complex into pandemonium. Emergency lighting ignites, painting the sleek surfaces with a haunting, blood-red glow. From afar, a menacing growl permeates the frantic silence—the promise of an approaching monorail, a sinister herald of what's to come, growing louder as it thunders into the platform with a pneumatic hiss.

Its heavy steel doors slide open like the jaws of a monstrous beast, and from within its metallic belly bursts forth Yūki Yakishina, the fierce matriarch of the Bosozoku yakuza clan, flanked by the final remnants of her ruthless gang. Their eyes burn with determined ferocity, their bodies tense with adrenaline-fueled readiness.

Without hesitation, they unleash a hailstorm of bullets, their violent greeting sending the two security personnel stationed on the platform into a panicked scramble for cover, one which is made futile by the storm of lead that cuts both men down.

Everywhere, the bunker erupts into bedlam. Scientists,

technicians, the agricultural workers tasked with operating the subterranean farms and vegetable cultivation facilities, all of them abandon their posts, fleeing to whatever shelter they can find in the sprawling complex. Those who are part of the security team attempt to mount a defense, positioning themselves along the corridors Yūki and her band pour down, but their efforts prove useless as they find themselves hopelessly outnumbered in the face of the Bosozoku onslaught.

In a dimly lit corridor, choked with the acrid smell of gunshots and fear, a lone security officer finds himself cornered. With shaking hands, he drops his weapon before raising them in surrender. The echo of the gun's clatter seems to linger in the air, a testament to his capitulation.

Yūki strides up to him, her eyes hard and demanding, her every step an embodiment of predatory grace. As for the man's eyes, they widen as she approaches, the bodies of his dead comrades scattered about behind her.

"Where is Mayu?" she snarls, her demand resonating through the corridor, as chilling as the red light that bathes them.

Terror flooding his features, the man nods. "I can take you," he vows.

"Then do it," she replies.

———

LIKE A SPECTER, Jin's silent shadow stalks through the apartment, slithering across the shoji screens, the smooth, cold pistol in his hand glinting in the muted light. Peter, his body bruised and battered from the month's previous engagements, feels the prickling tension build as the supposed calm gets set to transform into a battlefield, his back pressed into a nook in one of the walls, listening to the gentle rustle of Jin's clothing.

The game of life and death is afoot.

Silhouetted in the subdued light, Koji Tanaka hides in one of the bedrooms, listening carefully for any signs of the unfolding violence, his gaze locked on to the closed door of the room.

While Peter hides, a painful twinge radiates from his torso where the body armor managed to stave off the bullets. The impact has fractured at least two of his ribs, and each breath is now a labored chore. Another pang flares up in his right shoulder, still recovering from the bullet wound he received in Fuchu City. Nevertheless, Peter's seasoned composure doesn't flinch. He's been here before; this is just another trial he has to endure. Survival is his creed, and he pushes the pain deep into the corners, his keen mind set on one thing—disarming Jin.

Jin, an embodiment of silent menace, moves like a hunting leopard through the tastefully furnished apartment, methodically stalking his prey. But Peter is no ordinary quarry. He outmaneuvers, keeping to the shadows, using his knowledge of Jin's techniques to anticipate and avoid deadly encounters. Twice, he narrowly escapes being shot, his instincts and training buying him precious seconds as he almost walks straight out in front of the predator. One time, Jin sees enough of his target to fire two shots that barely miss before hitting a Katsushika Hokusai original woodwork print of Mount Fuji and tearing it apart.

As Jin probes, attempting to corner Peter with method-ical precision, Tanaka's heart thrums with anticipation, his ears pressed to the despairing sounds of his home. Each near miss, every bullet that finds the opulent hinoki wood instead of Peter, sends a ripple of frustration through him.

It is as Jin approaches a corner of a hallway that Peter seizes his opportunity. Springing from the shadows, he wrenches the gun from Jin's grasp, the weapon skittering across the polished parquet floor as they both lose grip of it.

With the advantage now gone, Jin switches tactics, adapting with an array of traditional Japanese martial arts techniques, launching into a flurry of attacks—transforming the scene from a hunt to a dance of death.

Jin's lightning fist comes crashing in, a move straight from the school of karate, designed to break bones. It finds Peter's arm, Azrael having put everything into getting the gun off him. The blow causes a sickening crack to resonate through the room and all the way up Peter's arm. It would've crippled most men, but Peter remains standing.

The real dance now begins, each move a response to the other. They exchange blows like two seasoned warriors, striking with precision and deadly accuracy.

His skill is immense, and he manages to land another brutal hit to Peter's arm, the crack of fracturing bone echoing in the vast room.

———

THE MAZE-LIKE CORRIDORS of the subterranean bunker resound with the sounds of emancipation. Previously sealed doors now hang ajar. Inmates wander aimlessly in the wake of this unforeseen freedom, all clad in uniform jumpsuits that mark them apart from the workers and security of Shinoshima.

Among these liberated souls is Michael, his expression dazed as he traverses the labyrinth, his body aching, his mind confused.

Lost in the sea of indistinguishable jumpsuits, a familiar figure catches his eye. Mayu. She is like a beacon in the tumultuous ocean of faces. Dressed in the same prison uniform, she stands distinct among the crowd, and when their eyes meet across the bustling hallway, an almost magnetic connection forges an immediate recognition.

An invisible thread pulls them toward each other, and the world seems to blur around them as they rush into each other's arms, their embrace a sanctuary amid the bedlam. "I'm so glad you're still alive," Mayu breathes, her voice laden with the weight of disbelief and relief.

Michael steps back, his hands resting on her shoulders. His eyes scan her uniform, a frown forming on his brow. "What happened?"

"Father found out I helped you."

"And he locked you away?"

His question, however, remains hanging in the air as their reunion is interrupted by the sound of a familiar name reverberating along the passage: "Mayu?!"

Mayu's hold on Michael loosens as she turns to the sound of her name, her eyes landing on a figure at the corridor's end. Time halts for a breathless moment, her mind laboring to comprehend the sight before her. The woman at the end is a figure from a distant past, a living memory—a specter of loss.

Mayu's heart stammers in her chest, and her mind races

to connect the dots. A decade and a half span between their last meeting, the gap filled with longing and sorrow. She had only been a child then, a seven-year-old girl who lost her mother. The realization dawns slowly, but when it does, it hits Mayu like a tidal wave.

"M-mother?" The word escapes her lips, fragile as a whispered prayer.

She relinquishes her hold on Michael, her hands sliding away as she gravitates toward the woman at the end of the corridor. With a rush of unleashed emotion, she bolts toward Yūki. Mayu's arms instinctively reach out for the woman who represents a past she thought was forever lost— all her lingering questions answered in an instant. Their reunion is marked by heart-wrenching sobs, the sound reverberating off the stark concrete walls, the two figures lost in their shared grief and joy.

Yūki clings to Mayu, her own body shaking with sobs as she holds her child—a child she believed dead—in her arms, cradling her to her breast for the first time in what feels like an eternity.

———

PETER WILL HAVE to draw upon his entire wealth of combat knowledge. Borrowing from the raw power and dexterity of Muay Thai, he lands a ferocious elbow strike into Jin's chest, using his good arm, the one without the fracture. He follows up with a knee strike, targeting Jin's midsection, exploiting the brief moment of his adversary's faltering balance. Each strike he makes carries the weight of his survival.

Jin counters. Peter anticipates the move. He mirrors the flowing, circular movements of pencak silat, dancing around Jin's advances, avoiding the onslaught of Indonesian martial arts.

For what feels like an eternity, they spar, Tanaka's underground apartment resonating with the sounds of their epic struggle. Every punch Peter takes, every kick he deflects, brings him closer to the edge. His body screams in agony, but his resolve remains unwavering. Mother and Magda didn't spend all those years tempering him into hardened steel for no reason.

Jin finds Peter's stomach with a tanden zuki punch, the sharp blow almost ripping all the air from his lungs. Peter counters with a swift jab to Jin's throat. Then, as the diminutive bodyguard staggers back, he hits him with a powerful roundhouse kick, each move punctuated by Peter's desperate resilience.

Jin flicks himself back and away, a look of resolve glowing on his face as he comes at Peter again. The latter incorporates the ruthless efficiency of Krav Maga, the ground-based finesse of Brazilian jiu-jitsu, and the fiery strikes of Muay Thai. The dance between the pair becomes more brutal, their movements more frantic, their merciless brawl painting a visceral picture of life and death.

As Jin comes at him again, a whir of limbs, Peter looks for an opportunity to pull him in. Taller and heavier, his advantage is in his frame. But to use it, he's going to have to pull the little guy in close. Easier said than done. Especially when his body is screaming out in pain, something that gets worse and worse with every move Jin lands on his wrecked body.

Peter's survival instinct catalyzes a sudden surge of strength.

As the bodyguard throws a kakato geri, also known as the "axe kick," at Peter's head, the downward kick delivered in a similar fashion to the swing of an axe, Peter slips to the side, grabs the leg under his left arm, clamping it there, and lifts the diminutive Jin up.

With the bodyguard pounding Peter's back with punches that ricochet through his bones, Peter drives Jin into the nearest wall, smashing the concrete and feeling the air punch out of Jin's lungs with the shock of the blow.

He wastes no time. Peter throws Jin onto the floor like he's garbage, and before the bodyguard gets a chance to climb back onto his feet, Peter is toppling onto him, pinning him down with an armbar that traps him, sapping the fight out of the formidable combatant.

With a final, desperate surge of energy, Peter launches a decisive attack. Using his free hand and his knees, he lands one punishing blow after another, his fist raining down, pushing Jin to his limits. Peter's adrenaline peaks, fueling a rush of frantic strength. He tightens his hold, forcing Jin into unconsciousness. The bodyguard's resistance finally crumbles, and Peter sends him into the void, holding on until he is sure he's gone.

Peter lets go and staggers back to his feet. He stands over the fallen bodyguard, breath heaving, body screaming with exhaustion and pain, but alive. Still alive.

In the bedroom, Tanaka listens carefully, a profound dread coiling around his heart at the cessation of the violent sounds. The once invincible puppet master waits there, his eyes wide in a cocktail of fear and disbelief. The realization that he might have just lost his primary line of defense sends a shiver down him.

———

Off the coast of Shinoshima, the US Navy, aided by the Japanese Coast Guard, surround the island. A whole array of crafts occupy the water. An Arleigh Burke-class destroyer; two Virginia-class Submarines; a Zumwalt-class destroyer; two Ticonderoga-class cruisers. The entire fleet armed with surface-to-air missile systems.

Ben Knight wants to make a point. The more guns, the more likely the armed men inside Tanaka's bunker will simply surrender. "Overwhelming muscle" was how he put it.

Led by US Marines, a fleet of landing crafts surge toward the island's quay, ready to infiltrate and take over.

Inside the chaotic scenes of the bunker, Michael, Mayu, and Yūki dash through the underground complex toward the monorail station. A disorderly, huddled mass of anxious souls—imprisoned test subjects and workers alike—are jostling to escape the fortress. The three of them squeeze through the frenzied crowds, Yūki leading the way, holding her daughter's hand, a determined and protective force.

The doors of a waiting monorail car stand open. Yūki ushers Mayu and Michael inside. The monorail's interior teems with people, their wide-eyed desperation reflecting off the glossy surfaces of the luxury carriage.

Once inside, Mayu turns to her mother. Yūki hasn't followed them inside. Instead, she remains standing at the door.

"I'm sorry, but I can't come with you," she declares, her voice barely audible above the din. "I have to go."

"Where?" Mayu demands, her grip tightening around her mother's hand. The confusion in her eyes gives way to dread as she reads the intent on Yūki's face.

"I have one last thing to do," Yūki says, her voice firm. An unspoken promise of vengeance is evident in her resolute gaze.

"No," Mayu pleads, clutching her mother even tighter. "I won't let you go. Don't leave me again."

Yūki's gaze softens. A hand touches her daughter's cheek as a tear rolls down it. Gently prying Mayu's fingers from her own, she says softly, "This is how it has to be, Mayu. You have to understand." Turning to Michael, Yūki implores, "Keep her safe." The silent vow that passes between them is profound. He nods, a grim understanding settling in his eyes.

As the monorail doors begin to close, Yūki slips out onto the platform. Mayu lunges forward, but Michael pulls her back, the closing doors ultimately blocking her path. She presses her hands against the glass, her breath fogging the surface.

Yūki steps back from the departing monorail, her expression becoming resolute and fierce.

As the train pulls away from the station, Mayu watches her fade into the distance, the monorail carrying them off from the mother she never knew she had. All the way until she did.

———

Koji Tanaka can only cower in the relative safety of his chamber. His formidable bodyguard, Jin, is dead, his meticulously crafted sanctuary overrun by invaders. Each passing second drips with the mounting mayhem that reverberates through his apartment.

His heart stops as the shoji door slides open, interrupting his thoughts. An all-too-familiar shadow spreads over him, yet he doesn't look up. He doesn't need to see her to know who occupies his doorway.

The imposing figure of Yūki Yokashina stands there. Her posture is of a seasoned warrior, and in her hand, the wakizashi short sword, twin of the one that Peter dropped to the bottom of the ocean, shimmers under the subdued red lighting.

For a moment, time seems to hang suspended. Then Tanaka looks up, his face a pale canvas of fear and resignation. Looking her directly in the eye, he appears to accept his fate. "Go on," he says, his voice a hollow echo in the thick silence, "Do it. Have your revenge."

"Do you remember," she says from the doorway, "your fencing lessons?"

He says nothing. Just stares at her with his sad, gray eyes.

Yūki isn't in the mood for an easy kill. This, the final act of her vengeance, will not be rushed.

On the wall hangs one of Tanaka's many antique katanas. Keeping her imposing eyes always on him, she advances to it, her steps quiet and measured, and smoothly unhooks it. She tosses it at his feet. He watches it land with a thud, and his eyes shoot back to her.

"Use it," she challenges him, her voice frosty. "Use it for once, Tanaka. I want our last moment together to be something more. I want you to defend yourself. When I was no more than your bodyguard, I saved you on three occasions. Now, for once, why don't you defend your own life?"

She gestures for him to pick up the katana and follow her into the living room. Reluctantly, Tanaka lifts the sword and unsheathes it, its cold steel unfamiliar in his hands. After all, it is no more than a decorative wall feature. But, still, it is a genuine katana, the edge of its blade razor sharp.

The living room becomes their arena, the two standing opposite each other, Tanaka clumsily wielding his katana as Yūki holds her wakizashi with an expert skill and precision honed over years of relentless training with her father Takashi, the Gun.

"Were you sad when you saw the head?" she asks, her voice cutting though the air as well as any sword.

He says nothing, his face merely twitching.

"You know you didn't have to kill Ryu," she goes on, referring to the man she had married in Hokkaido. The man who raised Mayu the first seven years of her life. "He never hurt anyone. He only ever loved us."

Tanaka's top lip curls like a snarling wolf's. Finally he speaks, his voice a low growl: "He took what was *mine*."

Yūki tips her head. Shakes it gently. "That's always been your problem, Tanaka. Greed. But you can't own the world."

The lip curls further up his face. His eyes bulge.

"Are you ready?" she asks.

He flies at her, brandishing the katana above his head as though he wants to chop her in half. He's so off-balance all she has to do is tilt her body to the side and step back a little.

He misses, carrying on in a stagger, until he gathers his feet and whirls around.

He lunges once more. Yūki's wakizashi darts around with the precision of a calligrapher's pen, cutting through the red air, nicking Tanaka's cheek with expert precision and opening up a two-inch gash that drools with blood. His clumsy attempts to counter only evoke her laughter, the sound cutting into him deeper than any blade.

She toys with him, her short sword a blur of quicksilver as it continues to leave minor cuts on his body, shredding his expensive clothing gradually to ribbons. Her sniggering mirth fills the room as she chases him, her amusement only growing as he futilely tries to strike back. He begins to whine in frustration, in being reduced to the punchline of a joke. Because to a man like Koji Tanaka, a man of immense money and power, this type of humiliation bites so hard he can taste it in his mouth.

He swings the katana at her. She spins away, and as she twirls, she flicks the wakizashi at him, slicing the very end of his nose clean off. Tanaka drops the katana, the metal making a clattering sound as it hits the hard floor, and grabs his face, his cupped hands instantly dripping with blood, his gray eyes going wide. Covered in a litany of leaking cuts and slashes, his clothing reduced to rags, he looks a pitiful sight.

"Pick your weapon up," Yūki tells him.

His flashing eyes flick up at her. But it is not indignation that flashes in them; it is outright fear. He is terrified of her. In a way, he always has been. First, it was her beauty that had frightened him, then her vengeance. Now it is her aura of invincibility and superiority in the face of his withered form.

"Please," he whimpers.

"Pick it up."

"Please."

An unguarded tear falls from her eye. Once upon a time, she had truly loved this man.

"I love you," he says, his eyes burning with an intense conviction.

She shakes her head at him. "Your love isn't real love, Koji," she says in a voice as cold as ice. "It is the love one feels for a possession. More about attachment and desire for an object than for a person. Driven by the satisfaction, pleasure, comfort, or status that a particular object provides. The form of love that you feel, Koji, is self-centered, less likely to involve sacrifice or deep emotional connection. It hinges on the value you ascribe to the possession and how it benefits *you* or makes *you* feel. Love for a person, on the other hand, is far too profound, complex, and dynamic for someone like you. It is a deep emotional bond, empathy, a willingness to prioritize another's well-being over one's own. You, Koji, are capable of none of these things. Your love is an attachment marked by desire, satisfaction, and self-centered enjoyment. When I left you, I was no longer in your possession. That was why you wanted to destroy me; and look where it has brought you: your destruction has come full circle."

Her eyes gleam under the red lighting.

"Now," she adds, "pick up the katana."

With trembling, blood-soaked fingers, he reaches for the sword, lifts it, cries out, and charges her. A smile illuminates her mouth as the dance of swords resumes its former pattern, Yūki evading him with ease, flicking him with the wakizashi, making him mad, bringing his frustration to the boiling point, laughing as he cries out in exasperation. It is then, when Tanaka's blood is bubbling in his veins, that Yūki feigns a mistake, creating an opening that Tanaka desperately lunges at. But it is a ruse; in that fleeting moment, she rips her kimono apart and shows her tattooed torso. There, amidst vibrant ink, is the intricate hell screen. An entire landscape of the men she's slain, immortalized in pain and agony. Kenji Kiobi, depicted as a sloth with a human face, is the newest addition to her macabre collection, the playboy lounging haplessly amidst hell's flames.

The sight of his fallen compatriots, the details of their faces expertly rendered on her bodily canvas of retribution shocks Tanaka into pausing the action of swinging the katana, losing his opportunity to strike her down. Instead, faced with this vision of hell, he drops the sword and falls to his knees. Completely broken, he raises his wringing hands up in supplication. To see what she has done to her beautiful skin, to the part of her that he most desired to own, to see such horror covering it now, breaks the final spoke in Koji Tanaka's wheel.

"You are not really a man, Koji Tanaka," she declares, standing over him, her wakizashi poised for the final blow, her bare, patterned flesh bearing down on him.

"Kill me," he begs in a weak voice.

A smile curls the edges of her mouth. "Broken," she whispers to herself. It is just as she planned. She only wishes her little brother, Tatsuo, were here to see it with her.

Tanaka's head drops, his gray hair, matted with blood, drooping down his chest, his beseeching hands remaining held up to her. "Kill me," he repeats.

But the final blow never comes. Instead, as US Marines storm the apartment, Yūki steps back from him, taking refuge in a corner of the room, when the men spot Tanaka from the doorway and head straight toward him.

One of the Marines unceremoniously lifts Tanaka's head by the hair, while the other uses a handheld biometric facial scanner to read his face. It takes a few attempts, since Tanaka's physiognomy is pretty shredded. The once all-powerful billionaire shows not a single sign of struggle as they perform the action.

The device beeps. "It's him," the Marine holding it says.

"Koji Tanaka," the other Marine announces, thrusting a slip of paper toward him, "we are arresting you on behalf of the International Criminal Court for crimes against humanity. We will now be taking you to a police precinct in Kagoshima on the Japanese mainland. Do you understand what is happening?"

But all the great industrialist Koji Tanaka can give in reply is two withered words: "Kill me."

In her corner, Yūki pulls her kimono back across her chest and sheaths her sword, its work done. As they fasten handcuffs around Tanaka's wrists, she walks away, the bitter sobs of her former lover trailing behind her.

The greatest punishment for a man like Tanaka is to lose everything. To have to live through his transformation from all-powerful megalomanic into prison inmate. Death, for a man like that, is a much worse proposition. Yūki would prefer he lives out the rest of his days in the hell of his own creation before he eventually joins the others.

The bitter sobs of the now broken Tanaka fade into the background as she steps out of his apartment into the rest of the bunker. Most of the people have either left or been rounded up by US Marines.

"Excuse me, ma'am," an American voice says as she walks along a corridor.

A Marine, young and stern-faced, steps into her path. His hand drifts toward the firearm hitched at his hip, his posture ready to enforce order amid the chaos.

"I need you to come with me," the Marine goes on.

Yūki goes to speak, but before she can utter a word, Peter is at her side. His eyes, like ice in a tundra, meet the Marine's stare with a silent warning.

"She's with me," Peter rasps, his voice a strained whisper, yet his tone leaving no room for argument. The Marine hesitates, glancing at Yūki then back at Peter.

"And who are you, sir?"

Peter says one word that sends a shiver up the Marine: "Azrael."

The Marine points his eyes at the ground. "Yes, sir," he says before stepping aside.

Only once they are several meters away does the Marine look back, his eyes lingering on them as they disappear along the corridor.

"Holy shit," the Marine says to himself. "That was him."

———

As the monorail carriage emerges from the depths of the bunker, they are met with the glaring light of day. The sunlight, filtering through the ashen clouds above, casts an ethereal glow over the rocky landscape of the island.

At the station, they leave the train and make their way to the quay. That's where most of the action is now happening. The stone harbor is bathed in golden light when they reach it, as well as swarming with US Navy and Marines and Japanese Coast Guard. They are busy processing the hundreds of people they've just pulled out of this place. There are scientists, security guards, general workers, farm workers, cooks, cleaners, scientists, and, worst of all, the ragged remains of the men and women Michael saw delivered to this hell on Earth for the purpose of scientific experimentation.

Peter's and Yūki's eyes search the bodies for their children. Michael and Mayu come into view, and when their eyes meet, their expressions become a blend of relief and shock, the weight of their experiences still palpable.

They make their ways to each other, and soon Yūki holds Mayu in her arms. Peter and Michael stand opposite each other, the signs of wounds all over their two bodies. Then, without a single word, both break and throw themselves at each other, their bruises throbbing as they pull the other into their arms.

"I'm sorry for leaving you here," Peter whispers into his son's ear. "I should have never agreed to any of this."

"We made it, didn't we?" the kid replies.

Peter breathes out. "I guess we did."

As the reunited foursome talk among themselves, Ben Knight breaks away from a group of naval officers and strides toward them, his eyes on Peter, reflecting a mixture of relief and respect. As he approaches, Peter spots him, and Knight gives a tight smile, a meager attempt to lighten the grim atmosphere.

Peter detaches himself from the others to meet the deputy director of the CIA.

"You did well," Knight begins, his voice gruff with admiration. "You and the kid. The world's a better place because of it. But there are more men like Koji Tanaka. More places like this that need shutting down. You think the two of you might want to become a permanent fixture?"

Peter's response is as swift as it is impassive. His frosty gaze never wavers from Knight's optimistic one, his expression guarded. In a dry tone, laced with the faintest hint of amusement, he replies, "I have at least two broken ribs, a fractured arm, two bullet wounds, and God knows how many bruises and cuts. I've been stabbed, shot, beaten, half-drowned, suffocated, choked, set on fire, imprisoned. The kid has probably had worse while he's been stuck here. So no. I don't think we'll be making this a permanent fixture. Just the promised remuneration will do, Ben."

The terse reply hangs in the air, leaving Knight momentarily speechless as he takes in the full extent of Peter's words. Dismissing the CIA officer with a final glance, Peter diverts his attention back toward his son, as well as Yūki and her own sweet reunion with Mayu. Then, once he's rejoined them, he turns toward the horizon, where the sun is falling beneath the ocean, marking the end to another adventure. One which has pushed both men to their limits.

EPILOGUE - PART 1

HOKKAIDO

IN THE SERENE SANCTUARY OF AN UNASSUMING wooden house nestled amid the untamed wilderness of Hokkaido, Peter, Michael, Yūki, and Mayu have found a momentary refuge—a place where they can lick their wounds and mend their souls from the battles fought and lost.

Their days now unwind to the rhythmic hum of nature, punctuated by leisurely amblings along the jagged, salt-kissed coastline and unhurried ascents up the neighboring foothills, the landscape dotted with cherry blossoms and Japanese maples, their leaves whispering in the breeze.

As dawn breaks, it illuminates Peter and Yūki, each cradling a steaming cup of coffee, their bodies sinking into the warmth of their kitchen chairs. The world outside the window seems to sway in a gentle waltz as an array of birds flit among the watching pines, their songs threading the air while butterflies dance from flower to flower in an endlessly colorful spectacle.

Absent from this serene tableau are Mayu and Michael, who are busy strolling along the rugged coastline.

Within the comfort of the kitchen, a tranquil silence stretches between Peter and Yūki. Their voices aren't needed; a television perched atop the fridge-freezer fills the room with its low drone, casting flickering images that sporadically illuminate the otherwise softly lit kitchen. Koji Tanaka's crestfallen countenance fills the screen, his downfall narrated by the steady voice of the news anchor meticulously listing his charges.

Tanaka, a man once brimming with power, now appears as a specter of his former self. His hair, once a resplendent steel-gray, is now a tangled, snow-white mess; his previously imposing frame is reduced to a skeletal silhouette. His frailty is stark, his dramatic weight loss painfully visible in the gaunt and hollowed face that eerily stares out from the screen. Guided into the daunting expanse of The Hague's International Court of Justice, his steps falter, and he leans heavily for support on the robust arms of the guards that flank him.

Yūki breaks the silence, her voice barely above a whisper. "I almost feel sorry for him." A pause lingers in the air before she adds, just as quietly, "Almost."

On a nearby beach, the soft murmurs of a conversation carry across the sea breeze, where Michael and Mayu find their sanctuary. Seated on the sun-kissed sand, Mayu unveils her childhood, a patchwork of bittersweet memories, marred by the void of her absent mother. Her intimate recollections interweave with the rhythmic lull of the black waves that roll onto the desolate stretch of sand, their steady cadence a soothing balm for the poignant revelations she shares.

"He made me believe that she was dead," Mayu confesses, her fingers absentmindedly tracing circles in the wet sand beneath them, "and all this time, she was led to believe the same thing about me. What kind of man does that?"

Michael says nothing. He merely squeezes her gently as they sit together, cuddling, his arm across the back of her shoulders, their backs to the gray remains of a fallen tree that lies on the sand. Their relationship certainly has gone full circle.

Simultaneously, ensconced within the rustic charm of their forest haven, Yūki unravels her own tumultuous past to Peter. The unvarnished truth of her encounter with Tanaka, the dehumanizing aftermath, her struggle to reclaim her identity from the clutches of despair, spills from her lips in a torrent of cathartic confession. The low hum of the television has been replaced by the tranquil sounds of nature, a serene orchestra that underscores their intimate exchange. They now sit entwined on the veranda steps, their gazes following the whimsical journey of clouds that mirror leaves drifting on a stream.

"Do you know how I escaped Shinoshima?" she inquires, her voice a delicate whisper against the rustling leaves.

"No."

"He let me go," she declares, a hard edge of disbelief etching into her tone. "Tanaka. He had his men clean me up, sedate me, and then they left me in Osaka. That was when I spiraled into a vortex of despair, a ghost wandering the streets, a woman possessed, tearing at her own disheveled hair. Eventually, I was detained by the police and confined to an institution. Ten years of living as a nameless shell passed until my brother, Tatsuo, finally found me. He saved me."

In the silence that ensues, no words are necessary on the subject of her dead brother. Peter has previously shared his own failed attempt to save Tatsuo's life before the fatal blow of the Israeli sniper. Their stories, fraught with pain and survival, entwine in the silent understanding between them.

"When he found me, I was lost," her voice goes on like a ghost's whisper. "Catatonic, they call it. A waking coma. I'd sit there, eyes open, staring into space, not a sound or movement. I'd chew and swallow food, but that was about it. I was trapped at the bottom of a well, inside a void, the world far away at the top. Even though I could perform simple tasks, like chewing and swallowing food, my mind was an isolated cave."

"And what was it that guided you out of that darkness?" Peter inquires.

"Talk of revenge," she admits. "During his visits, Tatsuo would bristle with fury as he relayed the rumors he'd heard about my ordeal. Even as I sat in my detached state, he couldn't contain his outrage at the horrors I'd endured. Little by little, his words permeated the veil of my coma. I began to register his tales of retribution, and his vivid imagery of me exacting revenge sparked an ember in me. It was as if my soul was gradually rousing from a deep sleep. His words were like a lifeline, tugging me back into consciousness—as though he were blowing air onto the ember to produce a flame. As I began to respond, contribute my own thoughts, for the first time in a decade, I felt the stirrings of action within me—of will to power. No longer a shell, a puppet at the mercy of another's cruelty, I realized that I could seize the reins of control, and with each word of vengeance that passed between us, I felt invigorated, becoming stronger and stronger."

Peter can almost see the flames dancing in her eyes, the embers of her will to live rekindled by the all-consuming desire for revenge.

Her words trail off as the sight of Mayu, bathed in the dappled sunlight filtering through the canopy of leaves, catches her eye. Her confession transitions into a soft revelation. "But now I have her," she says as Mayu and Michael draw closer. "Now I have a purpose that transcends my obsession with retribution. Now I have a reason to live—to protect, guard, and nurture my newfound family."

EPILOGUE - PART 2

As the sun descends and dusk reaches out with long, dark tendrils, stretching from the silhouettes of trees, Yūki stands poised in the heart of their little house, her reflection staring back at her from a dressing mirror. Her gaze lingers on the tattooed representation of the hell screen etched into her skin, its detail as sharp as her memories. The scene of damnation is laid bare: the six men condemned to eternal torment, and the final figure, Koji Tanaka himself, immortalized as a hungry ghost.

In the ink and skin, Tanaka kneels amid a feast, shoveling food into his gaping maw. But his eyes, wide and desperate, and his gaunt, skeletal figure tell a different tale: his eternal hunger and thirst forever unquenched. He is ensnared in the flames of his own greed, alongside his damned cohorts: the proud Watanabe, his face stripped of identity; Iwasaki, forever gnawing at his own innards; Shusaku, the mutilated eunuch; Myomoto, the sightless fool; Kiobi, nonchalantly languishing in the fiery pit.

Yūki is torn from her introspection by Peter's voice calling her name, causing her to swivel toward the door. "You joining us?" his voice rings out, calling her from the confines of the room. Buttoning up her blouse, she leaves her reflection behind.

The rustic charm of their outdoor dining area, nestled amid the rustling pines, welcomes Yūki. The low murmur of the ocean waves kissing the cliffs, carried to them by the soft breeze, sets a tranquil ambiance. A Japanese barbecue sits at the heart of their wooden table, plumes of steam rising from sizzling meats, filling the air with an irresistible aroma.

Peter handles the grill with Michael, Mayu, and Yūki gathered around the table, waiting in eager, hungry anticipation, the smell of cooking bringing saliva flooding into their mouths. Satisfied with the sear on some teriyaki ribs, Peter relinquishes his position at the grill and takes a seat next to Michael, Yūki opposite him, Mayu across from Michael. As they tuck into their meal, their laughter and chatter creating a warm, familial atmosphere, a figure materializes at the edge of their property.

An elderly woman, frail and disoriented, steps onto the dirt carriageway from the adjoining track. Her snow-white hair stands in contrast to her scuffed clothing, hinting at a long journey traversed. At least eighty years old, she exudes an air of vulnerability that tugs at the empathy of the diners.

Mayu is the first to spot her wandering toward them. As the sun sinks lower and the gentle hum of conversation pervades the evening air, she rises to welcome the lost stranger.

Only then do the others turn to the scene of the trepidatious old woman, her aged fingers playing with the strap of her handbag as it hangs from a shoulder.

"I'm sorry," the old woman says in Japanese when Mayu reaches her. "I was out walking and got a little disorientated. Can you show me the direction of Higashiura?"

"Yes, *Obasan*. It is back down this road."

She points, and the old woman follows the gesture, her eyes searching the stretch of undulating hillsides that spread out from their little haven.

"How far?" she asks with trepidation.

"About six miles, *Obasan*."

"Oh, my. I've gone the wrong way then."

"No need to worry. We can drive you to Higashiura if you can wait for us to eat."

"Oh no," the old lady protests gently, waving her away. "I wouldn't want to impose upon your meal."

"You won't be imposing. Come join us. You like barbecue?"

A smile flitters upon her lips. "Very much."

"Then come. There is more than enough for another."

They make a space for the old woman next to Yūki, asking her if she'd like to eat. "Just a little," she says. "Just to get my strength back from my walk." And soon the foursome have become a fivesome, the old woman nibbling on a piece of buttered corn.

"What were you doing out here?" Michael asks.

"I like to take at least one walk a day," she tells him with a nervous smile. "But this time I got lost."

"You're not from around here?" Peter asks.

"No. I'm from Osaka."

"On holiday?"

"You could say."

Her liver-spotted, wrinkled hands lift the corn to her mouth, and she smiles before taking a series of nibbles. When she drops the corn to her plate, the smile is back on her face, her old eyes tethered to Michael as he cuts into a piece of Kobe steak that is dripping in sweet teriyaki sauce. Her grin widens, and her eyes glow as he places the juicy piece of meat in his mouth and begins chewing, her expression mirroring the joyful one that illuminates the kid's face as he eats.

"That is so darn good," Michael groans with pleasure when he's swallowed.

"The best steak in the world," Peter says.

The old woman claps her hands together, making the others turn sharply to her. She seems almost overjoyed at the kid's culinary experience.

Placing a hand to her mouth, she apologizes. "I'm sorry. Is he your son?" she asks Peter.

"Yes."

"He reminds me so much of my own son. He used to like to eat."

"Did he?"

"Yes. He could eat one bowl of udon after another. I loved to watch that boy eat. He had an insatiable appetite for food."

"Where is he now?" Michael asks.

Her face grows dark, as though enveloped in shadow. Her smile drops, her eyes go dull. In a whisper she tells him, "He died."

"Oh, I am sorry to hear that," Michael says.

"He was such a good son," she goes on like a ghost.

"Always looked after his mother. Some said he was a bad man, but I always saw good in him."

A tear falls from the old woman's eye. She reaches for the small handbag she's brought with her and pops the catch open. They expect to see her hand emerge with a pack of tissues to dab her wet eyes, but instead, she produces a sharp object that gleams menacingly in the fading sunlight. She is quick for her age. In a swift, unexpected movement, she lunges at Yūki.

Chaos ensues. Before anyone can stop her, the knife has risen to Yūki's neck and is piercing the right carotid artery. She gets in a second blow before Yūki can grab the frail wrist, and before the rest of the table is out of their seats and everyone has a hand on the old woman as they're sprayed with a shower of blood and the old woman screams about her dead son, her beloved Kujira. And by the time they've got her bound and lying on her side on the ground, her white hair smeared in blood and muttering under her breath, Yūki is lying in her daughter's arms while Peter rips up his shirt and comes over her to tie it around the brutal wound that lies open on her throat. But before he can get there, her eyes go blank and Yūki Yokashina dies in Mayu's arms. The final victim of her own chaotic revenge, her soul is carried away from them on the cool breeze like a silent shadow.

Don't miss THE LAST RUN The riveting sequel in the Peter Black Thriller series.

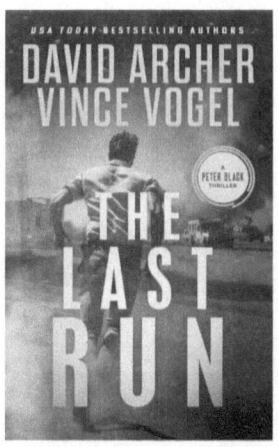

Scan the QR code below to purchase THE LAST RUN

Or go to: righthouse.com/the-last-run

NOTE: flip to the very end to read an exclusive sneak peak...

DON'T MISS ANYTHING!

If you want to stay up to date on all new releases in this series, with these authors, or with any of our new deals, you can do so by joining our newsletters below.

In addition, you will immediately gain access to our entire *Right House VIP Library*, which includes many riveting Mystery and Thriller novels for your enjoyment.

righthouse.com/email

(Easy to unsubscribe. No spam. Ever.)

ALSO BY DAVID ARCHER

Up to date books can be found at:
www.righthouse.com/david-archer

ROGUE THRILLERS
Gates of Hell (Book 1)
Hell's Fury (Book 2)

JACOB HUNTER THRILLERS
The Kyiv File (Book 1)
The Bogota File (Book 2)

PETER BLACK THRILLERS
Burden of the Assassin (Book 1)
The Man Without A Face (Book 2)
Unpunished Deeds (Book 3)
Hunter Killer (Book 4)
Silent Shadows (Book 5)
The Last Run (Book 6)
Dark Corners (Book 7)
Ghost Operative (Book 8)

ALEX MASON THRILLERS
Odin (Book 1)
Ice Cold Spy (Book 2)
Mason's Law (Book 3)
Assets and Liabilities (Book 4)
Russian Roulette (Book 5)

Executive Order (Book 6)
Dead Man Talking (Book 7)
All The King's Men (Book 8)
Flashpoint (Book 9)
Brotherhood of the Goat (Book 10)
Dead Hot (Book 11)
Blood on Megiddo (Book 12)
Son of Hell (Book 13)

NOAH WOLF THRILLERS
Code Name Camelot (Book 1)
Lone Wolf (Book 2)
In Sheep's Clothing (Book 3)
Hit for Hire (Book 4)
The Wolf's Bite (Book 5)
Black Sheep (Book 6)
Balance of Power (Book 7)
Time to Hunt (Book 8)
Red Square (Book 9)
Highest Order (Book 10)
Edge of Anarchy (Book 11)
Unknown Evil (Book 12)
Black Harvest (Book 13)
World Order (Book 14)
Caged Animal (Book 15)
Deep Allegiance (Book 16)
Pack Leader (Book 17)
High Treason (Book 18)
A Wolf Among Men (Book 19)
Rogue Intelligence (Book 20)
Alpha (Book 21)

Rogue Wolf (Book 22)
Shadows of Allegiance (Book 23)
In the Grip of Darkness (Book 24)

SAM PRICHARD MYSTERIES
The Grave Man (Book 1)
Death Sung Softly (Book 2)
Love and War (Book 3)
Framed (Book 4)
The Kill List (Book 5)
Drifter: Part One (Book 6)
Drifter: Part Two (Book 7)
Drifter: Part Three (Book 8)
The Last Song (Book 9)
Ghost (Book 10)
Hidden Agenda (Book 11)

SAM AND INDIE MYSTERIES
Aces and Eights (Book 1)
Fact or Fiction (Book 2)
Close to Home (Book 3)
Brave New World (Book 4)
Innocent Conspiracy (Book 5)
Unfinished Business (Book 6)
Live Bait (Book 7)
Alter Ego (Book 8)
More Than It Seems (Book 9)
Moving On (Book 10)
Worst Nightmare (Book 11)
Chasing Ghosts (Book 12)
Serial Superstition (Book 13)

CHANCE REDDICK THRILLERS
Innocent Injustice (Book 1)
Angel of Justice (Book 2)
High Stakes Hunting (Book 3)
Personal Asset (Book 4)

CASSIE MCGRAW MYSTERIES
What Lies Beneath (Book 1)
Can't Fight Fate (Book 2)
One Last Game (Book 3)
Never Really Gone (Book 4)

ALSO BY VINCE VOGEL

Up to date books can be found at:

www.righthouse.com/vince-vogel

PETER BLACK THRILLERS

Burden of the Assassin (Book 1)

The Man Without A Face (Book 2)

Unpunished Deeds (Book 3)

Hunter Killer (Book 4)

Silent Shadows (Book 5)

The Last Run (Book 6)

Dark Corners (Book 7)

Ghost Operative (Book 8)

JACK SHERIDAN MYSTERIES

A Cross to Bear (Book 1)

The Clay House (Book 2)

Into The Woods (Book 3)

The End is Nigh (Book 4)

A Step Into The Dark (Book 5)

Holier Than Thou (Book 6)

Streetlight City (Book 7)

An Offering for Sin (Book 8)

A Lark on the Wind (Book 9)

A Glass Darkly (Book 10)

Never Came Home (Book 11)

ALEX DORRING THRILLER

Agent 192 (Book 1)

The Hitman's Death (Book 2)

The Wrong Man (Book 3)

Who Dares Wins (Book 4)

The Highwaymen (Book 5)

The Ring (Book 6)

ABOUT US

Right House is an independent publisher created by authors for readers. We specialize in Action, Thriller, Mystery, and Crime novels.

If you enjoyed this novel, then there is a good chance you will like what else we have to offer! Please stay up to date by using any of the links below.

Join our mailing lists to stay up to date -->
righthouse.com/email
Visit our website --> righthouse.com
Contact us --> contact@righthouse.com

facebook.com/righthousebooks
x.com/righthousebooks
instagram.com/righthousebooks

EXCLUSIVE SNEAK PEAK OF...

THE LAST RUN

PROLOGUE

A BUNKER SOMEWHERE IN RUSSIA - 14TH APRIL, 12:37 (MSK)

IN THE DEPTHS OF AN UNDISCLOSED LOCATION, the president of Russia sits in a state-of-the-art underground bunker. Dominating the wall behind him, the Russian tricolor stands resolute and unwavering, its bold colors a striking contrast against the room's stoic grayscale. The banner casts a solemn shadow over the long, austere table where Vladimir Vladimirovich Putin sits alone, his presence lit by the somber glow emanating from an enormous telescreen adorning the wall in front of him.

Displayed on the colossal screen are the grim faces of his three main military chiefs, their expressions grave and their attention undivided, each burdened with the toll of a war spiraling out of their grasp. The silence in the room is deafening, interrupted only by the quiet hum of unseen air filtration machinery and the sterilized, measured steps of the bunker's carefully selected staff.

In their white uniforms, gloves, and face masks, they move with precision, carefully maintaining distance from Putin as they serve him breakfast. One aide places a steaming cup of black coffee next to the president. Another unveils a platter of warm croissants, their aroma subtly perforating the sterile air. They retreat with a courteous nod, leaving Putin alone with his breakfast and the faces on the telescreen.

"Gentlemen." He addresses the somber assembly standing attentively on the screen, his voice reverberating against the cold, stark walls of the bunker. "Report."

The generals exchange weighted looks before a hard-jawed man steps forward. His voice carries a heavy truth. "Mr. President, we've lost significant ground in Ukraine. Our position is rapidly deteriorating... At the current rate, we risk losing the war within the next year, thus ceding the territory we gained in 2014, including the Crimea. We also see Ukraine becoming a full member of NATO by then, thus placing Western missiles on our own borders."

A palpable silence falls over the room, the devastating words hanging in the air like specters. Putin finally breaks the silence. "What about conscription? Mass mobilization of all able-bodied citizens aged eighteen to thirty?"

The generals wince. One by one, they shake their heads. "A draft of that scale would cause massive public dissent," one general admits. "Furthermore, it would come without guaranteed success... and with the current state of our ammunition and equipment supplies... It's not a viable solution, Sir."

Putin steeples his fingers, his gaze darkening. He breathes in deeply, his mind racing. There's a moment of silence before he straightens up, his gaze hardening with resolve.

"Then we must take decisive action, gentlemen. Initiate Protocol X-9."

The order echoes in the sterile room, its significance palpable. No one argues or disagrees. The generals on the screen offer their silent nods, a grim acceptance marking their faces—which have lost all their color. Something terrible has just been set into motion, unbeknownst to everyone except Putin and his staff generals. The untouched croissants and untouched coffee bear mute witness to the weighty decree that has just been issued in the bowels of the earth, unseen and unheard by the world above.

CHAPTER 1

THE EARLY MORNING SUN CASTS A SURREAL GLOW over the bustling harbor of Red Hook Container Terminal in Brooklyn. The colossal silhouette of an oil tanker juxtaposes the calming hues of the dawn as a matte-black SUV navigates its way toward it through the maze of crates and machinery.

Driving is Michael Black. Beside him, his petite girlfriend Mayu observes the busy scene with wide eyes. Seated quietly in the back is Peter Black, his kit bag on the seat beside him.

His gaze lingers on his son and the woman beside him. He feels a pang of envy at their unblemished existence, their simple pleasures. He longs for the normalcy they have, a normalcy that he has never known.

Michael parks the SUV near the towering ship, twisting around in his seat to face his father.

"How you feeling about your first day as a tankerman?" he asks.

"Nervous" is Peter's reply. "Now remember," he then adds, his tone becoming serious, "I don't want you two getting into trouble while I'm away. It's four months. A long time. Long enough to get into plenty of trouble."

"We'll be fine, Dad," Michael reassures him. "Just don't work too hard, okay?"

Peter looks at his son, his pride evident. "I'm glad," he says softly. "Glad that we're all finally living normal lives. After what you've both been through, you deserve to live like normal people." The note of finality in his voice has them sharing a sobering silence.

"And you, too, Dad," Michael adds. Mayu nods beside him.

His voice shaking slightly, Peter adds, "You'll be in college by the time I get back. Both of you."

"We'll still be in the same city. Our new apartment will only be a half hour on the subway."

Peter tries to smile but merely looks glum.

"Look," Michael says, "don't go getting all sad on us. You don't want your shipmates seeing you like this on your first day. It'll be four months at sea, and then you'll be back for four months. We'll spend plenty of time together then."

Peter finally manages to smile. "I'm looking forward to that," he says, and they embrace across the car.

As he walks away from the SUV, his heavy boots crunching against the gravel of the weathered dock, he looks back once to see Michael wrap an arm protectively around Mayu.

It's the two of them now, he thinks. *She's his future. I'm his past.*

He turns, squares his shoulders, and walks up the gang-plank, the salty air carrying whispers of secrets and danger.

The inside of the ship is a stark contrast to its exterior—less maritime, more clandestine. The inside is practically deserted, and the men who inhabit the ship don't make eye contact with Peter, looking down the second they see him strolling their way along one of the narrow corridors that vein the vessel. No one asks for his papers, no one greets him, and no one tells him where to go. That's because Peter knows where to go. Because despite his son thinking he is going to be working an oil tanker these next four months, he is not.

Descending into the ship's belly, the first person to greet him is none other than Ben Knight from the CIA. The lanky man with a mop of white hair and dressed in a plain black suit extends his hand, his face adorned with a subtle grin.

"Good to have you back, Peter," he offers, his handshake brief and firm.

Guiding Peter through the labyrinthine vessel, Knight escorts him to a secluded office nestled within the tanker's hull, an aura of urgency permeating the air. Sliding into a chair behind a desk, Knight gestures for Peter to do the same.

"What have you got for me, Ben?" Peter inquires, leaning forward with an air of anticipation.

"How does a trip to Spain sound?"

"Sounds nice. What's in Spain?"

"Pest control."

"That's what I'm here for. Who's the pest?"

"Cockroach by the name of Ali Hossain. He's got previous with al-Qaeda, ISIS, and anyone else who needs to blow up a bunch of kafirs in the hope of progressing the international caliphate."

"Do we have his exact location?"

"Not yet. But we've got a lead. He's set to show up in Madrid. Our surveillance team has been tracking his crew. They're confident that the crew are planning something big in the city to mark the twenty-year anniversary of the Madrid bombing and that Ali Hossain will surface in the city within the next twenty-four hours to meet them."

Peter nods, a hint of a smile playing at the corners of his lips. "Sounds like an easy first day back if all I am is the trigger man."

"It will be unless something big comes up."

"Well," Peter responds, an air of casual indifference in his tone, "here's to hoping nothing big comes up."

———

AS THOSE PRESUMPTUOUS words linger in the stale air of the oil tanker, across the globe, a long-dormant network of Russian sleeper agents spring to life. Triggered by a single phrase, lives are disrupted and ordinary façades peeled away. A sequence of phone calls ignites a chain reaction. The message coming down the line is the same everywhere: "The dragon is released."

In the heart of Paris, within the clamor and aroma of a bustling fast-food restaurant, a man named Antoine receives the call. His supervisor begins complaining as he answers it, warning he shouldn't have his phone on him. All the while,

Antoine's hand hesitates over the sizzling grill, then drops the spatula. Without a word or backward glance, he strips off his apron and strides out of the restaurant, leaving behind the bewildered faces of his coworkers.

Half a world away, in the gleaming skyscrapers of Dubai, a businessman named Hamid is immersed in a high-stakes board meeting over the architectural design choice of a new shopping mall. His phone vibrates silently against the polished mahogany conference table. Excusing himself with a wave, he answers the call and steps into the corridor. Those same four words and he too is abandoning his post, his high-polished shoes tapping against the marble floor as he walks to the building's exit.

In São Paulo, a university professor named Helena stands in the middle of an engrossing lecture on the intersection between quantum mechanics and human consciousness. Her phone rings, the sharp trill cutting through her words as she explains Orch-OR theory. Pausing, she checks the caller ID and then answers, listening with a furrowed brow at the front of the auditorium. Four words later and she is placing the chalk on the blackboard and striding out of the room, ignoring the baffled looks of her students.

Down under in Sydney, a taxi driver named Liam hears his mobile chime through the speakers of his cab.

"The dragon is released." And the call goes dead.

Liam's passenger watches in surprise as the affable driver's face turns serious. "Gonna have to cut this ride short, mate," Liam says tersely, pulling over abruptly. He orders the fare out, then speeds off, leaving the bewildered passenger standing on the curb.

Across the Pacific in Atlanta, a seasoned cop named

Jackson sits in his cruiser, his partner chattering next to him. His cell phone rings, cutting through the idle banter. Recognizing the number, he answers. "The dragon is released," says the voice on the other end. Nodding, he hangs up, steps out of the vehicle, and begins walking away. His partner's calls fall on deaf ears as he disappears into the crowded street.

Thus, in cities scattered across continents, a chorus of seemingly inconsequential actions ripple through the mundane rhythms of daily life. Unseen and unknown, the sleeper agents have been activated. The dragon has indeed been released.

CHAPTER 2

RUSSIAN FEDERATION MINISTRY OF DEFENCE, MOSCOW, RUSSIA - 14TH APRIL, 13:29 (MSK)

ONE OF THE MEN WHO TOOK PART IN THE EARLIER conference call with President Putin sits alone in his massive, shadow-laden office. Russian Staff General Vasily Ivanovich occupies a huge wooden desk, burdened by stacks of documents, photos, maps, and a neat row of fountain pens. The high-ceilinged room carries a thick silence that is only broken by the relentless tick-tock of an antique wall clock.

Perched in his high-backed leather chair, Ivanovich keeps his piercing, eagle-like eyes fixated on the clock as his typically calm hand rhythmically taps a finger upon the dark wood of the desk, while his foot performs a nervous dance beneath the heavy furniture. The room feels charged and uneasy, and the decorated general's worry is palpable.

The clock strikes 1:30. Ivanovich springs to his feet. It is time. He moves swiftly to the door, his decorated chest catching a glint of dim light, and with a few hushed words to his secretary, he vanishes into the hallway, his mobile phone uncharacteristically left behind on his desk.

Half an hour of tense driving later, he leaves the cityscape behind and finds himself surrounded by the verdant countryside of the Moscow Oblast, studded with scattered dachas. Ivanovich pulls his car to a stop in front of a nondescript wooden dacha, its privacy protected by the dark canopy of the surrounding forest.

The staff general's heart hammers in his chest as he fumbles with the padlock. The ever-shifting shadows of the trees fan the flames of his paranoia, looking like men playing out imagined threats in the benign tranquility of the woodland. He can't help stopping and glancing furtively around every so often, the padlock key slippery in his sweaty palms.

His mouth parched, he steps into the small wooden cabin.

Inside, the décor is simple, an embodiment of rustic Russian aesthetics: rough-hewn log walls, faded but richly patterned rugs over oak floors, an iron wood-burning stove. His footsteps reverberate in the silence as he navigates his way to the kitchen. He pulls away a plain rug, revealing a concealed hatch in the floor. There is a heavy click as the hatch unlocks, and he descends into a dimly lit stone basement.

A workbench is pushed against one wall, cluttered with tools and mechanical bits and pieces. He pulls open a drawer on it, and his fingers close around a small burner phone. His heart feels like it might burst out of his chest as he powers it on.

He's no traitor, Ivanovich. No spy for the US. This

phone is, and was, only ever a precaution. Just in case there was a reason he needed a back channel. Now is such a case.

Summoning his courage, he punches in a number that he's never written down but has committed to memory. It is answered after only two rings. An impersonal, unmistakably American voice greets him on the other end of the line.

"Yes?"

"This is Pablo," Ivanovich announces, his voice bouncing around the basement. "It has happened. The dragon is free."

A pause, then incredulity colors the American voice. "No... Are you for real?"

"I am. So you Americans need to make your move now," Ivanovich says, urgency creeping into his voice. He feels cold sweat trickling down his spine.

"How far is it gone?" the American asks, a tick of worry in his voice.

"It is happening now, right this second, Knight! Don't you listen?!" Frustration and desperation bleed into Ivanovich's voice.

"But you said there'd be enough warning."

"He surprised us all. So you need to move. Now!"

He ends the call, and the echo of the last word "now" resonates in the chilly basement air, amplifying the urgency of the situation.

———

CIA HEADQUARTERS, Langley, Virginia, USA.
    14 April, 07:10 (EDT)

. . .

Sandy McLean, the director of the Central Intelligence Agency, is standing in her bathroom, toothbrush in hand, when her phone erupts into a ring. It's a disturbing intrusion in her otherwise peaceful morning routine. She spits out the toothpaste, grabs the phone, and answers, "McLean here."

"It has happened, ma'am," comes a voice she recognizes as Ben Knight.

Director McLean's brow is crinkled up. "What has happened?"

The words coming through the line send a chill down her spine. "The dragon is free."

Twenty-one minutes later, Sandy McLean races through the corridors of CIA Headquarters, Langley, her mind already working on the implications of what is happening right now across the world. As she reaches a set of double doors, she pushes through into a buzzing conference room.

The room is alight with activity; on a large screen at the front, the head of the FBI, the chairman of the Joint Chiefs of Staff, the secretary of defense, and the national security advisor are all present on a secure video call. Their faces are grave, the weight of the crisis palpable.

"Has the president been informed?" one of them asks.

"No, not yet," the secretary of defense replies, his voice heavy.

Director McLean takes a seat at the head of an oval table. Ben Knight is already three, having landed from New York only an hour before.

Leaning into him, she says, "Ben, please tell me your man in Sudan is ready."

"Our call time," Knight explains, "is eight Eastern Standard." He checks his watch. "Another forty-five minutes. He switches on the burner for fifteen minutes while he picks his kids up from school."

"And you can't get to him sooner?"

"No. The Russians are listening in to every other phone line."

"How close is he to getting a sample?"

Everyone in the room is looking at Knight, including those on the telescreen.

"He has the host containing Symbio-B."

"And are they capable of producing the protein?"

Knight nods. "But he'll need to send us his research data, too."

"Then he needs to move—ASAP," Director McLean says with some force.

Knight nods and exits the conference room, moving into a secure communications suite. There, he anchors himself in a waiting game that stretches into forty nerve-wracking minutes. Every tick of the clock amplifies his apprehension, mulling over whether his contact is sufficiently prepared. Their short phone conversations, punctuated by the chatter of the contact's daughter in the background, invariably portray the man as hesitant, a quiver of nervousness always present in his voice. Knight can't help but question—in this defining moment, will this man indeed be able to muster the courage needed to deliver when it matters?

The clock hits 8:00. His fingers fly over the keyboard, bringing up a secure line. He dials in a number, knowing that every second counts.

"Ibrahim, are you alone?" Knight asks urgently as the line connects.

The voice on the other end is hushed. "I'm with my daughter." Knight can hear the sounds of her in the background, the everyday noise of a little girl unaware of her precarious position.

"Ibrahim," Knight starts, his voice level, "I need you to move."

The panic is clear and immediate in Ibrahim's voice. "What?! No. I can't. Not yet. I mean, have you seen it here? We're minutes away from civil war. Me and my family are due to leave the city in the morning."

"Ibrahim, listen to me. You have to."

"But why?" There's a tremor in Ibrahim's voice, an undercurrent of fear. "You said we should take it easy, not arouse suspicion. A month, you said."

"We haven't got a month."

"Why?"

"Because the Russians are releasing it as we speak."

The line goes deadly quiet. Knight can imagine Ibrahim absorbing the information, the magnitude of what Knight is asking him to do, and the weight that has just been placed upon his shoulders. The weight of the world.

Finally, after a long pause, Ibrahim speaks, his voice more resolved. "Okay. Okay. I'm due in the lab in the next hour. I'll fetch the bacteria sample for you today."

"What about the host? Can you move them?"

"Yes. I will be with the host when your men come to take us."

"Then I wish you luck, Ibrahim," Knight tells him.

The line goes dead, leaving Knight alone in the room, the weight of the mission pressing down on him.

CHAPTER 3

FACILITY FIFTY-THREE, SUDAN - 14TH APRIL, 16:10 (EAT)

IBRAHIM CAN'T CONTROL THE SHAKING. THE AIR presses down on him so hard it feels like it's squeezing the life out of him. His heart pounds mercilessly in his chest, threatening to break out, and each breath he draws feels like swallowing shards of ice, every exhale a muted scream.

Beneath the harsh sterile lights of the laboratory, Ibrahim stands before a Class III Biological Safety Cabinet, an imposing monolith, his frantic heart matching the low hum of the cabinet's ventilation. Staring through the cabinet's glass screen, he is a man at the edge of a precipice, staring not just at the vials held within but into an abyss of invisible danger held at bay by the glass wall.

He slides his hands into the glove ports, the cold, detached touch of the metal handle through the rubber glove gripping his skin. The vial, a tiny vessel of devastation, rests within the cabinet, waiting.

Ibrahim's breath comes in ragged gasps as he maneuvers the mechanical hands toward the vial. Every so often, he pauses the delicate work, casting anxious glances over his shoulder despite knowing that he is alone and despite being in the camera's blind spot. Because get caught doing this and he is a dead man. And not just that: so too is his entire family.

Refocusing on the task at hand, his world shrinks to this singular, defining moment, a monumental endeavor demanding his entire concentration. Get this wrong and he could crack the vial, set off the detectors, the alarm system, and cause a shutdown protocol. End up stuck down here for the next three days while they perform quarantine. Not good. Not when you're trying to do what Ibrahim is trying to do.

The mechanical fingers close around the vial—secure, no crack. With extreme caution and precision, he guides the hands to deposit the vial into a shock-resistant case nested in the cabinet's drawer. His heart rebels against its bony cage, a wild creature seeking release as he nestles the vial within the foam padding and seals the case.

Withdrawing his hands from the gloves, relief seeps into his tense muscles. He moves to the adjacent drawer, eyeing the indicator light, willing it to flash green, signaling its unlocking.

And it does.

A newfound wave of resolution empowers Ibrahim. He seizes the case—the cold weight of it a grim testament to the lethal secret it harbors. Clasping it against his chest, he stows the case within his lab coat. The bulge beneath the pristine white fabric brands him a traitor, and he prays fervently that the guards monitoring the facility aren't scrutinizing the corridor cameras with any real vigilance.

Drawing on a threadbare courage, he steps out of the lab, trying hard to maintain the picture of an unassuming scientist. But beneath this façade, his insides writhe with terror. He feels as though he's balancing on the edge of a razor, one misstep away from falling onto the blade.

Ibrahim slips through the maze-like environment of the lab, straining to retain his composure. In the changing room, within the sanctuary of the camera's blind spot, he stealthily secures the container inside his work bag. In the elevator, he breathes a sigh of relief at being alone; maintaining his composure under the scrutiny of others would be a Herculean feat, given the explosive secret concealed in his bag.

Like normal, the guards don't inspect his belongings, and he seamlessly passes through the turnstile, the two men wishing him goodbye as he leaves. His responses are automatic, the entire interaction shrouded in an aura of unreality, as if he's ensnared in an unsettling dream.

Donning a pair of shades, he steps into the glaring desert sun, a lone figure navigating the desolate Sahara. To any observer, not that there are any all the way out here in the barren desert, it would look like the man in the nice suit is walking out of a small military compound made up of nothing more than a single stone building where two guards block a turnstile that leads to nothing more than an elevator. They would see nothing more than the small building and a large shed and think that these men were guarding no more than the forty-foot antenna sticking out the top of the place: a military radio antenna, if you ever happen to look it up. They would certainly know nothing about the giant seven-story laboratory buried a thousand feet below the surface.

Upon starting his car, the radio crackles to life. It is filled with news reports on the imminent scrap that's about to happen in Khartoum, an added layer of tension on all of this. But the real news isn't out yet.

Ibrahim's trembling returns as he waits at the fence of the compound for the automatic gate to open. It seems to take much longer for them to press the button today. He's never known it to take this long. A bead of sweat glides down his face, making the skin underneath itch and prickling him with dread.

Finally, the gate swings open, prompting a long-held breath to escape his lips. As the compound recedes into the distance in his rearview mirror, Ibrahim hastily dials a number on the disposable phone provided by his contact.

"Okay," he utters as soon as the call is answered. "I got it."

"Good," comes the succinct reply. "Now get the host and meet the extraction team at the airfield. And Ibrahim?"

"What?"

"You're a good man. Remember that."

His voice chokes with emotion. "Tell that to my family if they die because of me."

———

MILITARY TRUCKS RAMPAGE down the streets of Khartoum, as they have been for almost a week now. The rebel RSF have entered part of the city, all guns pointed on the good folk of Khartoum.

Ibrahim makes it back into the city much quicker than usual. The drive usually takes about an hour over the gravel road, the need to keep your speed down to no more than sixty due to the damage loose stones can do to the underside of the BMW. But today he doesn't care. Today the needle doesn't drop below a hundred, the sharp din of gravel hitting the car's undercarriage a mere whisper against the clamor of his immediate worries.

This is not how his life is supposed to be.

Dr. Ibrahim Bol, a towering figure with a mind as vast as the Sudanese savannah he hails from, is a living paradox. A child prodigy who traded the dusty landscapes of Sudan for the esteemed halls of Cambridge, his genius is both his identity and an enigma. Thriving on the adrenaline of scientific discovery, Bol's relentless pursuit led him to the uncharted realms of symbiotic research. His theories, once considered audacious, now thrive under the watch of his paymasters: the Russian Federation. With their money and the use of Facility Fifty-Five, he has been able to revolutionize our understanding of life itself. It is many of his papers and patents that have changed how we view bacteria, turning them from simple organisms into allies, partners, potential saviors—or potential killers.

Once past the White Nile, the inevitable clog of traffic he meets in the inner city presents a maddening obstacle. He stares helplessly at the obstinate knot of smoking, honking vehicles. Fear like a relentless tide washes over him, bringing back the trembling, and it's as if his blood is in such an uproar it's boiling in his veins.

A few blocks into the city, his wife's call pierces his anxious reverie.

"Amira?"

"Ibrahim, have you finished work yet?"

"Yes. Did you gather the children as I asked?"

"That's what I wanted to talk to you about. I forgot that Leila is at your parents' place today."

Ibrahim goes cold. Frustration flares. "I asked you to keep Leila at home," he retorts, the unexpected fissure in his plans threatening to widen.

"But she's only around the corner at your parents', Ibrahim. I can go pick her up now."

"No!" The word snaps out, frantic, his fear spiraling. "Don't leave the house. I'll pick her up. Stay put with Ali and Tariq. Do not leave the house."

Just as he's about to disconnect, she breaks the silence.

"I know I've asked repeatedly," she says, "and you've told me not to worry repeatedly, but please, Ibrahim—what's going on?"

"I promise you, by the end of the night, my love, everything will be clear. For now, I need you to trust me."

He ends the call, fear constricting his stomach like a coiled snake. Sweat trickles down his face, even with the BMW's air conditioning going at full whack.

Navigating through a tangle of city traffic, Ibrahim reaches his parents' house. At one juncture, he finds himself trapped behind an ancient T-54 tank, a gift from the Soviet Union decades prior. The monstrous relic of World War Two relentlessly spews plumes of black smoke, the rancid stench a bitter reminder of the impending threat of war.

He reaches his parents'.

As Ibrahim steps into the living room, guided by the maid, his mother's words puncture the tension-laden air. "You look terrible," she says.

Her face is etched with worry. Deep furrows accentuate her normally wrinkled brow. The television plays in the background, its screen displaying an ominous collection of images: army convoys, rebel soldiers, armored vehicles encircling the city, embassy evacuations. Lines of foreigners are shown boarding planes at Khartoum Airport, a last-ditch effort to escape before General Hemedti and his men storm the capital.

"Did you hear me?" his mother repeats, her voice piercing the room.

He shifts his gaze from the television to meet her anxious eyes. "I'm okay," he reassures her.

Unconvinced, she insists on assessing his health. Resigned to his mother's habitual fussing, he allows her to check his temperature and pulse, her lips drawn into a tight line all the while as she places a hand across his forehead before checking his pulse.

"Your heart is racing," she frets.

Blaming his anxiety on the overwhelming talk of war, Ibrahim tries to defuse her worries. However, her scrutiny doesn't waver. She switches off the television, plunging the room into a profound silence, her penetrating gaze never leaving his face.

"I'm okay," he tries to assure her.

"Well, you don't look it. You're ill."

"Mom, please," Ibrahim groans. "I'm in a hurry. Where's Leila?"

Sighing loudly like she always does when she's annoyed,

she replies, "In the garden with Papa."

She guides him back outdoors, into the vibrant embrace of the sun. They discover his father tucked away within the confines of a quaint greenhouse, diligently tending to a tomato plant. Beside him, Ibrahim's daughter, Leila, is playing her part in this humble act of cultivation. With an innocence only a child possesses, she assists her grandfather in repotting the plant, her small hands busily scooping in heaps of soil around the base, while the old man carefully supports the plant's delicate stem.

"Leila," Ibrahim calls out. "We need to leave right now."

The tiny girl raises her gaze, and her face brightens with joy.

"Papa!" she squeals.

Abandoning her task, she bounds over, the dirt from her small hands transferring onto his clothes as she throws her arms around him in an affectionate embrace.

"We need to get going," Ibrahim tells her as she pulls away to look up at him. "Your mother and brothers are waiting."

"Are you leaving so soon?" his father inquires, hoisting himself upright from his bent position. "Won't you stay for a cup of tea?"

The words hit Ibrahim like a ton of bricks. A thick lump forms in his throat. This will be his final encounter with his father in person. It wasn't supposed to be this way.

"I'm sorry, Papa," he says. "But Amira has dinner on the table, and you know how she is about being late."

His father smiles and nods, understanding a husband's plight.

With an urgency coursing through him, Ibrahim shepherds Leila out of the house and into his waiting BMW. As they drive away, he doesn't even check his mirrors to see his mother waving them off from the driveway.

A minute later, the sound of Leila's nursery rhymes fills the air of the car, a welcome respite from the grim news updates of the impending civil war. It is in the midst of her singing and dancing that a call comes in. It's Amira, her voice trembling as she whispers into the phone. The words "They have guns" are followed by a short, snatched scream before a male voice takes over the line.

The stranger's voice paralyzes him with fear. "Ibrahim Bol? If this is you, come home. Your family needs you."

The line goes dead, leaving Ibrahim in a state of terror, his heart pounding in his chest. He feels as if he's falling out of the sky.

Quickly composing himself, he stops the car at the side of the road and turns to his daughter. "Leila," he says as she stares at him, "do you know the way to Grandma and Grandpa's from here?"

The little girl nods.

"Are you sure?" he says sternly, giving her that look he gives Leila and her brothers if he thinks they may be lying.

She crosses her heart with a finger, a familiar tactic.

"How?" he asks to be sure.

She points behind them. "The alley. It takes you right there."

Ibrahim knows for sure she's done the journey with her mother and brothers a thousand times already in her seven years.

"Then I need you to go there. Not now!" he adds quickly as her hand snatches at the door handle.

She turns back to him.

"First," he adds, "I need you to trust me. Do you trust me?"

Leila nods immediately.

Ibrahim retrieves the case from under his seat and opens it. He removes the vial, looking at it a second or two. It is more than a liquid; it is the culmination of years of research, a microscopic army in a sea of hope. His fingers tremble as he takes a syringe and draws the precious cargo into it. All the while, the girl's big brown eyes stare at it.

"Leila," her father's soothing voice says, "I need to inject this into you."

"But I hate needles," the girl whines.

"I know. But you have to be brave." Looking her in the eyes, his expression as soft as he can make it, he says, "Can you be brave for Daddy?"

Her lip quivers, but she nods.

"That's my girl. It's going to be just like when Doctor Hammed gave you your shots. Okay?"

Another nod.

Ibrahim takes a deep breath. Every scientific principle he stands by, every ethical boundary he respects is now blurred in the face of a father's love. His gaze meets Leila's, her dark eyes wide and trusting. She understands little of her importance, only that she is the only one of her siblings who sometimes has to go to the lab to be tested.

As the needle pierces Leila's skin, she winces, a soft whimper escaping her lips. Ibrahim's own breath hitches in sympathy, the anxiety etched deep in his furrowed brow. There is no turning back now.

As the needle slides free, a solitary bead of crimson

emerges. Tenderly, Ibrahim wipes Leila's arm, soothing the pinprick wound.

"You really are Daddy's brave girl," he tells her. "Now you must go straight to Grandmama and Grandpa's. Do not stop. Do not look back. I am counting on you, Leila."

They hug one last time, and she leaves the car, Ibrahim watching her disappear into the alley. Alone now, he takes a deep breath, his heart heavy in his chest, and makes a quick call on his mobile.

"They know," he says when it is answered. "They are already at my house."

"Where are you?"

"Around the corner."

"Then turn around right now."

"I can't. They have my wife and sons. If I don't show up, I'll be condemning them to death."

"But we need the bacteria sample. The host. Without it, we're blind. This will..."

"Knight!" Ibrahim snaps. "You will get it. I have placed the bacteria into the host. I pray that my research is correct and that her unique genome will bind with the bacteria and give us the protein. If not, I have killed her."

"Who is the host?"

"It is my own daughter," Ibrahim replies with an element of regret in his voice. "She will be with my parents, Mustafa and Fatima Bol. Their address is 101 Al Abdi, Um Dalil. You need to move fast."

"Okay. I'll have the extraction team head there now. But I also need you to turn around right this minute. Go to your parents. Stay with your daughter. Wait for my team. Because we're going to need you, Dr. Bol."

"I'm sorry. I have to be with my wife and sons."

And with that he ends the call, swallowing down a dry lump.

A minivan is parked in his driveway as Ibrahim walks shakily to his front door. The oppressive heat and his overwhelming fear make him drop his keys multiple times along the way. As he enters the door, he's immediately seized by two waiting men, roughly hauled across his own hallway, and tossed onto the living room rug.

His wife and sons are on the couch, huddled together in infinite terror. Ibrahim lands awkwardly on his knees, his eyes fixing instantly on the terrified faces of his family. There is a man standing menacingly behind them who draws Ibrahim's attention. The man's red beret signals his affiliation with the Rapid Security Forces (RSF). Once a militia with links to the army, they are now in full rebellion for control of the country.

"Ibrahim Bol," the man announces in a threatening tone as he produces a piece of paper. "You have been placed upon a list."

Confusion sweeps over Ibrahim. "A list? What list?"

"A list of men who have betrayed Sudan. Whores of al-Bashir. Whores of al-Burhan. Betrayers of Sudan."

"You're not from the lab?"

The rebel commander furrows his brow at him.

"Did the Russians send you?" Ibrahim asks.

The man shakes his head. Pointing to the ceiling, he says, "God sent me. To revenge his people." Flapping the paper, he adds, "You have been found guilty of betraying the people of Sudan by working with its former government. By using your intellect for your own benefit while your people live in poverty."

"This *isn't* about the lab?"

"No, Mr. Bol. This is about your work for our corrupt government."

"But I was only an advisor. I was never in the government. I never even received payment."

"And yet you are still on this list," the man in the beret says, rattling the paper.

"And so what? I'm under arrest?" Ibrahim ventures, hoping against hope for a relatively benign outcome. But as the man rises and gestures to his men, a cold realization dawns on him. The men raise their AKs, and the room fills with a chilling proclamation.

"You, Ibrahim Bol, have been found guilty of treason!"

"No! Wait!" Ibrahim yells, but it's too late. The men cock their weapons and let loose a volley of bullets. As his wife and sons scream, the leader steps aside, and the men turn their smoking guns on them, transforming the family into bullet-riddled flesh.

———

AT THE EDGE of a dirt runway on the outskirts of Khartoum, four figures clad in tactical gear stand resolute against the biting onslaught of sand and heat. A Lockheed Martin C-130J Super Hercules, a monolith of gunmetal gray, stretches out behind them.

Bulging veins trace paths of anticipation along the men's sun-kissed forearms, hands tightly gripping the lightweight, battle-tested bodies of M4 Carbines. They stand there like silent statues, their minds and hearts racing with the pulse of the mission, ebbing and flowing with each tick of the unseen clock.

This is the extraction team.

The omens are poor: Trouble is coming. The horizon swallows the dying embers of the day, replaced by a brewing desert storm of dust and dread, painting the vast sky a muddy swirl of browns and grays. The road leading into the airfield is almost invisible. And not just that. The city has finally descended into open conflict. The air is thick with the crackle of gunfire and the thud of explosions, the undercurrent of a civil war resonating in the distant alleyways of Khartoum.

With the Internet down, all they have is an Iridium 9575 Extreme satellite phone. It suddenly shatters the oppressive silence, but due to the storm, the line is bad. Its static-laced message scratches against the eardrums of Jameson, the extraction team leader, as he presses his ear to the speaker and frowns, getting only fragmented words like "city," "target down," "retrieve," "daughter"—the words ghosting through the airwaves. The frown etching its way onto Jameson's face mirrors the confusion, the half-understood message doing nothing to alleviate the tension that has them all on a razor's edge.

"Repeat that, base. I didn't get it all."

His request for clarity hangs unanswered, swallowed by a relentless torrent of static—which is then interrupted by the sharp, distinctive crack of a sniper's bullet that slices through the gloom and finds its mark: Jameson.

The second the bullet hits, the rest of the team knows they're in deep trouble. Blood spouts like a fountain from the hole in Jameson's neck, his body collapsing heavily onto the hard dirt of the ground. The dust it kicks up swirls into the air.

"Move, move!" Alvarez, the point man, shouts, the urgency in his voice betraying his usually calm demeanor. The two other remaining men, Turner and Castillo, react immediately. All three of them half-crawl, half-run toward the yawning mouth of the Hercules' rear.

They scramble into the cover of the ramp as the thunderous barks of AK-47 gunfire, the weapon of choice for the RSF, fill the air, the bullets ricocheting off the Hercules' reinforced steel body, each one a deadly echo in the night.

Turner, a hulk of a man with biceps that look like they could rip the wings off a plane, turns back to provide cover fire, his M249 SAW light machine gun coughing out rounds. Castillo, the team's medic, drags Jameson's lifeless body up the ramp, his face a mask of determination and fear.

"Get us the hell out of here!" he screams into the mic of his comms, the words barely discernible over the cacophony of gunfire and the roar of the aircraft engines. The pilot, a seasoned vet, doesn't need to be told twice. The four engines of the Hercules burst into life, a monstrous, symphonic crescendo that drowns out the ongoing firefight.

The plane shudders as it lurches forward, the wheels straining under the load. The heat of the engines kicks up a dust cloud, which combines with the incoming storm and reduces visibility to near zero. But the pilot has done this a hundred times. He knows what he's doing.

Suddenly, a convoy of rebel pickups materializes from the dust, men riding on the backs of them, balaclavas over their faces, guns blazing as they lean them on the cabs.

Bullets ping off the plane's fuselage, each one a reminder of the deadly threat they are under. But the Hercules, as if alive and defiant, thunders down the runway.

Within moments, the plane is airborne, the ground falling away beneath them. The relentless gunfire follows them all the way up, a few bullets managing to find their mark on the underside of the plane as it rises beyond their reach. And they are away. They've escaped the jaws of death, leaving behind the chaos of the battlefield and an extraction mission gone terribly wrong.

As they glide into storm-ridden sky, Castillo lifts the radio to his mouth, his voice raw and ragged. "We're aborting! Repeat, we're aborting!"

Scan the QR code below to purchase THE LAST RUN
Or go to: righthouse.com/the-last-run

www.ingramcontent.com/pod-product-compliance
Lightning Source LLC
Chambersburg PA
CBHW030555180626
46816CB00005B/1555